Ginevra watche

'My agreement to w
pletely, and to carry
on one thing only.' S.
raised his eyes from the rim of his goblet and
looked steadily across at Ginevra. 'The
answer will be for you to decide.'

She frowned, utterly perplexed. 'Do you
mean *me*?'

He nodded and held her stare, seeing flickers
of alarm in her eyes. Without taking his eyes
from hers, he spoke. 'Alan, I want you to give
me the hand of your sister Ginevra in
marriage.'

Juliet Landon lives in an ancient country village in the north of England with her retired scientist husband. Her keen interest in embroidery, art and history, together with a fertile imagination, makes writing historical novels a favourite occupation. She finds the research particularly exciting, especially the early medieval period and the fascinating laws concerning women in particular, and their struggle for survival in a man's world.

THE GOLDEN LURE

Juliet Landon

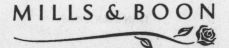

MILLS & BOON

MILLS & BOON LIMITED
ETON HOUSE, 18–24 PARADISE ROAD
RICHMOND, SURREY, TW9 1SR

*All the characters in this book have no existence outside the
imagination of the Author, and have no relation whatsoever to anyone
bearing the same name or names. They are not even distantly inspired
by any individual known or unknown to the Author, and all the
incidents are pure invention.*

*First published in Great Britain 1995
by Mills & Boon Limited*

© Juliet Landon 1995

*Australian copyright 1995   Philippine copyright 1995
This edition 1995*

ISBN 0 263 78996 9

*Set in 10 on 11½ pt Linotron Times
04-9503-97813*

*Typeset in Great Britain by Centracet, Cambridge
Printed in Great Britain by
BPC Paperbacks Ltd*

CHAPTER ONE

TINY rolls of wool-clippings were caught up in the gusts
of wind which sneaked through the wattle enclosures,
and fell in heaps over Ginevra's bare feet. Some caught
on the stakes and fluttered there like plumes on
knights' helmets. The only sounds to be heard were the
roar of the wind, lifting the sheep's distress calls up
into the sky and down across the valley, and the
rhythmic crunch and snip of the shears.

She had been there, watching and waiting while the
sun moved down little by little towards the hill on the
other side, and so far Brother David had barely looked
at her. The late afternoon sun glistened on his thick
arms as he deftly worked the huge spear-pointed shears
in and out of the sheep's winter coat, leaving even
ridges of pink and white on the body.

Ginevra watched the thick white roll work its way
down to the ground in a glorious heap of solid softness.
She understood that there was no time to waste; the
sheep could not be kept penned all night, nor would
the brothers want to leave the job unfinished. There
were more of them to be done on the morrow.

Brother David kicked the white roll gently to one
side and lifted the naked, struggling sheep to its feet.
He straightened up, noticing Ginevra at last.

'Still here?' he asked in surprise. 'Won't you get into
trouble?'

She looked at him with unreserved admiration, her
eyes revealing in one short glance all the adoration of
her seventeen years. 'I was just gathering a few herbs

and happened to see you. . .' she began, but David had already reached for the next sheep and tossed it expertly over on to its rump, his hands beginning their work with the shears on its neck.

'Better go. I'll be here until we've done this lot.' And he jerked his head in the direction of the next pen. 'Hey, Rob! How many more to go?'

There was no more to be said. No point in her staying. She knew that already she had been dismissed and, to all intents and purposes, was no longer there. She turned her head into the wind and looked at the sun, barely an hour above the tree-line. Picking up her sandals, and without another glance, she moved away down the hillside, welcoming the sharp jabs of bracken on her feet as a diversion from the painful ball of tears in her throat. Faster and faster she strode, then broke into a run and then a headlong gallop as her sobs of anger and humiliation finally broke out, keeping time with her pounding feet. The words fell out in a breathless growl. Why do I even think he knows I exist? Why do I care? *What* do I care?

There was no answer inside her, only the massive pain of being the one who cared for the one who cared not. This, she supposed, was the punishment for being where she had no business to be. For talking with a lay-brother. For attempting to distract him from his work. For allowing certain thoughts to enter her mind, and—oh, so many other things. She knew that her punishment was to be nothing to the person for whom she wanted to be everything.

She slowed down to a walk as the shorter, gentle grass now coolly caressed her feet, telling her that she had reached the beck separating her from the priory field. She stopped and knelt into the coolness while the pain eased away, and she allowed a last thought of him to flow into her mind and out again like the dark, silvery-pink water before her.

'Holy Mother of God,' she whispered out loud. 'Holy Mother, what have I to do? Tell me what I have to do. Tell me.' The silence echoed around her head as she waited for an answer. The rattle of water through the stepping-stones, the call of a lapwing and the hum of a late bee brought her thoughts back down to eye-level, and she looked across at the massive priory buildings and then at the stones leading like a dotted line across to the other bank. Was this to be a crossing-point in her life? Was it a barrier? Or a sign to move forward?

The buildings now glowed rose-coloured in the evening sunlight like an enchanted castle in a pool of golden grass. The arches, chimneys and rooftops, towers and gables clustered together in a solid huddle, strong and beautiful and faithful—like a person, she thought. Like a wonderful, steadfast and desirable person. She frowned suddenly, struck by the significance of her thoughts. Oh, no, this can't be the answer, surely? No, not this. Holy Mother, you know I could never be a nun. She shook her head vehemently and began to rise from her knees. No, this was impossible. Prioress Claire knew only too well how unsuitable she would be. A pupil of some twelve years, and a broderer too. Good enough to have taught most of the younger ones, but *never* a nun. The thought of joining the ranks of novices was one she had never entertained, not even fleetingly—though she had many times wondered, especially recently, exactly what life had in store for her. Apart, that was, from returning home to keep house for her two brothers.

As though to shock the thought out of existence, she grabbed her shoes and put one foot into the ice-cold water, then on to the stepping-stone. The pathway over

the beck needed all her concentration, for the stones
had been placed there by men with bigger strides than
hers. As she leapt on to the opposite bank her mind
was ready to re-focus on the fact that she was late.

Ginevra had been tending her herbs when Sister
Agnes had asked her to gather watercress and angelica
from the beck, and a bagful of tansies, which grew up
on the hill slopes. Glad of a chance to escape the priory
walls for even a short time, she had taken the wicker
basket and an old canvas bag and headed for the water.
The angelica stalks were thick and woody and had
resisted all her efforts strenuously until she had hacked
through them under water. Leaving the long stems and
frothy flowerets by the dripping basket of cress, she
had moved towards the hillside and the yellow tansies.
It was then that the familiar sound of tinkling bells and
the chorus of bleating had wafted towards her on the
wind.

All thoughts of duty and time forgotten, she had
raced up the hillside towards the sheep-pens, knowing
that David was sure to be there and carefully timing
her arrival so as not to appear flushed or breathless.
But for all the notice he had taken of her she might as
well have been another sheep. She had waited patiently
for some sign of recognition—a greeting, a smile—but
she was well outside his world and, as yet, Ginevra was
unaware that a woman's presence could be unwelcome
to some men. Brother David and Rob worked as a
team and she had no part of it. Nor, she felt, would
she ever, for he had never encouraged her shy, maid-
enly interest in him since their infant days together on
the manor.

The sound of the vesper bell floated across the field,
fuelling her fears. Collecting the watercress and angelica from the bankside and dashing towards the door of

their herbarium, she desperately hoped that no one would notice her re-entry, nor her tear-stained face. She hurriedly adjusted the unwieldy bundle under one arm, shoes and basket in the other, and turned the weighty iron handle of the door. Pushing against it with her back and easing herself through the gap backwards, she almost collided with the white-robed figure of Prioress Claire. A tall, well-dressed man was by her side.

Ginevra could not help comparing the unfailing composure of the prioress with her own agitation, wishing that they had been alone and uninhibited at this moment. It was clear that she was expected to break the silence, but in view of her dishevelled appearance, still damp, breathless and tear-stained, words seemed to her to be superfluous. So she waited, her hand on the latch of the door.

'Ginevra! Didn't you hear the bell?'

Before she could respond, the stranger stepped behind her, aware that there was a part for him to play. 'Permit me,' he said. His voice was deep and musical. Ginevra watched with curiosity as he closed the door firmly. His dress indicated wealth; the muscular body was shown to advantage in the perfectly fitting tunic of rich brown and black-figured brocade. A jewelled girdle glinted over slim hips, accentuating the width of his shoulders. A neat beard outlined the strong square jaw and the glossy black hair made a frame for the elegantly handsome face. But it was his eyes which Ginevra felt, rather than saw. They were steel-grey, direct and piercing, deep-set under dark straight brows, almost hidden in shadow except for a glint of light between narrowed lids. Extraordinary shock-waves travelled through her, and for an instant she knew the same unaccountable fear of a wild hawk before one who would be its master. Pointedly she withdrew her gaze, and brought her dazed mind back to the waiting prioress. Obviously some kind of apology must be offered.

'I beg your pardon, Reverend Mother. It took me longer than I expected to reach the angelica, and the watercress. . .' She looked at the wet patch appearing on her kirtle from the basket.

'And the tansies? Were we not to have had tansies too?'

'Tansies? Er, yes, I. . .er. . .' Ginevra looked at her arm, hoping that the bag left up on the sheep-pen might suddenly materialise alongside the basket. But it didn't. She knew that a lie would be worse than useless; before two pairs of eyes of such intensity, excuses had suddenly dried up at source. Ginevra noted that the stranger's eyes had not left her face, and felt suddenly as though her thoughts of David up there with the sheep had been laid bare for him to see.

Indeed, the noble guest *had* made a lightning assessment of the situation, had noticed the lovely, tear-stained face, the rich profusion of copper-brown hair. Like an elf, he thought, a beautiful water-sprite. Tears—and a lover, perhaps? The simple homespun working clothes in which she had been tending the herbs did nothing to disguise the slender, youthful figure, the firm breasts, long legs, neat ankles and wrists. Nor, he thought, had the winds of the hillside quite removed all the evidence of her quest from the mass of curls which had escaped from her braids.

'Ginevra. Go and take those to the kitchens. Then change, and come to my room as soon as you are ready.'

Keeping her eyes lowered against the knowing intrusions of the stranger, Ginevra dropped a curtsy of

obedience. But as she turned to go he stepped quickly
between her and the prioress and, bending as though
to pick something from the ground, held out his hand
to her. 'One moment, *damoiselle*. Allow me to restore
this to your basket.'

Ginevra turned in astonishment. She had dropped
no watercress. But as the prioress turned to go he
tucked something deeply into the wet green leaves,
meeting her eyes with his. He was no longer smiling.
She lifted her chin and held his look fiercely, annoyed
at this advance into her private dilemma. Then, on
silent bare feet, she swept away from him, aware that
her exit from the garden was being watched by narrowed grey eyes.

Once into the cool passageway between the herbarium and the kitchens, and well out of sight, she stopped
to examine the place where the stranger had placed his
hand. From deep down underneath several stems of
watercress her fingers eased out a small white ball of
wool-clippings.

Even without the accompanying slam of the door, the
line of her mouth and the angry gleam in her eyes
would have been enough to convince Rowenna of
Ginevra's annoyance. She knew her friend's volatile
nature better than most.

'Ginevra, where did you get to? Reverend Mother's
been asking for you. Have you seen her?' She stopped
suddenly, reading from Ginevra's face that perhaps
that was the cause of the annoyance.

'Rowenna, please help me get this lot off. I've got to
see her right now. Why are you not at supper with the
others?'

'Didn't want to miss you when you got back. I saw
you galloping down the hillside a little time ago. . .'

And she tugged Ginevra's kirtle off her shoulders and tossed it to one side.

'Have I got a clean one in the chest? Just look at my hair, Rowenna. What must they have thought. . .?' She realised before the words were out exactly what *one* of them had thought, and could hazard a guess at what the Prioress had thought too, though her face was habitually enigmatic.

'They?' said her friend. 'Who's *they*?'

'Who *are* they!' Ginevra stepped into the clean bliaud and pulled it up on to her hands. She grinned at her friend, but Rowenna continued unruffled.

'Well, who *are* they, then? She was alone when I saw her. Hold still, girl, I think this is back to front now.'

'She's got a man with her. A horrid man. Hope he's gone by the time I get there.' The thought of his masculine presence made her stand still in reflection for a moment while the memory of his eyes was superimposed on the wall of the stone-cold dorter. Why was she recalling the expression of his face while at the same time wishing not to see him again? She shivered.

'Come about the wool-clip, perhaps?' said Rowenna, helpfully, 'did he look like a merchant?'

'Ginevra rubbed her face with the damp cloth; the cold water and abrasive fabric whipped up an astringent retort. 'Yes. A trouble-merchant!'

'Ginny! You're not in trouble again, are you?' Rowenna stopped braiding the tangle of wild curls and pulled her friend round to face her. They looked at each other and a tiny frown wrinkled Ginevra's forehead. Then she smiled in reassurance.

'No, I'm just late again, that's all. Thank you for helping me, dear one. I'd better go now.' And she turned to the door. But Rowenna's voice halted her.

'By the way, where *did* you get to just now?'

Ginevra paused and shook her head slowly. 'Nowhere,' she said, closing the door quietly behind her. 'Nowhere at all, really.'

Her fears that they might not be alone were allayed as soon as she entered the Prioress's cool, austere room on the same side of the priory. A brief glance was all that was necessary.

The room was small and would have been crowded with more than two people in it, even though the only furniture was a high-backed wooden chair, a table, a prie-dieu in one corner and a small stool. On the table by the window a fine white cloth lay open, like a partly wrapped parcel. Ginevra had been in this room only a few times before. It had seemed to shrink as the years passed since her very first entry at the age of five. Then her mother had been with her too, and she had been tongue-tied and very afraid of being left with this white-clothed but gently spoken lady, even though she had been assured of twice-yearly visits to her family.

But the terrifying pestilence of two years ago had claimed both her parents as its victims, a tragedy which had not only robbed her of their love with brutal suddenness, but had also taken away the delights of her home visits, to which she had used to look forward with such joy. For now Alan, almost a stranger to her, had abruptly inherited all his father's duties on the manor and had made it quite clear to her on subsequent visits that he and young Royce needed no help from a convent girl fit only for fine embroidery, whatever her good intentions around the house and gardens.

'Ginevra. Will you be seated, please?'

Her curtsy had been acknowledged with an inclination of the head, but the gentleness of the invitation gave no indication of intent, for Ginevra knew from

experience that the Reverend Mother did not make it
easy for one to read her mind.

'You have been with us here at the Priory of Our
Lady of Aire for twelve years now, have you not, my
dear?'

'Yes, Reverend Mother.' Ginevra nodded assent,
wondering what this well-known fact was leading to.
Was the punishment for being late to be especially
harsh this time? A thought flashed through her mind,
too quickly to take the form of words, but just as
positive. She glanced towards the window opening on
to the same view as the dorter, further along from
where Rowenna had seen her come racing down the
hillside. And the stranger? The wool-clippings? Had
he decided to comment on this to his hostess?

If she knew or guessed the anxieties in Ginevra's
mind, Prioress Claire gave no indication, though she
had noted the glance. 'And now, Ginevra, you are
seventeen, and a young lady. Quite ready, I believe, to
take your place in the world.'

A pause and a look at Ginevra indicated that she
might reply, but for a long moment there was only a
bewildered look of incomprehension on the beautiful
elfin face. For her, the room was darkening visibly as
thoughts flowed and spiralled into each other like oil
and water. Her gaze roamed blankly round the small
room, and rested on pinpoints of light. Fine gold
threads peeped out from the white cloth on the table.

'Reverend Mother, are you saying that I must go
home?' she whispered.

'My child, there are many reasons why this has to
be. Since Sir Alan and the Lady Aileen died your
brothers have made do without you so that you could
complete your education. Now I feel we cannot allow
them to make this sacrifice any longer. . .'

'Sacrifice!' The word shot out before she could catch it. But on this occasion her interruption was tolerated with an almost imperceptible flick of the eyebrows. Ginevra continued, incredulous, 'Reverend Mother, forgive me, but you don't understand. My brother doesn't want me at home. He clearly resents my being there. He makes me feel like an unwelcome guest. Royce is too young to care. Since my parents died *this* has been my real home.' And her hand waved an arc into the tiny room. She covered her eyes to hide the new scene of domesticity which had just been thrust in front of her.

The prioress waited patiently for the hand to be replaced in Ginevra's lap, and looked at the stricken face, her heart's love flooding into the girl to whom she had been a second mother and tutor for twelve years. And now? And now circumstances had taken over once again, and the life of yet another girl was being dictated by fate and men in equal parts.

She shook her head and sat in the large carved chair, looking out of the window briefly. 'Ginevra, my dear, listen to me.' She brought her eyes back to the girl. Why was this time so especially difficult for her, after so much practice? 'Ginevra, there is a plan for all of us. You must believe me. Every move that God plans for us is in the right direction. I would not be revealing His plan to you if I did not believe in my heart that it was the right one. I understand more of this plan than you do, and you *must* trust me. There are many reasons why it is now right for you to leave us here at the priory and return to your home.'

Ginevra heard the words, but no more than that. Believe? What must she believe? Reasons? What reasons? What plan? What home? 'Does my brother know?' she asked in a dull voice.

'No, your brother has not yet been informed. One of the stewards will be sent to Scepeton Manor tomorrow to tell him, and you will go the day after.'

Still Ginevra's mind was a blank. 'What of my embroidery, Reverend Mother?'

'You have taught the younger girls well, and I have taught you all I know, Ginevra. They will be able to continue the work they're doing for the moment.' She looked at the package on the table. She had not answered the question, but Ginevra let it go.

For the second time that afternoon, on a day which had begun with so much warmth and sunshine, Ginevra's world turned cold and dark with numbness and pain. Standing before the prioress, she received her blessing with a bowed head and watched the gnarled hands disappear once again into the sleeves of the rough white habit, like rabbits scurrying down into a burrow for safety.

As the door closed behind Ginevra the prioress stood in deep contemplation for several moments, watching the evening light fade along the hillside. Her eyes travelled across to the yellow banks of tansies, and then upwards to where, in the distance, she could see the lay-brothers releasing the sheep from the pens in a flood of white, drifting downwards and dissipating like apple blossom in the orchard.

'Yes, it's time for you to go, little blossom,' she said out loud, and placed a hand lovingly on the package of gold threads brought by her afternoon guest. She smiled and turned to her prie-dieu.

CHAPTER TWO

THEY set off soon after Prime on a day which promised
to be fair and warm. The sun glowed rosily through a
pale green misty sky, like a peach floating in wisps of
gauze. It was not far to Scepeton Manor; John was
sure they could get there and back in time for sundown
if they started early enough, and the prioress had been
glad to comply with her steward's suggestion. She could
ill afford to do without three of her flock, even for one
day.

Rowenna had wept at their parting, but Ginevra's
thoughts had been too confused for tears and she had
been strangely silent, preoccupied, anxiety playing not
a little part in the wakeful hours of the last two nights.
She watched the white homespun back of Mother
Breda, the sub-prioress, swaying gently on the grey
mare in front of her as they picked their way along the
track to the bridge over the beck. John Hoby on the
bay gelding went on ahead while Sister Joan, the
sacristaness, was doing her best to manage the roan, a
battle of wits taking place over which of the two should
take command.

'Bless this animal, Ginevra, why can't he stick to the
track like the others?' Sister Joan pulled and kicked in
frustration. Once in the lead, however, progress and
peace were assured.

Ginevra settled down to enjoy the view of the sky
and the hillsides dotted with sheep, the warmth of the
new sun on her face and, most of all, the silence. Her
stocky dark brown pony of the fells was strong and

nimble and made a comfortable ride, even with her
bag bumping about behind her saddle. Not that she
had much to take home; two gowns and three bliauds
had been hurriedly washed and dried the previous day,
but they were serviceable and much-mended rather
than attractive. Money for new clothes had not been
forthcoming over the last two years.

The prioress had given her a tiny gold cross with a
ring at the top for a chain, with a special blessing for
her safety and protection, though on this glorious
morning it was difficult to see where any danger might
lie, unless it was of the moral variety. On impulse,
Ginevra swivelled round in the saddle to look back at
the priory for the last time, and then at the hills on
either side, the tiny white sheep now silently immobile
in their early-morning slumbers. She saw herself running up the hillside again, as she had done on that
particular afternoon, the sting of rejection now swinging her sharply back to the front again, setting her face
in the opposite direction and urging Blackie on with
her hands and heels.

The valley of the River Aire now lay before them,
flanked by steep limestone fells. The water glistened
like a winding silver thread in the valley bottom.
Ginevra moved Blackie up alongside Mother Breda's
homely figure, her gray mare's neck and withers level
with the ground, the reins hanging slack in the rider's
hands.

'Are you all right, Mother?'

'Why, sure I'm all right, m'dear,' she smiled. 'What
a day to be goin' home. We should be there in no time
at all at this rate.' And she grabbed at the reins as the
mare threw up her head at a rabbit which darted across
the track.

'Mother Breda, do you know why all this is so

sudden? I mean. . .' Ginevra faltered as the nun looked puzzled. 'I mean, why was this return home decided only two days ago? Couldn't I have been told sooner?'

There was a silence, broken only by the multiple plodding of hooves and the clink of iron shoes on stones. Then Mother Breda said, looking straight ahead, 'It's true, lassie, that you were not given much time to think about it beforehand. But it's a fact that we're going to have to send more people home before long.'

'More people? Do you mean the girls, Mother?'

'Aye, lassie. I don't quite know what it was that made Prioress Claire to send you home first. *That* she'll probably tell me when she's ready. But you know, it's getting more and more difficult to keep the priory going since the pestilence took so many of the sisters, and the lay-workers too. And then so many of the sheep got diseased last year, so the wool-clip is down again. And little money coming in.'

'But the girls' parents, Mother. Don't the parents still pay fees? Can't they be asked for more, to help out until things get better?'

'Ah, m'dear, the sickness hit everybody, not just us. All the girls' folks are havin' a bad time of it. Serfs runnin' away, demanding more pay because they know the lords have no choice. It's either that or no one to work the land for 'em.'

'What about my brother? Has he not offered to help out with a bigger fee, as my father did?'

'Your father was a fine man, Ginevra. We'll none of us forget his generosity. Of course, your brother's no doubt a good man too. . .' she added hastily, 'but the fact is, we haven't had a farthin' from him since Sir Alan and the Lady Aileen died.'

Mother Breda continued to look straight ahead, but

was aware of Ginevra's reaction of amazement. At last she looked at her, and noted the stony face, lips pressed together tightly against an outburst of angry indignation and hurt.

Mother Breda sidled the mare closer to Ginevra's pony and, leaning towards her, put a firm hand on her arm. 'Ye're not to be upset, lassie.' she said. 'Ye cannot judge people unless ye know all the facts. And no one can know all the facts except the people themselves.'

The facts, thought Ginevra bitterly, seem to be changing daily. What will the facts be, I wonder, when I arrive home? For the moment it was easier not to think, not to give in to speculation about her future, though the news of her brother's inability to pay her fees had sickened her. She sat heavily in the saddle, keeping abreast of Mother Breda, grateful for her company and for her silence.

They were on top of the hill now, having risen above the valley which wended in a curve over to the right of them. A steep drop down through the wooded hillside and into the cluster of huts known as Gargrave would take them about halfway to Scepeton. The sun was well up now and the horses were snorting with the effort as they drew to a standstill behind John.

'What about having a bite and a rest up here on top of the hill?' John turned to face them with rosy cheeks. 'The view is good from up here.' They sat for a moment, looking across at the ranks of misty blue-grey hills as far as their eyes could see, speechless with pride that they were a part of this landscape. The sheep, unconcerned by the intrusion, made tearing sounds at the rough, short grass, and the horses' legs shifted under their riders, reminding them to make a decision. Yes, a bite would be most welcome, they agreed, and the three women unpacked the hunks of oat-bread and hard cheese, and last year's apples. They munched together while John, his mouth bulging with food, pointed out the small town of Scepeton in the distance, just before the river went off to the right. Straining their eyes against the sun, they could just make out tiny puffs of smoke which pinpointed some of the outlying cottages.

Once through Gargrave and along the riverside again, it was not long before they caught up with more travellers, it being a Monday and the day when buying and selling of surplus produce could be done in the space in front of the castle. One jolly woman sat astride a flea-bitten fell pony, two piglets in a basket behind her being tossed from side to side like ships at sea. Another basket on her lap was piled with duck eggs in straw, and the two men with her kept up a banter in such broad dialect that Ginevra's spirits were lifted with each moment.

Their interest in her was apparent, for they lost no time in vying with each other to discover who she was and where she was bound. The woman, too, could not disguise her curiosity, noting her elfin beauty and graceful poise in the saddle.

'Scepeton Manor? Well, then, yer mus' be Sir Alan's lass!' said the elder of the two men. 'She mus' be Sir Alan's lass, Betty!' He repeated this discovery with delight to the woman on the pony.

'Shh! Sir Alan deed, yer fool! An't Lady Aileen, too! A wer reet sorry, m'lady, that yer fowks deed. Thi' were grand fowks. Reet kind, thi' were.' The woman, now discovering that they had a link, was happy to move closer to Ginevra's mount and personally direct the conversation. The men moved forward to chat with John, whacking two cows off the track on to the pasture of the riverside with a, 'Gern! Gerrup theer!'

'Aye, things 'aven't bin quite same wi' young Alan theer,' said the woman, consolingly. 'Ee's not like 'is father, is 'e? But 'appen 'is young wife'll sort 'im out, eh?' She leaned towards Ginevra, threatening to tip the basket off her lap, her wide smile showing gaps which outnumbered teeth.

'What?' whispered Ginevra. She reined Blackie in so sharply that the pony backed sideways, nearly unseating her. The woman halted on the track beyond and waited, looking puzzled, her smile fading. 'What did you say?' Ginevra whispered again.

'Holy Virgin! Yer didn't know, did yer? About 'is wife. It were only last week at t'market that I 'erd too, so it couldn't've bin long ago. P'raps three week?'

Ginevra struggled to keep her thoughts on a straight track, but they flew ahead and sideways like startled hens. Her hand covered her mouth as she gazed unseeing into the far distance, shaking her head, saying nothing. The woman leaned forward to take hold of Blackie's bridle, and led him on to close the gap.

'What is it, child?' Mother Breda's voice cut through the blankness of her mind. 'What's the matter?'

'Alan. He's got a wife there at home. Did you know?'

'No, lassie, I didn't. I would have told you if I had known.'

'But why didn't he tell me? Why didn't he send a message?' This time it was Mother Breda and Sister Joan who gazed into the far hills, for no sensible explanation occurred to them either, and their training as Cistercians told them that silence was preferable to empty words.

'Will there be more facts, Mother?'

'Aye, lassie, I've no doubt there will be. I think ye'll have to be prepared for that. Are ye strong?'

Ginevra nodded and dug her heels into Blackie's sides.

Through the centre of the small town, with its straggle of rough, heather-thatched huts and bustle of villagers buying and selling, the journey proceeded past the castle bailey and up into the open space of common land. Scepeton Manor was now only a short distance away, up on the wooded hillside east of the town.

Ginevra's thoughts were now as confused as they had ever been. It seemed to her that she was suddenly being drawn into some conspiracy of events totally outside her control.

Rough huts clustered along the track. Hens, ducks and geese littered the approach to the little stone bridge, moving away with affronted dignity as the clatter of hooves threatened to engulf them. The stone house stood four-square, deep into the hillside. Trees above and behind provided a leafy-green backdrop to the grey-white limestone while the paler orchard trees to one side shone brightly in the sunlight like a jewel in a darker setting.

Clopping hooves and the ring of iron shoes on the stone bridge alerted the Mallard household to the new arrivals, for no sooner had they halted on the cobbles than the heavy oak door was thrown open. A young woman emerged, whisking off an apron and thrusting it at the girl behind her. This, thought Ginevra, must be Alan's new wife. She was slightly shorter than Ginevra, though well-endowed with ample bosom and broad hips. She looked around twenty-five years old and her face was knowing and alert, framed by a spotless white wimple and veil. Her two blue eyes sought out Ginevra immediately, verifying what she had been told about her beauty. Smiling graciously, and greeting the more important guests first, she curtsied.

'Mother, this is an honour. I hope you're not too fatigued by your journey. And you, Sister. . .' She turned to Sister Joan, who was more than glad of the respite. 'You are more than welcome to our home.'

Our home, thought Ginevra. *Our* home? Mine, too, I wonder?

'And Ginevra! But how tired you look!' She held out her hands to her in greeting, and made a brief contact.

Her hands are warm and firm, Ginevra thought, but her eyes are cool.

Alan appeared behind them, looking older, now bearded and more time-worn than when they had last met at Easter-tide. 'Ladies, your pardon for not being first here to greet you. I was in the courtyard. Allow me to introduce my wife, Johanna.' He bowed courteously, and Johanna bobbed a second curtsy. Taking his sister by the shoulders, he greeted her last. 'Ginny. You're most welcome.' His kiss on her cheek was no more than formal, but his hands were firm. She would not mention his new marriage until he did, nor the new plans for her sudden return. She would behave as though nothing had changed.

'Thank you, Alan. It's good to be home again.' She looked around for signs of her younger brother. 'Is Royce not here?'

Alan looked enquiringly at Johanna.

'No, he went off to be with his friend, early this morning. But he'll be back by mealtime, I've no doubt.'

They all laughed, knowing the unerring accuracy of young boys' inner timing, and Alan led the way indoors.

John Hoby had paced the journey to perfection, for they were in good time for dinner, two hours before noon.

During the quiet but formally prepared meal, Ginevra was thoughtful, and took advantage of the others' conversation to observe, and to try to piece together some coherent whole. It was now quite clear that her earlier visions of taking over the running of the house and being of some long-term help to her brothers would now have to be revised. Not that she had any desperate desire to be head of a household, or to prove herself to be indispensable. On the contrary, though she had learnt various skills at the priory, the running of the household was a daunting challenge which she had anticipated more with trepidation than enthusiasm. However, the role of unmarried sister to a brother who was apparently in financial difficulties was not an enviable one. A poor dowry would not be much help. Only a life ahead of. . . Here, her thoughts drew a blank picture.

But the dowry? Could that be why he had married this young woman? She thought back to previous times during the last year. Of Alan's frequent visits to the Plunkettes' estate to see Elise, their eighteen-year-old daughter. What had happened there? she wondered. Had Sir William decided that he was not a good enough catch, with an estate depleted of villeins after the pestilence and no one to keep the demesne in good order? Johanna certainly gave the impression that she could run this place single-handed, but how big a dowry had she brought with her? Who was her family?

As if in answer to this very question, a young maid appeared in the archway at the bottom of the staircase, leading a frail old lady dressed in a blue gown figured with black. Her pale face reminded Ginevra of a piece oi wrinkled linen on which stitches had been sketched in pale threads. She watched in surprise as Johanna and Alan stood respectfully to accommodate her at the table and to make introductions.

'Mother Breda, allow me to introduce my mother, Elizabeth Benynge.' So, thought Ginevra, the family has come too, I see. For some reason Johanna omitted to introduce Ginevra to Elizabeth Benynge, but the old lady was not to be so uninformed about the new young face at the table, and took the duty upon herself.

'And you are Ginevra, I suppose?'

The omission had escaped Alan's notice, but not that of the two nuns. The message that Mother Breda sent to Ginevra along the table was clear. The tiniest flicker of an eyelid was enough for one who was used to interpreting signals instead of words.

'Yes, mistress.' Ginevra's voice was clear and confident. 'Yes, I am Ginevra. The second child of Sir Alan and Lady Aileen Mallard, and Alan is my brother. This has been my second home since I was sent to the Priory of our Lady of Aire to be educated when I was five. Are you on a visit here, Mistress, or do *you* now live here, too?'

The hoods dropped a little lower over the pale eyes but the glance did not waver. The lips pursed ever so slightly and then she blinked, slowly, like an owl, turning her head away as she did do. Ginevra peeped at Mother Breda again and recognised the sign of approval in her eyes, then carried on eating as though nothing had happened. She was sure that they could hear her heart beating and it took all her concentration to still the trembling of her hands. But the rest of the meal passed without incident, though neither Johanna nor her mother addressed Ginevra again.

* * *

The sound of hoof-beats faded away, and the three tiny figures grew even smaller as Ginevra stood waving on the cobbles. There would just be enough time for them to reach the priory before nightfall, God willing. She turned and walked into the house through the dark screens-passage which led to the inner courtyard, then turned into the great hall through the screens.

Johanna and Alan were talking together at the far end by the stairway arch, obviously arguing heatedly, but broke off as Ginevra entered. The old lady was nowhere to be seen. 'Ah, Ginevra, you'll want to see your room now,' said Johanna, as though Ginevra were a stranger to the place.

'I think I remember where it is, thank you, Johanna. Has my baggage gone up?'

'Ah, well, we've moved things about a bit, you see,' she went on quickly, to forestall any reaction from Ginevra. 'You're now in the second room at the top of the stairway.'

'I see. And who has *my* room?' Ginevra could already guess the answer to this, but saw no reason to spare Johanna an explanation.

'Ginevra,' said Alan, in response to a glance from his wife, 'we've had to make some alterations. Mistress Benynge has been given the one at the end of the passageway because it's bigger, and she has a maid, you see. You do understand, don't you?'

'Of course. I understand perfectly.' Ginevra's anger was curbed; she had no wish to provoke an incident, and knew that she must try very hard to smooth over any changes which had been made to accommodate the new elements of the family. For her brother's sake, she smiled. She expected she would have many years in which to come to terms with the situation. Meanwhile, she would refresh herself and then offer to help.

The room which had been assigned to her was next
to the big solar which overlooked both the hall and the
front of the house. Her old one was the second largest,
on the opposite corner at the end of the passageway,
and she quite understood why Elizabeth Benynge
would have preferred that to either of the two little
ones in the middle. Nevertheless, she was relieved to
reach the solace of a room — any room — where no one
could disturb her racing thoughts.

She leaned back against the studded panels of the
door and looked about her. This had used to be the
linen-room. She opened the doors of the huge oak
cupboard. It still *was* the linen-room! There, in neat
piles, were towels, sheets, hangings, pillow-beres, tapestry cushions, rugs and blankets, furs and linen table-
cloths — some of which she recognised. Closing the
doors, she noted the small bed and single clothes-chest,
the only other furniture there was room for in this tiny
closet, and which had obviously been put in there
especially for her use. She knelt on the chest and threw
open the casement window to let in the warmth of the
noon.

Outside, the grass grew profusely beyond the cobbles, and now encroached into every nook and cranny,
bestowing an unkempt and derelict air on the place.
Clearly the surrounding land had not been kept in trim
as it had used to be. Last Easter she had noticed that
the hay-cart left on the grass had lost a wheel; it was
still there in the same sorry state, and she wondered
whether it would be mended by the time it was needed
in a few weeks. She turned to sit on the chest and
began to rebraid her hair into one big plait. She must
get someone to bring her some water by and by. . .

* * *

As Ginevra reached the bottom of the stairway she could see that there was great activity in the hall, for Johanna had donned her apron again and was busily directing the laying of new rushes on the floor. At the same time she was giving orders about the candles in the huge iron holders lowered down from the rafters and overseeing the arrangement of new evergreen branches in the massive stone fireplace. She saw Ginevra at once.

'I wouldn't normally do this myself, of course, but we're so short-handed, and Alan can't spare anyone from outside. It's just as bad for him.'

'Is something happening?' asked Ginevra, wondering why there should be all this fuss *after* the departure of the two nuns, instead of before their arrival.

'Yes, indeed, something is happening,' said Johanna. 'De la Roche is up in the dales, overseeing his estates, and he's due here this day for supper.' She paused to clout a boy around the ears, scolding him loudly in exasperation. 'He's staying overnight, too, which is a nuisance, because now Royce will have to give up his room and sleep in the solar with Alan and me. If you hadn't been here he could have had the lin——' She stopped herself just in time. 'Your room.'

So, that was what the argument had been about. She wanted me to give up my room before I'd even got it! Ginevra smiled her sweetest smile at Johanna's discomfiture.

'Alan's only just remembered to tell me that the priory steward gave him the message yesterday—the nuns being here reminded him! I sometimes wonder what your brother's got up here!' And she tapped her temples in despair.

'But how would the priory steward know about it?

The priory is not de la Roche property; it belongs to
the Cistercians, like Fountains and Beesholme.'

'How am I to know how he knew?' asked Johanna
irritably. 'All I know is that this old lord is going to be
a mite displeased to see his land and property so run
down. It'll be a wonder if he doesn't turf us all out and
give it to somebody with some money to spend on it.'
And she bustled off towards the kitchen, her veil flying
behind her like a distress signal.

Ginevra sat on a bench by the wall and leaned back
against the oak panelling. She closed her eyes to the
activities around her and allowed the implications of
what Johanna had said to sink in. It appeared that
Johanna clearly understood the dire circumstances of
the manor estates, and so, thought Ginevra, presum-
ably she must have been aware of this when she
married Alan. What, then, had persuaded her to take
it on, knowing the risks involved, the lack of money?
Had it been desperation, in view of her age? And now
Sir Michael de la Roche was to see for himself the
extent of the problem. It would be no surprise to him
of course, as the sickness which had begun two years
ago had devastated the population, highborn as well as
low, and the effects on the workforce had been cata-
strophic, affecting castle, monastery, manor and hovel.

Ginevra thought back and tried to recall the time,
many years ago, when Sir Michael had been here
before. She must have been very young then, before
she was sent to the priory. Her vague recollection was
of an elderly gentleman, greying and severe, but with a
musical-sounding voice which had fascinated the little
girl so much more used to hearing the dialect of the
north. He must be quite old now, she thought, probably tired too, after his journeys round the dales.

The courtyard, like the hall, was being swept and tidied, and the stable block at the far side appeared to be preparing for a seige. Several horses were already tied up along the wall while men led out more to join them. Alan appeared, his hand on the rump of the grey being led out before him, his gown tucked up into his belt out of the way. 'Now, I want this cleared before the sun touches the chimney,' he shouted to the two lads, and he moved to the centre of the yard. 'And that's from where I'm standing now, see?' He bumped backwards into Ginevra and spun round. 'Oh, it's you! I'm trying to make some space for the de la Roche horses. We've been using the empty stalls for fodder, you see. What a business!'

He smiled sheepishly at her from under his sandy brows. His white-blond hair had wisps of straw hanging from it, making him look like a boy caught coming out of a haystack, and for an instant Ginevra was reminded of David, of his hair littered with wool-clippings. She wondered if he would ever notice her absence.

'I'm sure he'll be very impressed, don't worry.' She had meant it as a kindly reassurance, but was aware that it sounded faintly patronising. She would have to work hard at building up a new sibling relationship of easy talk, to be taken at face-value.

'Well let's hope so. Quite glad you'll be here at supper this evening to help keep the company entertained. Don't go away after the meal, will you? You can talk to him. Keep his mind off the problems. I expect he'll leave tomorrow. Now, lad. . .' He called to the boy with the horse, and strode away to give more orders, leaving Ginevra to say softer greetings to the chestnut mare she was used to riding whenever she was at home. It had obviously not occured to Alan,

thought Ginevra, that Sir Michael might want to discuss
the estate with him after supper.

The mare recognised her immediately and nuzzled at
her fondly. It was the first warm feeling of affection
she had felt since the departure of the two nuns earlier.
And the only one I'm likely to feel for some time, she
pondered, unless a miracle happens.

It was apparent that in the short time since her marriage Johanna's energies had been concentrated on the
inside of the house and only as much of the garden as
was needed for the daily supply of early summer
vegetables and herbs. Nothing much had changed here
since Ginevra's last visit, except that everything was
growing at an alarming rate, and that the workers had
dwindled from three to one.

'What happened to Giffen and Thomas?' she asked
the unfamiliar lad who was filling a huge basket with
leeks, peas, beans and small cabbages.

'Thi went off, mistress,' he said, barely looking up.
'Thi could get more up at t'castle in Scepeton, so thi
went!'

'What about their families? Are they still here?'

'Oh, no, mistress.' He stood up and looked more
closely at this singularly ill-informed person, puzzling
how anyone could not know. 'No, they've gone wi 'em.
Thi got werk up at t'castle, too. An' better pay.' He
carried on up the pathway to the bed of onions.

'But they're not allowed to leave here just like that,'
said Ginevra indignantly, looking at the overgrown
beds and then at the boy.

He grinned cheekily up at her, a bunch of slug-eaten
onions in his hand. 'Well, thar weren't a lot master cud
do abart it, wer thir?' And he went on with his work,

glancing at Ginevra's neat ankles as she picked her way past him towards the door of the orchard.

Without getting in the way of her sister-in-law, Ginevra made what contributions she could to the preparations, taking advantage of the overgrown herb garden to gather armfuls of lavender, sage, bay, balm and mint to sprinkle on the rushes in the hall. The pungent fragrance as the plants were trodden by the scurrying servants was refreshing, though Johanna made no comment on the improvement. Her arms were piled with scarlet and white linen cloths for the high table and, once these had been arranged to her satisfaction, and the great salt cellar placed in position, she was able to stand back and admire the effect.

It was while she was helping Ginevra with the beeswaxing of the trestles down the centre of the hall that Royce entered with his friend. His face lit up as he identified the copper curls of his sister, and in a few bounds he had enveloped her in a truly brotherly hug.

'Ginny! You're here!' he cried, his face glowing with pleasure. 'You're to stay this time, Ginny, are you not?'

She held his shoulders away from her and looked at his growing frame. Even since Easter-tide he had grown apace. Then he seemed like a chubby-faced child. Now, suddenly, his face was leaner, more defined, and she detected signs of manliness about his eyes and mouth already. Unlike either herself or Alan, Royce was dark and straight-haired, sturdy and large-limbed. He glowed with rude health, bringing with him the cool freshness of the moorland. Though their contacts had been of brief duration during his ten years, there was an affinity between them, a closeness of an indefinable nature which was much less apparent between herself and Alan.

'Yes, dear one. I'm staying. Introduce us, if you please.'

He stepped back, all dignified solemnity in an instant, and stretched an arm gracefully towards his young friend, who stepped forward, equally grave.

'Ginevra, this is my best friend, Alric. Alric, bow to my sister!' And he gave the lad a gentle shove in the small of his back. Entering into the spirit of the moment, Ginevra responded with a deep curtsy, and the three of them broke into childlike laughter at the sight of each other practising the ritual. The merry laugh warmed her heart in an instant, banishing the anxieties of the day. But Johanna brought them quickly back down to earth.

'Now, you young people, go up and change on the instant. Our guests will be here at any time and then supper will be served. You boys are to wait at table. Ginevra, you'll have to take your own water up today; I can't spare anyone. You boys, go and wash in the courtyard trough. Hurry now!' She dismissed them all, turning to the setting of the silver.

'Can't I help?' Ginevra asked, feeling suddenly like a child in the way.

'No, thank you. Except to remove that bundle of herbs from the stairway arch. I'm nearly finished in here.'

Ginevra picked up the lavender, southernwood and rosemary which she had reserved for placing in the clothes-chests, and went up the stairs. The decision about what to wear was not going to take very long, she thought. Nor did she expect that anyone was going to notice one way or the other.

CHAPTER THREE

In spite of her apathy about her appearance at the
main meal of the day, Ginevra could not help but take
a sensuous delight in washing herself and vigorously
combing her hair until it sparkled like pale copper. The
nuns had tried hard to banish thoughts of the body
from the girls' young minds, but to no avail as, in the
dark of the dorter, one could submit to the pleasures
of the mind with perfect ease. But the pleasures of the
body were, as far as Ginevra was concerned, merely
conjecture. There seemed to be so much, at this stage
of one's life, which was confusing—areas where
pleasure and pain seemed to become entangled and
indistinguishable.

She sighed, laid down the old ivory comb, and
plaited her hair deftly into two braids. Looping these
up on either side of her head, she silently mused
whether one day she might be allowed to borrow
Johanna's maid to create a more elaborate style. But
as it was her old fillet, the narrow circlet of gold given
to her on her tenth birthday, would have to be her only
adornment. She placed it over her hair and down on to
her brow, hoping not to look too unsophisticated to
their distinguished guest. Slipping her faded blue bliaud
over her shift, she took a long girdle of blue plaited
leather, crossed it round her waist several times and
tied it over her hips. A quick peep in the tiny scratched
mirror told her that there was little else she could do.
She was ready to go down.

From the open window, the sound of voices died

away from the front of the house, the clop of many
hooves now continuing round the side of the house to
the stables at the back. She peeped out and watched as
the procession passed under her window, little wondering that Alan's frantic preparations had been so urgent.
The retinue was big enough to take over the whole of
his stable.

A huge black stallion was being led by a groom in
green and black livery, closely followed by a train of
pack-horses laden with the baggage of the de la Roche
party. Clothes, food, wine, money, fodder and docu-
ments—everything that would be required over the
month-long visit to the out-of-reach estates high up in
the dales. Obviously a covered wagon would have been
a hindrance rather than an asset. But no mere straggle
of travellers was this. Every man wore the same livery,
with a tiny gold shield emblazoned on the breast and
back, and every horse was trapped out in the same
decorated harness, rugs with green and gold borders,
the de la Roche monogram in every corner. Clearly
this was a man of great style.

The lovely face withdrew from the casement, wearing a bemused expression. With grooms and servants
better dressed than she was, the master was sure to be
quite a peacock, who would not be impressed by a
country mouse like her.

The group was standing by the screens at the far end
of the hall talking, while Johanna, now dressed in
yellow, fluttered to one side. Alan, neat and stylish in
dull gold, was talking with a tall, elegant man, black-
haired and strikingly handsome.

Ginevra held on to the stone archway for support.
This is not possible, she thought. I'm dreaming. The
guest turned, picking up the direction of Alan's gaze,

and faced her. Then she knew that, without a doubt, this was indeed the man in the herbarium—Prioress Claire's guest. Unconsciously a slender hand stole up towards her cheek in a gesture of uncertainty, and then to her breast, holding it there over a heart which was suddenly pounding out of control, tightening her lungs. She walked towards the group as though in a dream, with no thoughts except that here was some complex mistake which she had no power to understand.

While her mind was whirling in space her eyes needed only a fraction of time to note that, once again, he was wearing brown and black, but this time they were the clothes of a traveller. The short brown leather tunic outlined his deep chest and narrow hips; the woollen cloak thrown over one wide shoulder caught thick locks of black hair in the folds of its hood. His long muscular legs were encased in black *chausses* and high, soft leather boots, presenting an image of power and dominance.

Alan was speaking 'Sir Jais, allow me to present my sister, Ginevra.'

'I am honoured, *damoiselle*. To meet two lovely ladies in such a short time is more than I deserve.' He smiled at her, his even white teeth contrasting sharply with the bronzed skin and black jawline beard. His eyes were glinting in conspiracy.

Somehow Ginevra managed a curtsy, and as she rose his hand went out to support her, holding her steadily with strong fingers, deliberately raising her hand high to lift her eyes to his. She looked into the deep, piercing gaze again.

'You are welcome, sir. But did we not expect Sir Michael? Is he unwell?' Her voice was unsteady.

'I am Jais de la Roche. I lost my father two years ago of the pestilence, as many of us did.'

'My condolences, sir.' She removed her hand from his and, feeling herself freed, moved away to one side. The pounding of her heart was slowing, though her limbs felt suddenly useless. He had not mentioned their previous meeting, and she wondered if he intended to keep it a secret between them. She hoped desperately that he would not let slip the circumstances of that afternoon.

But this was ridiculous, she thought. She knew that her inexperience of men put her at a disadvantage, but surely one need not be so affected by every man who turned up as a guest? But his eyes were too knowing, his body too arrogant and graceful, the touch of his hand too strong. Once again she was assailed by that feeling of affinity with a wild bird being lured to the wrist by a falconer, and she decided that while he was staying here she would keep well out of his way. She would have to go through the motions of politeness during the evening, of course, but after that she could disappear behind some newly discovered but critically important occupation. She wished that she had been able to bring some embroidery away with her. That would have been the perfect antidote.

It was a credit to Johanna's skill as mistress of the house that she was able to organise such a meal at short notice and, with a minimum number of servants, have everything running so smoothly. Ginevra was impressed, and made a mental note that once the guest and his servants had gone on the morrow she would try to discover how and where these skills had been acquired.

With Elizabeth Benynge on Alan's left and Sir Jais on Johanna's right, Ginevra felt that she had a good chance of remaining an observer rather than a participant. But she was not to be let off so lightly. During the ritual of the main meal—the finger-washing and drying, the carving of slices of game on to shared trenchers, the pouring of wine into goblets—there were ample opportunities for Sir Jais to engage Ginevra in snatches of conversation. His nearness as he leaned towards her disturbed her and she found that her normally healthy appetite had disappeared.

'*Damoiselle*, you are not eating?'

'No, sir. I think I need time for reflection more than food. I've had an eventful day.'

'I know you have.' His grey eyes caught the flash of wariness in hers.

'And you showed no surprise at seeing me here?'

'I am not in the least surprised.' His mouth twitched and Ginevra was suddenly furious that he appeared to be enjoying the prospect of recalling earlier embarrassing events.

'You know nothing of the circumstances, sir, I assure you,' she retorted, her voice as icy as she could make it.

'Alas, you are mistaken, *damoiselle*. I know more about the circumstances than you imagine.'

His face was close to hers, but she would not give him the satisfaction of moving away. If he was pretending that he knew about her visit to Brother David because of the tiny piece of fleece in her hair, well, he would have to do better than that to unsettle her. She felt his eyes on her while she struggled to find a reply that would put an end to this ridiculous conversation. Turning to face him she opened her eyes wide, adopting the most innocent expression she could muster, and looking at him sweetly said, 'One cannot possibly make a judgement until one knows all the facts. And no one can know all the facts except the people concerned.'

He threw himself back into the carved guest-chair and let out a peal of laughter from deep down in his chest, his white teeth flashing in merriment. When the chuckling had subsided he leaned forward once again. Tilting his head towards hers, he countered, 'Then I shall make it my business to find out all the facts, *damoiselle*!'

Ginevra was annoyed, and could not conceal it from him. 'Do you always have the last word, sir?' she snapped.

'Yes, Ginevra. I do. Always.'

She blushed and turned away, reaching for an apple from the bowl beyond. Her teeth bit angrily into it with a loud crunch and she knew that he was watching her, smiling.

Later on, when only the silver goblets, the ewers of wine and the huge silver salt-cellar remained on the table, and when the rest of the diners in the hall had withdrawn to the far end to talk, those at the high table rearranged themselves on both sides. Mistress Benynge had retired to her room and young Royce and his friend, after their duties at table, had gone to the kitchen to eat. Only Alan, Johanna, Ginevra and Sir Jais remained to discuss the estate, as had been requested.

'What you may not be aware of,' Sir Jais was saying to Alan, 'is that the tenants of those two manors died without leaving anyone in a position to look after them. And, since you are the nearest of my surviving tenants, it will have to fall to you to run them alongside your own until I can find someone else. They certainly can't be left any longer, or we shall find them occupied by the Scots one of these days, and *that* will be a difficult position to resolve.'

Alan looked sideways at Johanna and moistened his lips. 'Sir Jais, in normal circumstances I would be glad to have the benefit of two more manors but, as it is, I am falling far behind in my upkeep of this one alone.'

'I know. You owe me rent over two years.' His voice showed no sign of compromise.

'That's right, I do, sir. The situation seems to be getting worse instead of better. The wool-merchant won't give me credit for next year's clip in advance. Says it's too unreliable at the moment. I honestly don't know where the money's to come from, and that's the truth of it.'

Sir Jais sat back in the chair and moved his long fingers up and down the stem of the goblet, not answering directly. 'How did you manage to pay Ginevra's fees, may I ask?'

There was a silence while all four, knowing the answer, waited. At last, Alan merely shook his head and looked at the table. Johanna put a hand over his and Sir Jais turned his eyes to her, questioning.

'I brought a dowry, Sir Jais, but it was not substantial. Mostly tied up in lands. But there are so few people left to work them now that we haven't been able to cut our corn for two years, nor plant it.'

'And we lost our bailiff and the steward, both. And now more mouths to feed. . .' put in Alan, and his glance fell on Ginevra, almost accusingly.

Ginevra placed her hands on the table and pushed back her stool, humiliated beyond endurance by this catalogue of well-known disasters. She would not listen to any more, nor see her brother squirm before this man's stony face. But, before she could move away, an iron hand came down hard on her wrist and held it to the table. She pulled sharply, and gasped at this unexpected restriction of her freedom.

'Sit down, if you please *damoiselle*. This conversation concerns you, too, as part of the family.' Sir Jais did not look at her, but his face was grim and there was to be no argument.

Ginevra sat down again and the grip was slowly relaxed and withdrawn, but for some reason she left her hand where it was, watching the white finger marks slowly change to red.

'What about young Royce?' continued Sir Jais, looking at Alan.

'Yes, well, that's another thing.' Alan looked over his shoulder to make sure that the lad was not within earshot. 'It's always been understood that he would go into the Plunkettes' household when he was ten. But recently Sir William's been putting me off when I reminded him of the old agreement with my father. I suppose it's because of the money situation,' he finished lamely, looking at Johanna again. 'I don't know what to do about Royce. I haven't found a way of telling him yet.'

'And Ginevra?' said Sir Jais in the same voice. 'What can Ginevra do?' There was silence again.

This man's arrogance has gone far enough, she thought. Why should *I* have to account to him for what I do? She looked at him from the corner of her eye and saw his profile outlined against the dark-tapestried wall beyond, arousing inexplicable feelings of rebellion and a slight fear. As though to banish them, she made a quick movement of impatience, resenting even the thought of having to speak in her own defence.

His head flashed round in the same moment, and his eyes locked with hers, forbidding her to leave. She glared at him, eyes sparking, weighing his challenge, testing the ground.

'I can embroider,' she said in a deliberate voice, choosing the one of her skills that she believed he would value least.

'Is that all?' The question was put softly.

'No. It's not *all*. But everything else I can do is, apparently, just as useless and inadequate, and hardly worth mentioning.'

'I see!'

'Yes, I'm *sure* you do!' she retorted, her eyes still fierce.

Sir Jais glanced at her and then at Alan. 'And a dowry? Was there no provision for a dowry by your father for when Ginevra marries?'

Alan made a grab at the ewer of wine and poured some into his goblet, splashing it on to the white cloth. He took a gulp and then held it tightly on to the table with both hands, trembling a little. His eyes were hollow and sad as he looked across at Ginevra and his voice was barely a whisper. 'There was money put by, yes. But I had to use it a year ago.'

Ginevra let out a long, slow, audible sigh and her jaw clamped tightly shut. She looked down at her hands clenched together on the table and then relaxed, her shoulders drooping.

'Not even enough for a novitiate at the priory?' Sir Jais's question was put quietly, almost as an after-thought.

'That's enough!' Ginevra snapped. She sprang upright, her eyes blazing with anger. 'That's *quite* enough! There is no *question* of my becoming a nun, nor ever has been!'

To her surprise a smile played about his mouth, and his eyes glinted narrowly in appreciation. He nodded very slightly, looking at her. 'No, I didn't for a moment think there was,' he said softly. And this time he let her go.

* * *

Neither the excitement of the day nor the discomfort
of the bed prevented Ginevra from sleeping as though
drugged. It was far into the night when Johanna, Alan
and Sir Jais finally retired, but Ginevra heard nothing,
not even the giggles and pleadings of the two young
boys as they asked to be allowed to sleep downstairs in
the hall on a huge pile of furs. Mutual consent was not
hard to come by; servants were there to keep an eye
on them, if need be.

The sun was well up and streaming through the open
window when Ginevra woke at last, and she lay there
drowsily while the events of the previous day flowed,
jumbled, into her mind. One hand moved towards the
wrist which had been held so firmly and she brought it
up to see what effects there were. A line of four small
bruises showed along the inside and one more on top.
'Brute!' she whispered. 'How dare he command me in
my own home?' But the mocking eyes and cool gaze
stayed in her thoughts as she threw off the blankets
and washed herself from head to toe.

There was no sound from the next room, and she
wondered how soon Sir Jais would be leaving. Perhaps
he had already gone. A curious feeling of emptiness
accompanied the thought, and she looked again at the
marks on her wrist, cradling it between her breasts
while she saw again his hands and strong profile.

Downstairs, the hall had been cleared and cleaned,
the trestles and benches neatly placed along the sides,
and servants were replacing the silverware in the huge
cupboards under Johanna's careful eye. 'Good morning. Did you sleep?' she asked Ginevra amiably.

'Thank you, I did indeed—for much longer than I'm
used to. I think I was tired.' Ginevra sat on a bench
alongside, watching Johanna lock the cupboard doors
and wave the servants off towards the kitchen. She

replaced the key-chain under her apron and sat down by Ginevra's side, her hands playing with the neatly turned hem. She hesitated, looking sideways.

'I thought you were very courageous last night,' she ventured suddenly.

Ginevra turned to look at her, hardly believing what she had heard. The face beside her suddenly seemed less fierce, less aggressive. The voice had softened somewhat, too. Was this the same Johanna as yesterday? The Johanna she had thought of as an adversary even before they had met?

Johanna felt her long gaze and turned to her. 'I don't want us to be on opposite sides, Ginevra. I'd much rather we were friends than enemies, and it's clear to me how much you care for Alan. I love him so much, you see. . .' She bit her lips together and turned away. 'They told me how very lovely you are, and then when I saw you I felt I'd never be able to compete, that you were sure to be high and mighty. And so I thought I had to assert myself straight away. But I realised last night that I don't have to do that, that you're as embarrassed by this whole business as I am, Alan having made a mess of things so quickly after his father. . .' She came to a halt, watching her hands twisting the corner of the apron into a tight roll.

Ginevra quickly covered the twisting hands with her own and stroked them gently. 'Johanna, you and I both got it wrong from the start, didn't we? I saw you as competition, too, because Alan hadn't bothered to tell me of your marriage. . .'

'He forgot *that* too, the great ox!' expostulated Johanna. 'Just as he forgets most things. And when I found out he hadn't told you I thought it was because he was ashamed of me!' Her voice dwindled to a whisper and her eyes filled with tears.

'Ashamed of you?' Ginevra squeezed her hand and shook it gently. 'Not even my mother could have served up a meal like yesterday's supper at such short notice. I thought you were superb, and I'd made a note to find out how you do it!'

The two women laughed together, shaking their heads, and Ginevra continued, 'And as for being lovely that's only a matter of opinion. The truth is, I've never seen myself all the way down. Or even from side to side, for that matter—I can only see one eye or one nose at a time.' They laughed again, both of them wiping moist eyes with Johanna's apron. 'What did you mean about my being courageous? I was furious! That conceited oaf. . .'

'That's what I mean! I don't suppose he has many people standing up to him like that. I'd have liked to do the same, but it wouldn't have helped Alan if I had, so I kept quiet. As a matter of fact. . .' She stopped while Ginevra looked at her enquiringly. 'As a matter of fact, he was much nicer after you'd gone.' She stole a glance at Ginevra's wrist. 'Are those bruises there?' Ginevra held out her wrist to be examined. 'Mmm!' she said. 'He's very masterful, isn't he?'

Ginevra snorted. 'Well, he's gone now, I see, so that's that!'

'No, he hasn't!'

'What?' Ginevra turned to her sharply.

'He hasn't gone. He and Alan have gone off round the demesne to look at things. We talked a long time last night after you'd gone, and he seemed to have a lot of ideas about how he could help.'

For a moment or two Ginevra's heart beat like a blacksmith's hammer. He was still here. She would see him again. His eyes, hands. . . Quickly she pushed the thoughts aside, forcing her heart to return to its normal pace. Fool, she thought. He's on business. Remember?

'He said he would need to stay another night. Said he had some proposals to make. Of course, he's sure to want something in return, but I'll be damned if I know what more we can do that we're not already doing.' She looked round the hall as though in search of ideas. 'Come on, we'd better get a move on. It's a fish day today and I've got to check, or they'll not bring enough in.' And she got to her feet, smoothing her apron down.

'One thing, Johanna,' said Ginevra and she turned and waited. 'Your mother—she's very fierce, isn't she? Doesn't she like me?'

'Oh, don't let that bother you, Ginevra, she's grown crabby over the years. She's very ill, that's the truth, so I couldn't leave her alone. I had to bring her and Alan didn't seem to mind.'

'Of course not,' said Ginevra. 'Neither do I.'

Johanna smiled warmly, and immediately the two women had their arms around each other in a hug of mutual comfort.

The day was quickly eaten into by household tasks and preparations for meals. With so many extra mouths to feed, Johanna's skills were stretched to the limit, and Ginevra could only marvel at her capacity for organisation, well aware that her own inadequacies in this department would not have stood the test. She was now allowed to help in numerous small ways. Johanna discovered that one of Ginevra's abilities was as a herbalist, with well above the usual knowledge which any woman was expected to have in the use of herbs for culinary and medicinal purposes. She made an infusion of lemon balm and honey for Mistress

Elizabeth, which her maid took up to her, and she gave some to Johanna to try.

'Ah, what else have you put in here besides the balm?' Johanna sipped the warm honey-coloured liquid again, slowly.

'Shall I tell you? It's anise seed, pounded. For calm nerves.'

'Well, then, we'd better have a potful ready for after the meal. Have you made enough?' And the two women snorted and giggled in easy companionship.

This time Johanna had arranged for musicians to perform during the meal, hoping to demonstrate that even in hardship the Mallards knew how to entertain guests in the proper manner, though she would have liked to have jugglers there, too. But none had been heard of, or seen, for at least a year in these parts, so there was nothing to be done except hope that the de la Roche party would be impressed by the food and the hospitality.

In spite of her discovery that the pantries were not as well-stocked as they might have been, nor the larders, Johanna was nevertheless able to devise patties, pies and stews of every variety, containing fish of six different kinds. Vegetables were presented in delicate sauces, even using the succulent new cabbage leaves to make parcels with a custard sauce poured over.

For the tables Ginevra had made leafy garlands of ivy and ox-eye daisies which they laid along the edges of the high table. The effect was fresh and pretty, lending a festive air to the grandeur of the huge hall with the lofty oak-beamed roof and heavy old tapestries.

She was upstairs in the passageway when the party arrived in the courtyard amid clattering hooves and

barking dogs and the shouts of the grooms. She could
not resist peeping through the small window on the
inner wall of the passageway which overlooked the
courtyard, to see what was happening. The two men
were dismounting, Alan's blond mop showing white in
the late afternoon sun and Sir Jais's black mane swept
back from his face by the wind. Alan, though not small,
was a head shorter than his guest, but fine and lithe
like herself. More the greyhound type, they had always
agreed. Sir Jais was more like a wolfhound, Ginevra
thought—lean, powerful, muscular and elegant, but
formidable. Graceful in repose but ferocious when
aroused. Well, she hoped never to see him like that,
and he would be away tomorrow. But she could not
help wondering what today's explorations had revealed
and how he thought he could help. She hoped, for all
their sakes, that he would offer some useful suggestions
without the humiliating repetition of last night's
interrogation.

The question still remained about his reason for
being with the prioress at Our Lady of Aire on that
afternoon. She did not intend to ask him directly, for
that would surely indicate that she had been thinking
about it, and he was quite sure enough of himself
without any encouragement from her. His, 'Yes,
Ginevra. I do. Always,' and his intent look had brought
a blush to her cheeks which had made it patently
obvious to what *he* was referring, even though the
question which had provoked it was less specific. She
hoped that no such banter would come her way at
supper today, for she knew little about either recognising it or dealing with it. Such are the pitfalls of a
convent education, she mused, turning away from the
window.

In spite of anxieties regarding her personal role in

the household and in the future, Ginevra felt that her
relationship with Johanna had now been resolved
beautifully, bringing again to mind the advice of
Mother Breda about making judgements, which Sir
Jais had found so hilarious. Once this man has gone,
she thought, I shall be able to settle down to some
definite plan. Until then. . . .

His voice was heard in the hall below, nearing the
stairway, and in a flash she had let herself into her tiny
room and closed the door, her heart pounding. Would
she ever be able to control it?

CHAPTER FOUR

THE meal was a success. Johanna was more at ease and
looked glowing in a soft pink madder-dyed wool gown,
causing Alan to glance at her appreciatively more than
once during the evening. He appeared ruddy, and
happier than on the previous evening, and lost no time
in taking his part as the gracious host, having been
primed by Johanna not to forget any of his duties and
to make sure that the two boys attended the guests
with good grace and deference.

Sir Jais sought out Ginevra as though he too was
trying to redress the balance of last night. His calf-
length green bliaud was of an intricately figured brocade with borders of goldwork, a cypher of gold on his
breast and a gold jewelled girdle over his hips. With a
glow in his cheeks and the black hair brushed high off
his forehead, Ginevra thought he looked magnificent,
and found it difficult to adopt the air of nonchalance
she had been practising in the privacy of her room
moments before.

The cypher on his breast caught her eye. 'Did a
friend work this for you, or a relative, perhaps?'

'I wondered if you might notice, *damoiselle*,' he said,
smiling at her. 'A relative of mine did indeed work it
for me, many years ago. An aunt.'

'It's particularly fine, sir. Much better than anything
I could do.'

'That's not what I was led to believe, Ginevra. I was
told that you are the best broderer in gold that this part
of the country holds.' He watched her reaction like a

hawk, and her startled glance told him that she was alert to the dangers of recognising a mutual relationship which she did not want to dwell upon.

But her curiosity, roused by the compliment, lured her on. 'The Reverend Mother told you that?' she said in a low voice, with a quick look to the side to make sure that neither Alan nor Johanna could hear.

He nodded. 'The Reverend Mother is a very astute lady. She recognises a rare talent when she sees it.'

It was on the tip of Ginevra's tongue to retort, Then why did she get rid of me with such haste—was Alan the only one not to be able to pay his fees? But at this point she could not bring herself to delve any deeper, and so she looked down at her silver plate, aware that this had stirred up yet another batch of questions to add to all the others. But there was one question which could be asked. 'If you already knew of my embroidery, why, pray, did you ask me what I could do last night?'

'Let's say that I was curious to know how much you would co-operate in resolving your brother's dilemma. One needs to know how each member of the family rates its own abilities before anyone can help them. I wondered how highly you rated your skills as a broderer, and now I know.'

She realised that he was trying to make her feel uncomfortable, to put her at a disadvantage in view of her contemptuous admission that this was her only skill. She was not to have known until now that he appreciated the craft. Did this man always have the upper hand? Damn him! Did he take her for a fool?

Sir Jais well understood the reasons for the perplexed and angry frown forming between the delicate arches of her brow. He would have given much to be able to tell her more, but the ground was already shaky and his steps would have to be placed with extreme care if the bird was to be lured without losing too many feathers in the process. One or two hackles had risen already, he realised, because of his overwhelming desire to tease her, to make her flare up and reveal those flashes of fire in her eyes. But a strong hand and much patience would be needed to tame this one. The prize, he thought, would be worth all the effort. And he turned to accept a tiny frosted fruit from Johanna and congratulate her on a memorable feast.

The time for more talking came after the tables had been cleared and the musicians had gone. This time Ginevra and Johanna had decided, by unspoken agreement, to sit together opposite the men. Alan looked across at his wife and stretched out a hand to touch hers in reassurance while Sir Jais looked at Ginevra over the top of his goblet and wondered if he had ever seen anything so exquisite in all his thirty-one years. He knew that the next move was going to be critical. Even he could not predict with absolute certainty which way the bird would fly.

'Were things as bad as you expected?' Johanna looked across at Sir Jais.

He set down his goblet with care and regarded her openly. 'Yes, things *were* as bad as I expected, Mistress Johanna, but I believe that there are many things which could be done to put them right. Some remedies will be short-term, some will take much longer, and I don't think any of us will find them comfortable until they begin to work.'

His voice, thought Ginevra, is very like his father's— low, deep and musical. Sitting opposite, she was able to study his face as he spoke, and to watch Alan, too.

As this could hardly involve her, she could afford to relax, and observe.

'What have you in mind, Sir Jais?' Alan asked, making an effort to sound willing and positive, though he found it difficult to see how anything could be done without huge expense.

'Let's first deal with the things *you* can do. The villeins can hardly do a decent day's work, either for you or for themselves, unless they're given better conditions. They're living little better than animals down there in the village, with hardly a good ox-team between them and the land barely good enough, or *flat* enough, to plough up, anyway. And the land that *is* good enough is yours, and *you're* not getting it sown. It's clear that some rethinking's needed here.' He looked at Alan and Johanna intently, his steel-grey eyes glinting in the light of the newly lit candles.

Ginevra was fascinated by the way he spoke, moving his long, eloquent hands to emphasise the points— strong hands, and powerful.

He continued. 'There are plenty of big cots down there left empty now, since the pestilence, with crofts going to ruin. Let the others occupy them and spread out to grow more food for themselves. Let them cut into the forest edges for extra tillage——'

'You mean *assart*? Without payment?'

'Heavens above, man, yes! They can't pay you at the moment, but they'll certainly repay you by staying alive a bit longer. And another thing—pay them for the work they do on the demesne in *cash*, instead of in kind. And when they do boon work at harvest, too. That way they can buy what it is they need. They need to regulate their own lives; that's why you're losing so many of them!'

Alan was leaning forward now, taking this in with

interest. 'It makes sense, yes, but how do I pay them when money is so short?'

'I'll come to that, but meanwhile there is more that can be done. They need access to the woodland. No, I don't mean that stuff that they can reach by hook or crook from the boundaries or wherever, but good timber to build and repair houses and chattels. God knows, the woodland is extensive enough, and those poor devils are not going to harm it by taking just what they need.'

'Do you mean allow them to use the saw-pit as they need to?' asked Johanna. 'That saw-pit hasn't been used for some time by the look of it.'

'That's what I do mean, Mistress Johanna, and not only that, but let them gather firewood from the woods, too. There's plenty that needs clearing out of there. And let them have what small game they can catch, too; they need meat and skins just as we do.'

Ginevra was riveted with interest. It was obvious that Sir Jais had missed nothing in his day's scouting of the estate.

'But we've lost our bailiff, you see,' said Alan, 'and it'll be very difficult to put all this into practice without some kind of overseer.'

'If you were to accept my proposals, *all* of them, I would be prepared to leave you my own bailiff until you find a replacement.' Sir Jais looked at Alan intently. 'But this will depend on your agreement.'

'Would he keep the farm accounts?' asked Johanna. 'We couldn't expect to borrow your steward, too.'

'Yes. You and he could do it between you. You've shown yourself to be more than able at managing affairs, mistress, you could do the accounts for the estate, too. Now, my next proposal is this: as we've seen, it's obvious that the men who are left can't tackle the ploughing, sowing, reaping and repairing as well as all the work for *you* that they have to do—that's why nothing's being done properly—so the sensible thing to do is what the Cistercians do at Fountains.'

'Sheep!' The word bolted from Ginevra's lips like a startled sheep from a pen. Sir Jais glanced at her with a slow, amused blink, and she coloured.

'Sheep,' he repeated.

Alan stroked his beard, thinking how much easier this would be, especially on the poor ground. 'It only takes one or two men to look after fields of sheep, that's true,' he said. 'But where do I buy sheep with no money?'

Sir Jais poured more wine into his goblet and took a sip. 'That brings me to the things I can do,' he said, looking at them and glancing at Ginevra. 'But what I do will depend on what *you* agree to do. Let me elaborate. As I've said, I will leave you my own bailiff to help as long as he is needed. And I will pay his wages.' Alan looked at Johanna and smiled. 'I will fund you enough money to pay the villeins for shepherding, and for boon work, whenever you need them. No more payments in kind. All their surplus produce they can sell. This payment will continue until you can make the sheep a profitable concern.'

Johanna put her hand on Alan's and gulped. She was close to tears.

'I will buy as many sheep as are needed for the land on the estate—the bailiff and you can work that out. You'll have to get a lot of those useless strips enclosed and use only as many as you need to for oats.'

'And my debt of two years' rent? What about my debts?' Alan was speaking quietly, gripping Johanna's hand.

Ginevra saw that he was shaking. Sir Jais sat back in

his chair, and Ginevra watched, puzzled. Was this where he wanted some agreement?

Johanna broached the silence at last. 'You spoke of our agreement, Sir Jais. Did you mean agreeing to pay the debts first?'

'My agreement to write off your debts completely, and to carry out all my proposals, rests on one thing only.' He spoke very slowly and clearly while the three faces watched with intent, wondering what it was that he required for such generosity. He raised his eyes from the rim of his goblet and looked steadily across at Ginevra. 'The answer will be for you to decide.'

She frowned, utterly perplexed. 'Do you mean *me*?'

He nodded and held her stare, seeing flickers of alarm in her eyes. Without taking his eyes from hers, he spoke. 'Alan, I want you to give me the hand of Ginevra in marriage.'

There was a profound silence. Ginevra felt a dull thudding in her breast; she was not sure that she had heard the words correctly. Could she have mistaken him? But his eyes told her that she had not, for they held hers coolly, without wavering, implacable and resolute.

She gave an almost imperceptible shake of her head as though to wake from a strange dream, but his eyes never left her face. No dream, but reality. She was indeed being used as currency, to buy Alan out of his financial difficulties. The scheme was outrageous!

Unable to believe that this was even a remote option, but some malicious trick, she gripped the table as though reaching for an anchor and pushed herself back into her chair. 'Alan, no! No!' She looked wildly at her brother, who was sitting rigidly transfixed, looking at Johanna with wide eyes. He turned to Ginevra with the same wide-eyed stare and she could see the look of interest dawning behind the blankness.

Again, she cried, 'Alan! No!' the panic in her voice now showing. She was trembling as she turned to Johanna like an animal at bay, grabbing her arm and shaking it urgently, as if to wake her from sleep. 'Johanna, please! You mustn't let him! Johanna! Say something!'

Johanna leaned forward to speak, her voice hesitant. 'Sir Jais, do we understand you correctly? Are you seriously asking Alan's permission to take Ginevra away with you, to live as your wife? And this in return for all your proposals?'

'As usual, mistress, you have understood me perfectly.' The grey eyes were narrowed and watchful. The hands perfectly relaxed on the arms of the chair.

Ginevra sprang into action. With a bound she shot away from the table, like an arrow from a bow, to escape the implications of this preposterous demand. So this was what it was all about! The generosity. The grand benevolence. The saviour of the estate. The cheat! How dared he use her as a bargaining tool? How dared her?

'No! I tell you! This is *outrageous*! I will not be used in this way!' She was white and trembling with anger, totally oblivious of the interest from the other occupants of the hall.

'Ginevra,' said Alan, 'we can discuss it. . .'

'Discuss what you like but leave me out of it!' she yelled.

Johanna stood up to put an arm round the distraught girl's shoulders, but Ginevra wheeled away to the end of the hall and out through the screens, leaving all eyes but two looking after her in concern.

Johanna sat down again opposite Sir Jais's impassive face and looked at Alan.

'She's not going to accept it,' said Alan, shaking his head mournfully. 'She'll never accept anything like that.'

Johanna was not so sure. 'Why do you say that, Alan? Do you really know her that well?'

'We've grown apart, if that's what you mean. I can't deny it. And I've used her ill—parting with her dowry and all. But now she'll feel doubly ill-used, and I can't say I blame her. She's a sensitive wench.'

'How highly does she value the manor and the estate?' asked Sir Jais, leaning back in his chair.

'She values the family, and she knows the seriousness of the position, but she's never had the thought of marriage brought so close before. Living in a convent for twelve years hasn't prepared her for *that*, the way a yeoman's daughter is.' He looked at Johanna and squeezed her hand, a fleeting smile in his eyes. His sigh hung in the air. 'Perhaps I ought to go and find her. . . to explain. . .'

'No! Let Mistress Johanna go to her when she's had time to cool off. Then I'll go to her myself.'

'Lord, sir. Don't *you* go to her! She'll tear you to shreds. I know what her temper's like, and you're our guest!'

'I can handle her. It's best if she doesn't have too long to think about it.'

Johanna intercepted the decision. 'Don't you think you should give her a little more time?'

'No, mistress. I don't have any time. I must leave tomorrow. It may be months before I get up this way again, and our agreement rests on Ginevra's accept-ance. No more, no less.'

'But isn't it a little unrealistic to expect her to agree

to such a proposal at short notice? She's unused to the ways of men, sir.' Truly, Johanna thought, Ginevra's acceptance would save the situation now threatening the future of the estate, but at what price? Could anyone reasonably expect a woman to decide an important question like this at a moment's notice? And her an innocent convent girl, too? She shook her head.

'It may appear unrealistic, Mistress Johanna, but greater decisions than this have been made at short notice to save a homestead and family. And as for being unused to the ways of men, well, that problem will take care of itself, I believe.' His look was so final, his logic so unanswerable that neither Johanna nor Alan could reply to it.

'Perhaps I should go and speak with her,' said Johanna, and both men stood as she left them.

'You have a very capable wife there, Alan.' Sir Jais poured himself a little more wine. 'Now, let's discuss the details, shall we?'

'You mean. . .? Details? You're so sure of the answer, then?'

'Of course. She would not have reacted like that if she'd thought there was nothing to think about. And as long as she thinks that there is, I can persuade her to agree.'

'You think so?' Alan looked more hopeful.

'I know so!'

Outside in the orchard the air was gentle and balmy, the sun now a rosy glow through the branches of the plum trees. Tiny clouds of midges danced in the last light of day, and the kitchen cat on the wall watched with mild interest as the figure ran through the trees, sobbing with distress and trembling violently. In a shadowy corner by the wall, Ginevra sank into the grass, pulled the golden fillet from her hair and drew her knees up to her chin. Rasping sobs broke from her tight chest, then the flood was loosed and she cried as though her heart would break.

Gradually her shaking body eased, the sobs slowed down, and she leaned against the stone wall, feeling its coolness against her hot back. The moon was still pale in the evening sky and she noted its serene beauty, absorbing some of its stillness into her breast.

'To be bargained with,' she growled between ragged breaths. 'To be used as payment as though I were a sack of flour, or. . .or a hen! And he expects that I'll embroider his clothes, does he? He thinks it might be useful to have a broderer around. And he can tell everyone his wife is the best broderer in the north! Wonderful!' Now words were replacing tears, tumbling out after days of confusion and uncertainty, tumbling through her hair and hands as she angrily twisted the hem of her gown into a knot. 'Well, I'm not. And I won't!' she whispered through clenched teeth. 'Alan can find a breeding-sow to pay him with.' Tears welled up into her eyes once more, blotting out the figure of Johanna, who sped silently through the grass towards her.

'Ginny! Oh, Ginny!' Johanna knelt in the grass by her side, using her brothers' pet name for her. 'Do you want to talk to me?'

Ginevra shook her head. 'No, Johanna. No, I don't.' An arm went gently round her shoulders and the two friends leaned against each other, the elder one gently rocking and soothing like a mother.

In contradiction to her words, Ginevra could not contain her fury. 'It's so undignified, Johanna. To be *used*! I'm a person. With feelings. Doesn't he understand that? Surely he can see that I'm not to be traded for someone's debts, just because I could be useful to him. I know arrangements like this happen, Johanna, but surely it doesn't have to be like this, does it? Alan doesn't want it like this, does he?'

Johanna's silence caused Ginevra to draw away and look at her sister-in-law's face in the fading light. '*Does* he, Johanna?' She was incredulous.

'Men are not like us, Ginny. They only know what they want and how to get it. They don't concern themselves too much with what it feels like. And, when they suddenly see a way of getting what they want on terms that are favourable, they don't waste precious time observing codes of chivalry. They pounce.'

'Are you talking about Alan. Or. . .him?'

'Both of them.'

'But I'm the one who has to make the decision,' Ginevra said, anger surfacing once more. 'And whichever way I decide, I lose! Is that fair?'

'Are you sure you'd lose, Ginny, if you married him?'

There was a silence while Ginevra struggled to understand her.

'What do you mean, Johanna?'

'Are you not a little in love with him already? You know that marriages like this happen all the time. It has to be like this for us. We're part of the property. But one can usually discuss it in a businesslike manner after a meal.'

Ginevra was indignant. 'Oh, Johanna. I can't bear the man! You've seen how arrogant and domineering he is. He's shown just how devious and scheming and ruthless he can be——'

'And he's shown how much he's willing to pay to get you, too,' said Johanna, cutting her short. 'It's often the other way round, remember.' Sir Jais had asked for no dowry, no settlement. Nothing.

'But he only wants to make use of me to adorn his clothes, and to keep some kind of hold over you and Alan—can't you see that?' She would not make it easy for herself. The newly discovered longings of her body must not be allowed to have a say in this affair; they were too untried, unreliable, unwanted.

Johanna laughed softly and ruffled the coppery curls. 'Idiot!' she said. 'He could buy a good broderer ten times over if *that* were all he needed. He wouldn't have to marry her, or him, would he?'

Ginevra heard Johanna's argument, but still refused to give it a place, knowing that it did not suit her own brand of logic. It might be too near the truth, and to admit it might give this trespassing stranger yet one more advantage over her. No, she would not fly to that lure. She untwisted the knotted hem of her bliaud and looked at it.

'What do you think I should do, Johanna?' she asked in a low voice. 'I don't believe for a moment that he cares anything for me, and I care *nothing* for him. But I don't know what to do. You and Alan can't do without his help.' More sobs rose to the surface as she spoke.

'I can't advise you what to do, Ginny. The decision rests with you. You have all night to think about it. He'll be going tomorrow, with or without you.'

'He said that?'

'Yes. But I'm quite determined that Alan shall not put pressure on you to accept if you feel that you can't. Are you going to come inside now?' She got up and brushed her hand down the pink gown and arranged her white wimple.

'No, I'll stay here awhile and come in through the

side door. Goodnight, Johanna. . . It was a lovely
meal. . . I'm sorry it ended like this again.'

They embraced, and Ginevra turned to lean on the
plum tree, listening to the first hoots of an owl in the
trees beyond the house and watching Johanna slip
through the gate at the front end of the orchard. She
turned to the tree and wrapped her arms around its
trunk, her mind still in a turmoil of conflicting thoughts
and emotions. What had Johanna said? Was this awful
ache in her breast—this fear, this anger—was this how
love felt? Wasn't it supposed to be blissful and happy,
sweet, gentle? And yet the image of his eyes burning
into her as he said those words stayed with her. His
wide shoulders—such strength—the determined jaw
and firm mouth—and his lips, how would they feel?

But with no experience of a man's body, nor of the
way his mind worked, there was little on which to build
her imaginings, no yardstick by which to measure her
own emotions. Her feelings were in total confusion—a
desperate wish to discover, conflicting with an equally
desperate wish to fight and flee. The longings of her
body surfaced, undefined but strong, only to be pulled
down again by her fear of the unknown. Her scanty
knowledge of how things should be did not allow that
there could be other ways, more unpredictable ways,
even violent ways of entering a state of loving. Now
she had been assailed too suddenly. The sight, sound,
smell of him had stormed her still girlish dreams and
turned her, overnight, into a woman, lighting her
daydreams with a flood of reality and rendering the
brightness too uncomfortable to bear. A man was for
fantasy, she thought, for illusion. The reality was
frightening, far too frightening, and she wanted none
of it.

She clung to the tree, pressing her cheek against the

rough, lichen-covered trunk, feeling its rigid firmness through her gown. She saw his face imprinted on her closed eyelids, his eyes sparking into hers—cool, grey, masterly. To live within arm's reach of this man for the rest of her life? Impossible! No!

She pushed the tree away from her and turned. There, standing just a little way in front of her, hands hanging by his sides at perfect ease, head erect and looking directly at her, was Sir Jais. Her hands flew to her breast and she glanced to see which way would provide the easiest means of flight. But he had seen the glance and his body anticipated the move before she could decide. In one stride, he was in front of her, with his hands on the low branches at each side of her head, and now there was no way for her to turn without brushing against him. His masculine nearness, so new to a girl of her inexperience, was like a torch burning through her thin gown, setting fire to her will and robbing her legs of all strength. Her eyes full of apprehension and anger, she could see the angle of his fine cheekbones and jaw in the pale moonlight. She saw the straight nose and firm lips, relaxed but unsmiling.

'Why the tears, Ginevra?' he asked quietly, not moving. She turned her head away sharply, looking stonily beyond his wide shoulders into the darkened sky. She remained silent. Why should she be required to explain how she felt to this insensitive brute? He must *know* why the tears.

'Answer me,' he said.

Stung by his insistence, she faced him defiantly, grabbing at the tree behind her, hoping that the feel of its rough bark on her hands would ground her fear of him and give her some strength to hold on in this contest, for surely she felt that it was an ill-matched one.

'They were tears of anger, sir, not pity, I assure you.'

'Anger? Are you angry to receive an offer of marriage, Ginevra?'

'I did *not* receive an offer of marriage,' she retorted, fire flashing from her eyes and glinting in the moonlight. 'I received an ultimatum. Either to see my brother lose the manor or to spend the rest of my life with someone I dislike intensely. Just to embroider his clothes for him! What kind of an offer is that, may I ask?'

'You may well ask, *damoiselle*. I am not used to making offers of this magnitude. But I believe it is a fair one, in the circumstances.'

'You asked my brother, not me!' she spat out, her hair tumbling angrily over her face. 'And I am not my brother's property to exchange for his debts!' She brushed her hair away with a trembling hand, held a fist to her mouth in a childlike gesture of distress, and a hot tear of anger stole down her cheek.

Sir Jais removed his hands from the branches and held her fist away, wiping the tear with one finger. He was now so close to her that she could feel his breath as he spoke. 'I think that Alan was not asked to exchange you in that sense, Ginevra. I am presenting to all of you a way out of your difficulties. After all, as the owner of the property, I am willing to invest in it. This keeps things in the family. Would you not prefer it to be that way?'

She felt his nearness through her woollen bliaud, and desperately wished to escape from its effect on her. His hand, still holding her clenched fist, was pushing all sane thoughts from her mind. 'You are still using me as currency!' It was all she could think of to say.

He touched a copper curl on her shoulder and wound it round his finger. Smiling into her eyes, he teased her gently. 'And what a currency! Newly minted!'

His flippancy infuriated her and she twisted herself away from the tree, resolved to put an end to the discussion. It was obvious to her that if he would not see the situation from her point of view, there was no more to be said. But if she had thought that he would step back to let her go she had misjudged him. She had walked away from his company three times already, and that was not to be repeated yet again. She found that she was now being held tighter by his hand on hers. All teasing was gone from his eyes, and she was being obliged by the firm finger under her chin to look at him. She had never before been held so by a man.

'I am offering you my home and security, Ginevra.'

'In return for *what*, sir?' Her eyes glared into his.

'I have need of your skills,' he said, his mouth set and grim. No mention of regard, nothing about caring for her, no tenderness. How could Johanna possibly have thought that she might entertain the idea? In love? Nonsense! She would be glad to see him go!

'But I, sir, have no need of yours!'

The wild throw-away words had been intended to disarm him, but it was too late to realise that they could have the opposite effect. As though a spring had suddenly been released, his grasp on her wrist tightened as he drew it in hard to his chest. She pushed at his shoulder as she was seized by the mass of hair at the nape of her neck and her face pulled to his. Her lips parted with the shock and the pain, but she was held immobile, helpless.

'I must disagree with you yet again, *damoiselle*. There is at least one of my skills that you very much need at this moment.' His mouth came down hard on

hers, blotting out the sky, the moon, the newly born
stars, the sounds of the night.

Her first impulse was to fight, but her hair was
gripped firmly by his relentless hand and there was no
strength left in her now. She felt nothing but his mouth,
his lips searing into hers, and the hard pressure of his
chest against her. At last the kiss softened, and he
raised his head from hers, letting go of her hair and
supporting her as she fell limply against his shoulder
with a whimper. She had ceased to think. The impact
of his brutal kiss had robbed her of all reasonable
thought and now she could only clutch at his arms to
keep herself from falling.

Thoughts which had been confused before were now
blurred and grey, sinking into the darkest corners of
her mind like shadowy ghosts. The hard pressure of his
body, the pain of his hand in her hair and on her wrist,
the searching of his mouth on hers were all she could
remember. They had nothing to do with decisions, only
touch, taste and smell—physical sensations which had
never before been stirred in this way. She found the
experience, after all that had gone before, had drained
her will, sapped her strength, breached her defences.
She could not look at him.

'Oh, no! I don't know. . . Please. . .let me go. . .'
He held her until she had regained control of her legs
and stopped trembling. 'Please, let me go in now. I
can't think any more. . .'

With her hand in his, he led her out of the orchard
and round to the front of the house.

Aware of her dishevelled appearance, she stopped
him by the entrance to the great hall and pulled away,
alarmed. 'I can't go through there to my room,' she
said in an urgent whisper. 'The servants. . .they'll
see. . . I don't want them to see me like this. . .' She

looked up at him in the gloom of the passageway, hoping that he would understand without the need for more words. Her eyes pleaded, but his grip on her arm did not relax. His proud head went back and the power of his firm hand flowed through her. He shook his head.

'Ginevra, I do not creep into my own property through a side door, especially at night with a lovely woman. The servants' thoughts are no concern of ours at this moment. Come!' He looked down at her and held out his hand gracefully, like a courtier.

She placed her hand in his obediently, and he led her without haste through the parting groups of servants and grooms, who shot respectful glances in their direction, but not a sound was heard.

Johanna and Alan had retired to their solar, and preparations were being made for sleep as Sir Jais escorted Ginevra up the stone staircase to the door of her room. Turning her by the shoulders to face him, he saw her large brown eyes in the dim glow of the candles on the wall. She looked exhausted by tears, but now more calm and dignified.

'Look at me, Ginevra.'

She lifted her eyes to his, too tired to refuse, too worn by arguments to raise more ammunition. He noted her aquiescence with a nod. 'You will give me an answer in the morning. If my offer is accepted——' he looked at her intently '—if my offer is accepted, we shall depart for York tomorrow. Things will then begin to improve for Alan and Johanna.'

'And if your offer is not accepted?' She tried one last weak attempt at rebellion.

A smile tweaked at the corner of his mouth. 'Good-night, *damoiselle*.' He opened the door of her room and she felt a gentle but firm hand in the small of her back.

Johanna had thoughtfully left two candles burning on the chest and by their light Ginevra took her polished mirror and stared at herself. Lovely? Both of them had said so. She looked long and hard at her worn face, her swollen lips and tousled hair, then shook her head slowly and closed her eyes. Nothing made sense any more. These were her last thoughts as she fell on to the bed and curled up like a child. Then sleep came.

In the next room Jais listened for the sound of movements, and then lay for a long time staring up at the flickering shadows made by the candlelight on the beams above him. His thoughts were of her soft body and the mass of rich lustrous hair in his hand as he had kissed her, of her fire, her volatile passions which would not be easy to understand, nor easy to handle. But he would make her come to him, one way or another, just the same.

CHAPTER FIVE

THE habit of waking at first light had not deserted
Ginevra so soon. She was aware, on this bright summer
morning, that new vibrations were quivering inside
her, that everything had changed within the space of a
sunrise and a sunset. She tried to remember what had
happened, and on which day, and how. Sitting in the
narrow bed, the memories of last evening flooded back
into her mind, painfully jumbled with a delicious
sweetness. With her two hands pressed tightly beneath
her breasts she savoured the moment of remembering,
seeing Sir Jais's head bending to hers and feeling his
hand on the scruff of her neck. One hand stole round
underneath her hair to explore, rekindling the pain and
pleasure of his grip, and to her surprise she became
aware of a liquid melting sensation in her thighs. She
drew her knees up beneath her chin and tightly hugged
them together while she toyed with the images before
her, playing them over to herself like the favourite bars
of a minstrel's song.

Gradually other memories crowded in, reminding
her of the decision she would have to make. 'You will
give me an answer in the morning. . .' This was enough
to propel her out of the daydream and into action.

'Don't be too sure,' she muttered under her breath
as she stripped off yesterday's clothes and flung them
into a heap on the bed. 'Don't be too sure that I'm
going to fall in with your well-laid plans. I have my
own plans too, I'll have you know.' Precisely what
these plans were, Ginevra had not yet decided, but

71

that didn't interrupt her reasoning at this point. Why should it? She would think of something, no doubt.

The lid of the chest creaked as she groped inside for a clean bliaud, and the thought occurred to her that marriages to very wealthy men could provide women with unlimited numbers of clean clothes every day. Slipping on her last clean shift, she realised that she would have to attend to the problem of clothes before very long. The soft cream woollen bliaud was all she had left to wear. She looked around her for the gold fillet; it was nowhere to be seen. In exasperation she realised that it must have been left in the orchard, dropped from her hand when. . . Damn the man. Slipping her shoes on and leaving her hair loose, she slipped quietly out of the room.

The kitchen cat lay in her arms like a baby, playfully tapping her curls as she carried it into the orchard. She laughed at its antics.

'That's better, I think.'

She gave a start. The cat leapt and somersaulted on to the ground, leaving Ginevra's arms empty in the air. Sir Jais was leaning against the same plum tree where the two had had last night's encounter, his arms folded across his chest. She could not help noticing that he was wearing his travelling clothes, and how shapely were his muscular legs in the brown *chausses* and soft leather boots.

'You here!' Ginevra exclaimed.

'As you are, *damoiselle*. Have you come to give me your answer?'

The idea that she had come to search for him, and here of all places, was too ridiculous. Did he really think. . .? Her eyes opened wide in astonishment. 'No, sir, I have not! I came only to look for. . .' He was holding up her gold fillet, a smile of pure mischief on his handsome face, dappled by the early morning shadows. 'You *knew* what I had come for,' she snapped.

He cocked his head to one side, watching her. 'I'm not sure which I like best—the laughter or the fierceness. But I must not anger you so early, must I? In case you change your mind.'

'You are mistaken, sir. I have not yet given the problem any thought.' She stood motionless in the damp grass, feeling very vulnerable with the slanting rays of the sun directly illuminating her face while his was in dappled shade. She would not move to collect the circlet of gold from him, but she knew that he would enjoy watching her walk away, delighting in her chagrin.

'Is it such a problem, Ginevra?' He turned the circlet around in his hands.

She would not give any answer to his question. Either way would leave her open to a quick response which she was fully able to anticipate. 'I must speak with Alan and Johanna,' she said, and she turned to go, totally at a loss how to handle the situation. Why did he always seem to have the advantage of her? she wondered, annoyed with her own inability to be as calm and relaxed in his presence as he apparently was in hers.

'Your fillet. Will you allow me to put it on for you?' She made no answer, nor did she move from the spot, but half-turned towards him and waited. He came towards her and lifted her chin very gently with one finger, until she was obliged to look at him, then he placed the gold circlet over her thick sparkling hair and down over her brow. 'There,' he said softly, leaning back a little to judge the effect. 'Finest English gold-

work. Are you still very angry, Ginevra?' He looked
searchingly into her eyes and waited until she could
form a suitable reply.

She sighed, and looked away into the distant hills,
still covered in early morning mists. His question
prompted her to assess her emotions once more, but
she found it impossible to be direct. Confusion, bewil-
derment and fear swirled around her still, even in the
pure light of dawn, and this could not be expressed
easily, if indeed at all, to a man who was expecting a
straightforward answer to a simple question. Even if
she had been able to explain herself, *would* she? To
this man? A stranger? Surely these feelings were so
private, so tenderly new, that to drag them out into the
light of day would shrivel them, dry them up before
they had been given the chance to take shape? No, no
sense in trying to explain the subtle nature of her anger
to a man like this. How could he possibly understand?

'I don't know *what* I am. I don't even know who I
am. I only know that I'm being passed from one place
to the next before I've had a chance to draw breath.
Other people appear to be directing my life before I've
had a chance to direct it myself.' She remained gazing
across at the misty hills as the sun turned them to
mounds of gold, and went on speaking, as though to
herself. 'I love this place. I would have loved to have
been allowed to spend my childhood here, but that
choice was not mine to make. I suppose I have gained
in other ways, but I'm not sure how right it is to remove
someone from the rest of the world, year after year,
and then plunge them back into it again, expecting that
they'll know all about it, about people, about
things. . .'

'What things, Ginevra?' He watched as she turned a
little towards him, her eyes moving slowly upwards

from his feet to his shoulders, lingering on his throat, his mouth, and finally his eyes. Her glance dropped as it reached the summit and she turned away, embarrassed that he had so easily read her thoughts and yet relieved that she had no need to give them voice. 'You have advantages that many others do not have, Ginevra. You have intelligence to learn quickly. You have courage and good health.' He did not mention her beauty, knowing that she would not regard that, at this moment, as being in her favour. 'It would not take you long to adapt to a new life; you were about to make that change, anyway, when I put my proposals to your family. This new one simply moves things on one more step. Don't regard changes as barriers, Ginevra. They're really more like stepping-stones.'

She turned and looked at him sharply at these last words. Stepping-stones? The image in the priory fields only a few days ago came clearly into focus. Water, lit by the rosy glow of dusk, swirling around the stepping-stones leading across to. . .the herbarium door. . . where he was. . . Yes, *he* was on the other side. Her face swung round to face towards Airedale and the priory, her body slowly following, erect, tensed, alert to the vibrations in the air between the image and herself, drawing it to her once again for a second impression. Quivering with receptivity and forgetting to breathe out, she stood, absorbing the message. Stepping-stones, not barriers. The image had told her this, but she had not understood then.

Sir Jais waited in silence, sensing her inner struggles, her readiness for flight like a wild bird. He wondered how far he could press her. She turned at last, letting out a huge lungful of air slowly as her eyes met his, and he felt that the crisis was passing, that a resolution

was imminent. This was the moment to press home the
advantage.

'Of *course* others will direct your life, if you allow
them to. If you're afraid of change, stay locked up in
the hills, safe in your burrow.' He saw that he had hit
the mark as she responded in a flash.

'And you, sir? You would direct my life, if I allowed
it?'

His voice was suddenly harsh. Challenging. His eyes
held a dangerous gleam. 'I would direct *your* life,
damoiselle, whether you allowed it or no!'

A surge of excitement tinged with fear bolted
through her limbs as she remembered the force of his
kiss and his hands on her, the support of his hand as he
led her through the hall, uncaring and bold, despite the
stares. Rational thought seemed far away. Something
else quite inexplicable had taken its place, something
which knew no rhyme nor reason. For several moments
she was lost in time, her eyes searching his for a sign of
compromise, of weakness. But every line of his face
told her of ruthlessness, dominance, mastery. Without
a doubt he would use every means to direct her life;
she was quite sure of that.

She was never able to explain, either then or later,
the strange impulse which took hold of her. As though
in a dream, she took his right hand in hers, and
removing the golden circlet from her head placed it on
his upturned palm. She watched his grey eyes darken
as they met hers, and knew that he had understood.

In reply, he removed a huge gold and topaz ring,
and taking her right hand in his own placed it on her
betrothal finger. It was so large that he had to close up
her slender fingers to stop it falling off.

'Say the words, Ginevra,' he said quietly.

'I. . . I don't know what I have to say. . .'

'You say, "I, Ginevra Mallard, vow to take thee, Jais de la Roche. . ."'

'I, Ginevra Mallard, vow to take thee, Jais de la Roche. . .'

'". . .to be my husband, when the time comes. . ."'

'. . .to be my husband, when the time comes. . .'

'". . .and thereto I plight thee my troth."'

'. . .and thereto I plight thee my troth,' she whispered, trembling.

'And I, Jais de la Roche, vow to take thee, Ginevra Mallard, to be my wife, when the time comes, and thereto I plight thee my troth.' His arms went round her, gently this time, supporting her, and his mouth was tender in a long slow kiss which made her swoon with its sweetness. She drew a ragged breath against his mouth as it ended, her eyes still closed.

'I'll make you pay for this,' she whispered. 'I swear I will.'

He tightened his arm about her slim waist and a low rumble of laughter began in his throat. 'Do your worst, *damoiselle*.' The words were growled against her hair. 'Now do your worst.' He released her, and tucked the golden fillet down inside the open front of his chainse, next to his breast. Then, taking her hand, he led her out of the orchard.

She found her brother and sister-in-law in their solar, sharing a brief meal before continuing their daily tasks. They greeted her with surprise.

'I came earlier to your room to find you,' said Johanna, rising to welcome her with a hug. 'But I supposed that you must be outside in the garden.'

'No, I've been to the orchard to look for my fillet.'

Alan glanced at her head and frowned. 'You haven't found it?'

'Well, yes, I found it, and then. . .' She paused. 'Then I lost it again!' she added in a rush, knowing that it would make no sense.

Johanna looked sideways at her. 'Come and have something to eat.' She ushered Ginevra to a stool and pushed a small round of bread and some honey towards her, pouring some milk into a beaker. 'Now, what's all this about? Did you fly off the handle again, last night, at Sir Jais?'

'You knew he'd spoken to me, then?'

Alan spoke. 'Ginny, I wanted to talk to you myself last night, to tell you how sorry I am. This whole business is. . .' He stopped, lost for the words to describe how he felt. The impression of inadequacy that he knew he presented was too acute for him to explain. 'But Sir Jais stopped me. He said it was best if you didn't have too long to think about it. . .' He caught the frowned look of warning in his wife's eyes as she broke quickly into his words.

'And so we haven't had a chance to say that you mustn't feel that we want you to go. If you're really so much against the idea of marrying Sir Jais, we'll find a way round it. . .somehow.' Her voice was kind, but lacked conviction.

'Don't say any more, please.' Ginevra brought her right hand from underneath the table where she had been concealing it, and opened her palm flat out in front of them. The ring glowed warmly in the early light of the morning. She twisted the stone over on to her knuckles. 'It's too big for me,' she whispered as she looked at it, 'but Sir Jais has told me that he will have one made to fit me properly.'

Alan and Johanna were speechless as they tried to take in the implications of the ring on Ginevra's hand, but Alan's thoughtless words still sounded in her head.

'He said it was best if you didn't have too long to think about it.' And she wondered what else Sir Jais had said before his secondary assault on the ramparts. He must have found it a relatively easy conquest, she thought angrily. All over. Vanquished within a few hours! How he must be congratulating himself on his victory after the final skirmish this morning. Was this really the way men regarded the business of winning a woman's hand? They pounced, Johanna had said. How right she was!

Johanna was puzzled by the defiant look on Ginevra's face, and mistaking it for resignation she was quick to sympathise. 'Oh, Ginny! I'm so sorry. Truly, I'm sorry it had to be like this. Was he very objectionable? He didn't threaten you, did he?'

Alan jumped up, knocking his stool backwards with a clatter. 'If he threatened you that's an end to it, right now! *Did* he threaten you, Ginny?'

'Shh! Please.' Ginevra put a restraining hand on his arm. 'No, it was not like that at all. He was not discourteous. Really!' And she remembered again the feel of his hard body as he had kissed her. 'Damn! Damn the man!' Her little fists came down hard on the table with all her force. 'Damn him!' she shouted. The wooden platter and earthenware beakers jumped, making ripples of light on the smooth surface of the milk.

Johanna guessed what had taken place and gestured with her head to Alan to leave them alone. He picked up his belt and leather tunic and went out, closing the door softly behind him. Women's talk, he supposed. But what a relief that things would now be put in order. The estate would be properly managed and, with luck, begin to make a profit again. He headed towards the courtyard to find Sir Jais to congratulate him. Easier to talk to men, he thought to himself as he walked down the passageway with a lightened step.

The two women regarded each other across the table, their eyes speaking volumes. Gently, Johanna's hand stole across to Ginevra's and enclosed it warmly, opening the way for words.

'What have I *done*, Johanna? What *have* I done?'

'Do you want to tell me about it, pet?'

'I just suddenly felt that it was the right thing to do. By the Holy Rood, Johanna, I don't know why.' She shook her head and her eyes searched Johanna's for a possible reason. 'He talked to me of stepping-stones. . .'

'Stepping-stones?' The voice was incredulous.

'Yes, stepping-stones rather than barriers. Changes. . . You know. . .'

Yes, Johanna did know. She understood and nodded.

'Then, oh, I don't quite know what was said, but I challenged him, and he took up my challenge. I should have known he would. He was so fierce. . .and yet so strong. Reliable. Secure. Somehow it seemed just right to put myself in his hands. . .' She spread out her hands on the table helplessly. 'I took off my gold fillet and put it in his hand. I had no ring to give him, but he understood what I was doing. And straight away he gave me the ring from his hand. He had no betrothal ring either, Johanna, so he couldn't have been any more prepared than I was. And then we joined hands and repeated our vows to wed each other when the time comes.'

'And then you kissed?'

'Yes. Why? Is that important?' She had a feeling that it was.

'Yes, it *is* important, Ginny. What you have made is
a contract to marry at some time in the future. You
could, if you both agreed, legally break the contract,
unless. . .'

'Unless? Unless what?'

Johanna looke down at their hands entwined before
them, and her fingers caressed Ginevra's in uncertainty. 'Unless your vows are consummated. Then
they're irrevocable.'

Irrevocable? Consummated? The words fell weigh-
tily into the sunlit stillness of the room, swinging
backwards and forwards in Ginevra's mind like lead.
She pulled her hands away and gripped the table.
'Consummated, Johanna? Do you mean. . . ?'

Johanna regarded the perplexed face before her, and
realised that this young woman knew even less about
the ways of men than she had already suspected.
'Ginny, there's no need to be afraid. Yes, that's what
it means. You go to bed together. Alan and I did it
that way before we were married, which is why, I
suppose, he forgot to tell you about the wedding. It
isn't all that important compared to the betrothal and
the consummation, you see. Only the tying of the knot,
that's all, in church or wherever. Some folks don't even
bother to go *that* far. But the consummation makes it
legally binding, Ginny. You have to know that.'

'Then he's going to want to. . . ! Oh, Johanna, I
don't know what happens! I've never been able to
discover.' Her voice was already tinged with panic.

'Listen to me, pet. It isn't appalling. When you love
the man it's wonderful. . . Oh, damn!'

A knock sounded at the door and Alan poked his
head round, grinning from ear to ear. 'May we come
in now?'

They groaned inwardly and rose to meet the two

men, knowing that this was, at least for the time being, an end to their conversation. Compared to last evening's discordant meeting, however, this quartet was more in harmony. While healths were drunk, and congratulations given, handshakes and kisses exchanged, Ginevra stood quietly, the new thoughts of her recent conversation with Johanna now aligning themselves alongside Jais as though trying them on like a new suit of clothes. His two kisses—one brutal, one tender—were still fresh in her mind. What more was there to know? she wondered, looking at him through her lashes. He was quite relaxed—obviously he had no concern for what lay ahead—his handsome head thrown back in laughter as Alan spoke to him, his long fingers spread across his slender hips above the tooled leather purse-belt, strong and elegant. How would they feel? she mused.

As if in answer, one hand reached out and gently took her wrist, possessively easing her to his side. Ginevra met his gaze boldly.

'We have to make a start within the hour, Ginevra. Are you ready?'

'Ready? No, sir, indeed I'm not! I haven't even begun!'

They laughed. 'You see how it will be?' said Alan. 'They're never ready when you are. . .for anything! Better get used to it!'

Jais's eyes twinkled at her embarrassment. Her brother's meaning could not fail to be understood. 'I intend to get the abbey by suppertime. We shall have to move soon.'

'Johanna will arrange for food to be packed, I know, and Ginevra. . .' Alan smiled at her kindly. 'I'm having your chestnut mare made ready for you. You can take her with you. She's yours!'

Ginevra kissed him warmly in thanks, and went to her room.

'Now,' said Jais, 'about young Royce. . .'

All at once the cobbled courtyard seemed to be a mass of animals and humans as young Royce and his friend Alric bounded in to see the preparations and to claim their ponies from the stables.

'Don't be taking Ginevra's chestnut mare,' Alan shouted to them. 'She's going to be needing it soon.'

They brought out the ponies, which had been out in the fields for the last few days, and tied them to two spare rings in the wall. Throwing the saddle across the back of his pony, Royce caught Alan's eye, but ducked out of sight to catch the girth under the pony's belly. Something in that look made the elder brother suddenly wary. He walked over to the lads.

'Where are you off to, exactly?'

'We're on an errand.' Royce looked sheepish.

'Where?'

'To the priory of Our Lady of Aire, if you must know.'

The words caught the ear of Sir Jais, and he turned to join Alan, full of curiosity.

'Why?' said Alan. 'What business do you have at the priory?'

'I'm afraid I'm sworn not to tell you,' Royce replied, doing his best to look at his saddle with a stony face, now aware of the attention he had atttracted from Sir Jais.

'Then you need not break your oath,' said Sir Jais, and as quickly as lightning pulled Royce's leather pouch and strap over his head and arm before the lad could resist.

'No, sir! Please do not, I promised Gin——' He

stopped and looked at his friend. Alric shrugged and shook his head. From the pouch Jais extracted two sealed letters of folded parchment, and held them up for Alan to see.

'One for the Prioress Claire, and the other. . .for David!' The two men exchanged looks. Alan was perplexed, but not Sir Jais. 'Well, I see no reason why you should not take this one, my lad,' he said, handing the pouch and the letter for the prioress to Royce. 'But as for the other, don't worry, I can deliver that very quickly myself.' And he tucked the letter to David into his own pouch and walked back to finish his business. *Now* what is the wench up to? he wondered, smiling to himself. What game is this that she plays?

Ginevra smiled too, from her vantage point in the upper passageway outside her room. The window overlooking the courtyard had given her a perfect view of the little scene down below and she was secretly delighted that her quickly hatched plan had given Jais something to think about. 'Well done, Royce,' she murmured as she watched the two lads trot out.

She turned to go down to the hall with Johanna, giggling. 'It worked. Now we'll see if he's so cocksure about things.'

'Ginny, you're playing a dangerous game. You don't know what he'll do when he's angry, and that's not a very subtle way of finding out.'

'Heavens! What could he do? There's nothing in it. I told you. Never was.'

'He could beat you!'

'Beat me?' Ginevra halted on the top step. The idea that he could be so angry, angry enough to beat her, had not occurred to her. Would he? 'You don't think he would, do you, Johanna? Really?' Her voice had lost its lightness now.

Johanna turned and looked up at her with eyes wide open, serious and honest, and her voice was quiet and grave. 'Some men do, you know. Had you not thought about it, Ginny?'

Ginevra sat down slowly on the step, her hand on the stone-cold wall. A shiver ran down her spine, raising the hairs on her arms and head, sending tremors into her thighs like a cold wintry breeze. She hugged her arms across her body, remembering the pain of his hand in her hair, his vice-like grip, his fierce look before he had kissed her so brutally. And she knew that Johanna was right, that *she* understood Sir Jais and his kind in a way that Ginevra herself did not— yet. For the second time within the space of a day Ginevra asked, 'What shall I do?'

Leaning against the wall, Johanna took a long look at the girl she had come to admire and felt pangs of pity for her innocence. A convent education of twelve years was hardly the grounding one needed to cope with a man of Jais de la Roche's character. Though, in truth, he had willingly taken on a handful in Ginevra, too. An interesting couple, she thought, almost smelling the scorching of wills.

'I think you'll find, Ginevra, that if the worst comes to the worst you'll know what to do. Don't anticipate problems. Be aware, but don't summon them up like demons to plague you.' She could see that the girl was full of doubts and anxieties. So would anyone be, being moved along at this pace. She regretted that she had drawn attention to the possible outcome of Sir Jais's anger and, cursing herself for a clumsy fool, went on down, leaving Ginevra deep in thought.

How long she sat on the cool stone stairway with her thoughts, Ginevra had no way of knowing. It was as though, at the moment of departure, something still held her back, forbidding her to leave.

Alan had appeared, briefly, to tell her that all was now ready, that her luggage was in place, that Sir Jais was waiting, and she had assured him that she would be with them presently. But she had not moved. The darkness of the stairway was like a heaven, cool and quiet, a place where the bustle and hurry of preparing for a new life could not intrude.

A figure blocked out the light at the bottom of the stairs and her heart lurched, sending messages to fly while there was still a chance, but knowing that it was already too late, that his long legs would reach her even before she had turned.

He spoke very softly, a whisper almost. 'Ginevra, come!'

'I can't!' she whispered back. 'I can't!'

'You're in your burrow, Ginevra. You told me earlier that you'd decided against it, that you had courage enough for the change.' He was moving very slowly towards her, speaking gently, as though to a frightened animal. 'Are you afraid?'

She would not say so, but her eyes glowed in the dimness, telling him of her unease. 'You're a stranger to me. And you're expecting me to quickly pack my bags and go with you and a whole lot of other strangers——' she waved her arm towards the hall '—to heaven knows where, just because you and Alan think it's a good idea. Well, *I* don't think it's a good idea! Go away! You disturb my peace!'

She heard the low chuckle and saw his teeth gleam as he came towards her, placing one foot on the step at her side. His face closed to hers and she felt the hard stone wall behind her head. Her hands shot up to ward him off but he caught her wrists and held them together

behind her back. Then, slowly but firmly, he lifted her
to her feet and pressed her against the wall. Their faces
were level, his eyes glinting directly into hers, twinkling
with amusement.

'I disturb your peace, *damoiselle*? Good. Then if I
were to disturb you yet more, we might be able to
begin our journey at last. Do you think?'

She struggled against him, but her feet on the narrow
step had nowhere else to go and she was held firmly as
his lips moved to take hers. Her wrists were released
at the same time, but it was too late. His kiss melted
all thoughts of resistance, both physical and mental.
Like a rich wine, it suffused her veins with a glowing
warmth and her mouth with the taste of surrender;
long and deep and unceasing, it took away her will, her
doubts, her intransigence.

At last he released her, and she saw the grey eyes
regarding her so closely that she thought he was going
to repeat it. 'Now, Ginevra. Are you ready to go with
me?'

She nodded, subdued.

He waited for a moment, reading her eyes, then,
holding out his hand to take hers, he repeated his first
command. 'Come!'

Out in the bright sunlight, as the cavalcade waited
impatiently to be away an almost audible sigh of relief
rippled through the company as Sir Jais led Ginevra
through the stone porch. She was still subdued as she
bade farewell to Johanna and Alan, hugging them
silently while holding back the tears to be losing a new
friend so soon. But the light banter between Alan and
Sir Jais eased the tensions while the liveried servants
looked on, amused but respectfully silent. Ginevra was
swung up into the saddle—now polished to match the
bridle—the mare's mane and tail braided with green

ribbons, the glossy coat like burnished copper. Jais's huge black stallion towered above them, rolling his big dark eyes and snorting with superiority to impress the mare.

Ginevra watched Jais spring lightly into the high roomy saddle and take his reins deftly, confidence written in every line of his body. His deep kiss still tingled on her lips and she could not help but wonder how a man could be so unaffected, so nonchalant after that. Had he done it so often? Was it something and nothing to him?

'Ready, Ben? Dickon? We'll be off, then!' And, with a last quick word to the bailiff he was leaving behind, he allowed the two head grooms to get the cavalcade under way, the clattering hooves almost drowning out the sound of the last farewells. At his side, Ginevra turned in the saddle to wave until the low branches of the bend hid her family from sight and, at last, set her face towards the east, and York.

As though sensing her preoccupation with thoughts of change, Sir Jais stayed alongside to talk to her, pointing out herds of deer on the edges of the wooded hillside and a tiny waterfall in a high ghyll, like a fine silver thread. Hares went hurtling across a field and hawks and the odd eagle hovered above the fells, looking for prey. Their journey eastwards was, he said, one which without pack-horses would have taken them only one day at a good pace. But as they had started off rather late, he intended to make a more leisurely progress and stop for the night at Beesholme Abbey, where the party had stayed on their journey into Airedale. They should reach there, he thought, by supper-time.

'You ride well, *damoiselle*. Have you had the mare long?'

'About four summers, sir,' Ginevra replied, stroking the chestnut neck. 'Will I be able to keep her near me?'

'Indeed, you will. My Negre has already taken a fancy to her.'

Ginevra had already noticed the sidling and prancing going on between the two, aware that it was only Jais's strong hands and legs which prevented the stallion from taking the odd bite at her mare's neck every so often. She laughed in agreement, looking sideways at the huge black beast, thinking how appropriate it was that they were both mounted on animals of their riders' colouring.

How alike they look, she thought, these two black beasts—how proud and fearless. In response to her thoughts, she pulled herself erect in the saddle and fingered the gold cross around her neck, given to her by the Prioress at their parting. Inappropriately, she wondered how she might fulfil the oath which she had made after her betrothal. Plenty of time to think of something, she thought.

CHAPTER SIX

PLENTY of time, indeed, were plenty of time needed. But here she was, sitting astride her frisky mare, both of them raring for a good gallop, the open moorland in front of them and on every side. What could be easier? She knew this country better than Sir Jais or any of his men, knew that once through the narrow winding gorge, where rocks rose high on one side and almost vertically down on the other, the track led through a small dark forest and out on to rough moorland. This was common land, belonging only to the villagers in the area. This was the limit of her knowledge, for this was the extent of the lands belonging to Scepeton Manor. By noon, she supposed, she would be obliged to excuse herself and seek a private place away from prying eyes, and by that time they should be in just the very spot. She smiled, almost seeing herself flying freely across the turf, alone, unencumbered by strangers.

Her smile did not go unnoticed for, despite his nonchalant air, Jais was well aware of her ability to plan some way of escape; it went hand in hand with her courage, her still smouldering anger and her good horsemanship. Somehow, he felt, he would have to put their contract on a more permanent basis as soon as possible, for he was sure that the situation had been explained to her, just as Alan had mentioned it to him during the course of their discussions. And yet. . . He glanced sideways at her. And yet. . .she was a virgin, tender and sensitive for all her fiery ways. It was not his way to ride roughshod where a gentle hand would achieve more in the long-run. Outright brutality was not the way to tame the bird.

The climb up to the narrow gorge was long and arduous for the well-laden pack-horses and progress was slow, but once they had embarked on the narrow track on the other side of the steep hill there was no place for them to stop. Dark, fern-covered slopes scattered with mossy-brown boulders of millstone grit rose above them on the right while the valley dropped away steeply to the left, then rose up again on the other side. On the skyline the bare rocks glowered at them, cutting out the sun and bouncing eerie echoes back to them. Progress was just as slow going downhill as it must have been coming up, and so the rewards of rest and food were welcomed with puffs of relief on the open ground before the forest.

'Come, *damoiselle*.' Jais held out his hands. Loosing her feet from the stirrups and throwing her leg forward, she allowed herself to be lifted down while the mare was led away to be tethered. 'Sit here.' He placed a sheepskin against a boulder for her, and she sat obediently, taking the chance, while he spoke to his men, to look around her at the possibilities. This was the ideal place, she was sure. She would wait until they were all at rest, and then take the mare and fly.

Johanna had packed a splendid feast, all the more acceptable for being in the clear open air which lent an extra succulence to the little meat and vegetable pasties, the cheeses and last year's fruit, the oatcakes and slices of cured fish. After the silence of eating came the barely concealed belches and leg-pulling, mingled with a few fake snores, the men knowing full well that nobody would be allowed the luxury of sleep so soon.

Ginevra wished that this had not been so, for it would have made things easier.

Seeing that Jais was still eating, his arms resting on his knees, she felt that this was the ideal time. She stood and brushed the crumbs from her gown.

'I trust that you will excuse me, sir. I need to be private for a few moments.' And she turned to move away. To her consternation Jais immediately stood up, casually leaving his food aside, to follow her. She stopped, nonplussed. 'No, sir. I need to be. . . .' She pointed towards the forest. This is absurd, she thought, I'm not even going to get near the mare with him alongside me. Perhaps he did not understand. 'I need to be alone, sir!' She spoke low but clearly, standing in his path. Surprisingly, he took her arm in his hand and turned her to walk towards the shade of the trees, and she was marched along before she could wrest her arm free of his grasp. In two strides she knew that he had seen through her ruse and a spurt of white-hot anger overwhelmed her. His cleverness, her impotence! Damn the man! She veered violently away from him and towards the mare. She would *not* be deflected in this high-handed fashion! But he was fast, and once again she was caught in his iron grasp and whirled round to face him.

'No, Ginevra!' His expression was adamant.

She chose to pretend to misunderstand him. 'You mean, I can't be private? Anywhere?'

'I mean, *damoiselle*, that you don't need your mare with you on this occasion, and I mean that you will have *me* to protect you. I hope my meaning is clear?'

She was furious. Her eyes blazed with anger that her plan had come to nothing and that he should have anticipated her. It was just as galling that she would now have to suffer his presence, even though her chance of escape from him had been removed.

'I do not need *your* protection, sir!'

But now it was his turn deliberately to misunderstand. 'Very well, I'll get some of *them* to protect you instead.' He nodded his head towards the group of men, beginning to turn towards them.

Ginevra caught at his arm. 'No!'

He stopped and waited, his expression still implacable. 'Well?'

There was no more she could say. Her plan had failed and clearly he was not going to leave her alone. He knew that she understood that. She turned her back on him towards the forest, and waited for his next move with her head bowed, toying with the end of her girdle. She felt a gentle hand on her back, moving her forward.

'Go on. Get on with it. I shan't look.'

She chose a site a few yards away behind a thick holly bush, keeping an eye on him as he turned sideways on, arms folded and legs wide apart. Brute! she thought. Insensitive brute! But the words had a hollow ring, for she knew that he was playing the same game as she, only one step ahead. And for that she could not help but respect him.

She rejoined him, silent but proud, and seemingly carefree, stooping to pick a dainty wood-anemone which she twirled in her fingers. For a moment he watched her superficial interest in the little white bloom, then carefully removed it from her fingers and fixed it into the lacings at his neck. 'Thank you, *damoiselle*, I shall treasure it.' A glance through her lashes told her that he was smiling. 'Now, you go on ahead and make yourself ready to go. I'll catch you up.'

As she walked away from him, his words echoed in
her mind. Catch me up, will you? Well, we'll see who
catches me up next time, Sir Jais. You can't win every
game, surely. Not *every* game.

With her back to the preparations, Ginevra re-
adjusted the white wimple around her head and neck.
The water in the icy-cold beck tumbling down through
the gorge had made her face and fingers tingle with
freshness, at the same time bringing back childhood
memories of play in the sparkling sunshine and shimmering pools, damming up the flow with pebbles only
to breach it again to watch the dramatic torrent burst
through. It all seemed so far away now. What had
happened to push it back into her life? she wondered.
And what lay ahead? She looked along the track
winding through the forest, sniffing the air for a new
taste, recognising the pungent resinous smell of pines
and bracken. Then, strangely, as though to counterbal-
ance these senses, images of gold embroidery intruded,
so real that her fingers itched to touch the cords and
threads again, to lay the silk and gold along the rich
velvets like streams of liquid metal, and watch them
build up into rivers and torrents.

She closed her eyes against the longing, snapping the
images back inside her memory like the lid of her
workbox. She turned and saw Jais, standing watching
her between narrowed lids, head thrown back.

He had noted the smoothing and fingering of her
cream bliaud by the restless hands at her sides and
could sense something of the conflicting emotions
flowing through her, knew that her anger was still
barely under control. The last little episode had
reinforced his suspicions that she would try to fly before
the net tightened, and his assessment of her courage,
combined with her desire to remain free, assured him

that she would certainly try again while there was still time. Whether merely to cause him annoyance, to make good her vow, or to make a genuine bid to release herself from a permanent situation which had thrust itself upon her too soon, he was not so sure. But, for whatever reason, he would let her fly for a while to release some of the pent-up energy. If thirteen of them couldn't bring her back, well. . . ! He smiled and walked towards her. It was time to move on.

There was a general feeling of relief as the party emerged from the dark forest. The sound of hooves had been muffled by layers of soft pine-needles and mud, throwing haunting bird-calls into sharper relief. Now the bright light lifted their spirits, shimmering over the moorland ahead in the early noon, opening up the sky to a wild expanse of sheep-strewn grass where birds swooped and called in alarm at their passing.

But Ginevra's spirits were not yet lifted. I will not be swept along this damned track, her inner voices growled. 'Best if you didn't have too long to think about it', indeed. Well, maybe *you* won't have too long to think about it either, Sir Jais. She noted his move up to the front of the cavalcade to speak with the leaders and she was barely able to suppress the tremors of excitement at the thought of freedom ahead.

Free! Free! Free! The word took hold of her, transferring its signal to her hands and legs. In an instant the chestnut mare had pricked her ears and responded to the new tensions in her rider's body, as willing as her mistress to taste the fresh moorland air in her nostrils. Ginevra felt the surge of power in the haunches beneath her and gripped hard with her knees as they plunged away off the track and into the heather.

Head low, hands high up on the mare's braided neck, Ginevra urged her on with heels and voice. 'Go, go! Free—I'm free!' Her heart sang as the turf sped past under the flying hooves. 'Go on! Faster, faster!'

She did not hear the shouts of alarm behind her on the track, only the wind rushing past her. But Jais had already issued orders to keep moving as he wheeled away in long easy strides to follow at a distance. He had been ready for the manoeuvre and now a smile played about his eyes as he watched the pale form flying off into the distance.

'Well, we were wondering how long it would be, were we not, Negre? We'll let them fly, then we'll bring 'em back.' The great horse flicked a neat ear in response and snorted in enjoyment, settling down to an easy ground-eating canter. 'Steady, boy. We don't need to catch 'em yet.'

Down the slope of the moor Ginevra and the mare went at full tilt, legs and hips swinging as they dodged across the narrow beck at the bottom and up the other side. With only the wild moors before her, she had no thoughts, no fears, no demands or expectations; she saw only space, felt only silence, wind, speed, power and exultation, tasted and smelled only clear, clean freshness. Her hair was whipped out of the white linen wimple, leaving it to billow around her neck below a cascade of copper curls. Even her hair was free. Knees gripping, weight forward, hands light on the reins, Ginevra laughed as they covered the ground, dropping down carefully into gullies and easily up the other sides, scattering startled sheep, disturbing grouse and plover.

Now the ground rose gently upwards to where gnarled hawthorns coupled with huge boulders as though for mutual protection, and beyond them, on the low skyline, Ginevra could see a cluster of large standing stones, like a group of people deep in conference. She slackened the pace to an easy canter as they approached, dropped the reins and, sitting well down in the saddle, raised her arms towards the sky, like a bird stretching its wings before flight. With head thrown back, she rode freely like this towards the stone circle, until the mare, lacking proper direction, came slowly to a halt and stood waiting. Ginevra leaned backwards against the high saddle as far as she was able, her chestnut hair touching the horse's flanks and merging their colours. A change of legs tipped her gently, and she sat up, moving forward into the circle of stones.

She saw that there were nine, equally spaced except for a gap where one had fallen. As she turned to count and examine she saw the mare's ears prick forward, her nostrils flaring, then heard her whinny. Shading her eyes against the expanse of sky, she strained them into the distance and saw, with intense suddenness, what had been blotted from her thoughts since she had left the track. Walking at an oblique angle across to her right was the figure of Sir Jais on the black stallion, looking for all the world as though on a leisurely country ramble. Had he seen her? Had he heard the mare's whinny?

Her hands clenched on the high pommel of the saddle; she was aware that her heart was pounding with anger and trepidation. She manoeuvred the mare with heel and knee to place a tall stone between herself and him, watching for a sign that he had noted their position. But he was looking ahead, away to her right, and appeared to be passing them by. Ducking low, she moved round, stone by stone, as he passed below them on the slope of the hill until the top of his black head disappeared from sight below the turf-covered brow. Her solitude now shattered, her flight checked, she sat still, racked by uncertainty, infuriated by this intrusion. She would give him time to go on, and then proceed herself—but in which direction? Where?

She waited for what seemed like a lifetime. But again the mare's acute senses gave Ginevra warning as the head swung round with a snort, jerking her to attention. With a start, she whipped round in the saddle. There, immediately behind them, at a standstill, was the black stallion and its rider. Behind them? How on earth. . .? Fury gripped her.

'Go away!' she yelled at him from the top of her lungs as she moved the mare round to face him. 'I'm free, don't you understand? I'm free! And I'm not going anywhere with you!'

He did not answer, but his white teeth flashed a smile of pure enjoyment. The very way he sat his horse struck dread into her breast—dread at the sheer raw power of the pair compared to herself and her dainty beast, nimble though she was. Without a visible sign from his rider Negre moved very slowly towards them, but Ginevra had already gathered her reins ready to bound away. In one moment, she whirled the mare around and kicked her heels hard into her flanks, spurring her to one gigantic leap over the fallen boulder and out of the stone circle. She missed the grin of approval on Jais's face, both for the skill of the almost standing leap and for the direction of her flight, for she had exactly followed his intended course.

Now her exultation was replaced by the rage surging through her arms and legs as she hurtled down the hillside towards the first gully. This side was steep and her first approach in the opposite direction had been further along, where it was shallower. Should she risk

it? No, it would slow her down to take it here, better
to go alongside. But she was forbidden a change of
direction, for as she swung away Jais was heading her
off with ease, and she was forced to turn back again
and plunge down the bank, across the narrow trickle of
brackish water and up the other side. To her horror, as
she reached the opposite bank, she saw them take a
flying leap from one side to the other with hardly a
pause in their stride, bringing them closer than ever.
With a cry of alarm she swerved to avoid them, but Sir
Jais and his mount had hunted together for many years
and both understood the ways of the quarry. They
responded simultaneously to every move, and for every
change of direction Ginevra made, they matched it as
though reading her thoughts. He stayed to the right of
her, moving her over towards new ground which she
had not crossed on her outward flight, and it was not
long before the tiny figures of the cavalcade appeared
on the distant track.

Instantly, on a surge of mutiny, Ginevra swung
sharply away, hoping to slip past Jais while his big
mount was on the wrong foot, but in one stride they
had closed the gap and she glimpsed his laughing eyes
as he leaned from the saddle to grab at the mare's reins
with one long arm. She was forced to a standstill,
shouting with impotent anger and humiliation.

'No! No! Leave me alone! Let go!' She pulled hard
at the reins to wrench them free as he came alongside
her, her temper now unleashed against this intrusion
into her freedom. The mare, receiving conflicting
demands from different sources, reared with a snort of
irritation, pawing the air with her forelegs. Ginevra
grabbed at the beribboned mane and neck, gripping
tightly with her knees against the saddle, and as the
mare came down again glared at Jais in white-hot fury.

'How *dare* you stop me? How *dare* you?' She made as if to dismount, but he leaned forward and grabbed her arm in a grip of steel.

'How dare I, wench? You may well discover what I dare if your temper doesn't cool immediately! Look over yonder.' He jerked his head to one side and she saw his meaning. They had come round in an arc and were now well within sight of the men on the track, who had halted and were watching the proceedings with interest. 'If you dismount, *damoiselle*, I shall catch you and beat you soundly, right here in full sight of the men. Do you want me to do that?'

Her breasts were rising and falling with anger and the exertion of the ride as she read his face for true intent. His fearsome expression gave her not the slightest doubt that he meant every word of what he said. His eyes said so. She dared not take the risk.

'Now. Do you want me to lead you back with your reins in my hand and your hair everywhere? Or would you rather replace your wimple and ride freely along-side me? The choice is yours.' He could see the struggle taking place within her, her jaws working to hold back the sobs of frustration rising in her breast. Her eyes looked up at the sky and the diving sparrowhawks. As a falconer watched an untamed bird, he understood her fury at being brought back to the wrist in mid-flight. He waited without speaking as the angry tears ebbed away, then spoke more gently. 'Come on, little bird. You've flown far enough for one day. You escaped me, and I recaptured you. That's a win for both of us. Isn't it?'

The tension finally slackened and her rigid body eased again into the saddle as, without answering him directly, she retied the linen wimple around her tumbled hair, tucking the stray curls inside. He kept hold of her reins, noting the slim waist and graceful curve of her back, recalling her superb riding across the moor. Now she faced him, once more in order, and held out a hand for her reins without a word, rebellion still simmering below the surface. For a long moment their eyes were locked in combat, Ginevra's still glaring and resentful, Jais's like cold steel, unyielding, demanding her submission.

With a quick flicker of surrender her head lowered, and she looked down at her empty hands on the pommel, biting her lips in uncertainty. 'Good,' he said, his mouth showing a quiver of approval. He held out the reins to her and she received them with a softened glance. Together they turned the horses' heads towards the track. There were some well-hidden looks of amusement and several knowing winks as the team moved forward again, but no one spoke. It was noticed though, that Sir Jais remained by her side for the remainder of the journey.

She peeped sideways at her companion. It was clear that she was learning more about him every moment, for this day alone had taught her more about the complex ways of men than she had learnt in a short lifetime. And yet some women were already mothers by this age. Which was better? she wondered. Had it not been for her parents, anxious to make the right connections, then she might by now have been one of those seventeen-year-old mothers, knee-deep in the domesticity of a country manor with a husband away on the King's service for much of the year. Heaven forbid! She looked at him again, sitting proud and erect beside her, his black forelock lifted by the wind, a fuzz of black fur showing at his throat above the lacings where the wood-anemone now hung limply. Yes, for all his fierceness, he was preferable to some of the immature or over-mature specimens to whom some of her contemporaries at the priory had been offered year after year. She remembered the tears, the pleas, the stories of threats. No, at least this man was not objectionable in *that* way. She glanced at his mouth and a shiver ran through her. Indeed, he knew how to hold a woman and melt her with his touch.

But still, his method of conquest was totally unacceptable. She rallied her argument. Totally unacceptable. She was still being passed on like a piece of merchandise after a highly dubious means of obtaining her consent. And for that undignified and degrading transaction she would make him pay. Changes? Stepping-stones? Rubbish! A bridge would have been more dignified, and a real choice of whether and when to cross it! Oh, yes, she would make him pay.

'Are you familiar with Beesholme Abbey, Ginevra?' The question broke into her musings at a relevant point for she was, at that moment, wondering how the accommodation for the night was to be organised. It was as though he had read her thoughts.

'No, sir, I have never been this far from our estates before. This country is new to me.' Now that the moorland was behind them, the thickly wooded valleys were less desolate and dramatic, cosier somehow, and friendly with the soft hush of the breeze in the pines.

He turned to look at her. 'We stayed overnight there on our way up to the dales. The abbot, Father Gregory, is a dear man; he knew my father well. And he knows the Prioress Claire, too.' He awaited her reaction at the mention of their mutual acquaintance.

'Yes, I know he does.'

'You knew?' The surprise showed in his voice instead

of in hers, to her quiet amusement. She did her best to sound casual, struggling with a smile that threatened to surface, keeping her eyes fixed between the mare's ears.

'Yes. I know that he and the Prioress Claire know each other.'

'Did he visit Our Lady of Aire, Ginevra?'

'Only once.' It was so tempting to make him dig for every scrap of information, she thought, wondering why it should matter to him why or on what grounds they knew each other. It would not be too difficult to draw some conclusions, but she supposed that when one knew the facts it was never easy to understand why others should not know them too.

'Recently?'

She could not contain herself, so patent was his curiosity. The smile which had bubbled under the surface now broke forth, bringing with it a pent-up explosion of laughter. With her head thrown back, her merry laugh tinkled up into the air like bells, lighting Jais's face with astonishment. This was only the second time he had seen her laugh and he was captivated. Her lovely even teeth grinned at him mischievously, her eyes twinkling, infecting him on the instant.

'Tell me, *damoiselle*,' he laughed. 'What is it that I am too dim to work out for myself? Ah, wait!' He held out a hand before she could answer. 'I think I might know. It's to do with embroidery, am I right? Embroidery for the abbey? Done at the priory?'

Ginevra bent over to adjust a loosening ribbon on the mare's mane and looked up at him as she tied it. 'It was many years ago when Father Gregory and his sacrist came to Our Lady of Aire. And I met them, but they would never remember me. I simply showed them some of the work we were doing in the workroom because they wanted a silk altar-frontlet with a decorated border, I remember. It was the first one they'd ever had, because the Cistercians had only recently allowed decoration of that kind. Well. . .' She looked up at his interested face '. . .well, it takes them a bit longer to catch on up here, you know.' She laughed. 'Then, because they didn't have an embroidered chasuble, or a cope either, we made them, too. As gifts.'

'As gifts? You mean, Prioress Claire *gave* them?'

'Yes. She gave them. I thought you would have known; the Cistercians are not allowed to commission *that* kind of thing. . .to wear. Only, they *can* accept gifts. So we made them.'

'No wonder she's finding it difficult to make ends meet,' he mumbled under his breath, and went on rapidly before she could question his information. 'And did you work on the embroideries personally?'

'Oh, yes, of course. I was about thirteen summers, I think, and the Reverend Mother put me in charge of the group. I remember it well. Rowenna worked on them, too. We had such fun!' She smiled secretly to herself.

'Fun, Ginevra?'

She hung her head a little, to stifle the laughter.

'Well, having an important commission to work on was always a good way of getting out of all the church services, you see. . .'

'Ah! So you had extra time to work on the embroidery?'

'Well, that was the idea. But Rowenna and I would steal out. . .' Here her confession came to a halt, and she bit her lip, looking up at him with laughter in her golden-brown eyes.

'Tell me, wench. You stole out. . .?'

'. . .and went to watch the lay-brothers at work!

They didn't see us, of course!' she was quick to assure him but the laughter spilled over again and her teeth parted to admit the gusts and chuckles that had, once again, built up under the weight of the memories.

'And that's how the altar frontlet came to take twice as long as need be?' He grinned at her escapade and at her merriment.

'Well, not exactly. We simply worked twice as fast at other times. Some of the nuns were so slow that our normal speed was twice as fast as theirs, and our double speed was four times as fast!'

Jais let out a bellow of laughter, shaking his head at their scheming devices. It was in his mind to ask her about Brother David, but he was loath to spoil the rare moment of harmony with such a question, knowing how it would annoy her. It would wait for another occasion, he thought, for now Beesholme Abbey was in sight at last.

CHAPTER SEVEN

FROM the distance of the track, Ginevra felt that they
could be approaching a small walled city, for she was
totally unprepared for the size of the place. As they
turned the leafy bend, overhung with curving ash
boughs, the immense huddle of buildings was lying
below them in a secluded valley, surrounded by for-
ested hills and crags, like a sleeping child in the circle
of its father's arms. The massive, obviously masculine
abbey, with the snaking shadowy river flowing behind,
was many times larger than Our Lady of Aire. Masculine in appearance, perhaps, but solid and vibrant with
life for all that. Wisps of smoke already rose from
several of the buildings, and tiny figures of men moved
about on their daily business among the pathways and
in the yards, with only the occasional whinny of a horse
or the bleat of a sheep to disturb the tranquillity.

As they clattered through the cobbled entrance of
the gatehouse the echoes changed key to a higher
pitch, and Ginevra's growing doubts about her appearance, her lack of a maid and her exact place in the
scheme of things found a different level of urgency in
her mind. Suddenly it became imperative that these
problems should be resolved before meeting her hosts
for the night.

'Sir Jais. . .?' Her voice was urgent. Fearful.

'*Damoiselle*?' Jais, seeing that there was something
troubling her, immediately took hold of her horse's
bridle and led her to one side, waving the party on past
them. 'Go on to the guest-stables, Ned!' he called,

moving Negre to face her, knee to knee. 'You are troubled, Ginevra, are you not?'

'Sir, this will not do!' she said. 'I have no maid to attend me and I am not suitably dressed to appear as an honoured guest, as you are. And. . . I. . . Oh, dear. . . I have hardly had time to become acquainted with my new position, and even now I'm not sure how I stand in relation to you. What am I going to answer if the abbot should ask me?' She dropped her reins and spread out her hands in a helpless gesture at the ambiguity of her situation.

'Little bird, hear me!' He leaned forward and took one of her hands in his, shaking it gently until she raised her eyes to his smiling ones. 'We have much to discuss. Perhaps we'll find time to talk after supper. But meanwhile, take my lead. You are seeing problems where there are none. You have no maid. Neither have I brought my valet along on this occasion. There is nothing remarkable in that. The fact that you are not wearing the most sumptuous gowns will find favour with the abbot, I know, and I shall not be richly dressed either. But, even if I were, I would not attract the least amount of attention with *you* by my side.' She looked up at him shyly, and was obliged to smile at his gallantry. 'As for your standing in relation to me, it's quite simple. You and I are betrothed, are we not? Don't be surprised at the arrangement. . . They were only expecting one of us on the return journey, not two. But it makes no difference, no one will be in the least put out. Just take my lead. Will you do that?'

She nodded, somewhat relieved by his assurances and his obvious control of the situation. Clearly her unease had not escaped him. What a strange mixture this man was, delighting in stirring up her anger at one moment, and at the next doing everything possible to assuage her misgivings. What was she to expect next? she wondered.

Brother Cuthbert, the merry-faced guest-master, had seen the arrival of the de la Roche cavalcade and was ready to meet them at the entrance to the guest-house as they approached. One of Jais's young grooms came racing towards them as they dismounted and they were soon being warmly welcomed with not a hint of unsettled surprise.

'You are most welcome, Sir Jais. We've been expecting you these last few days, but clearly you had much business to attend to.' He beamed at Ginevra.

'Brother Cuthbert, allow me to present my betrothed, Ginevra Mallard.'

'Mallard? Why, then you must be one of the Scepeton Mallards. Your father, Sir Alan, stayed here more than once. You are doubly welcome, *damoiselle*.'

Ginevra dropped him a respectful curtsy, and she felt Jais's hand taking hers, noting his look of approval. 'Thank you, Brother, you are kind.' Her shy smile made the old man's eyes twinkle like bright stars, peeping out from beneath a cloud of bushy white brows. As he led them up the outer steps of the cool stone building and into the interior Ginevra sensed the pervading peace closing off all outside effects, their voices and steps reverberating on the solid walls as they passed along the upper passageway.

'The abbot asked to see you in his parlour before supper, Sir Jais,' Brother Cuthbert was saying, 'but he has Father Robert, the abbot of Fountains, staying with us on his yearly visitation, and that's why all our guest-rooms are occupied. But,' he hastily added, 'we kept yours vacant against your return, of course.' He opened the door with a hefty iron key from his girdle and ushered them into a comfortable room looking towards the abbey. It was on the tip of Ginevra's tongue to ask where *her* room was to be found, but the monk's words warned her that the question had better not be put at that moment. 'Take my lead,' Jais had said, and a quick look at him assured her that her silence was appropriate.

'Thank you, Brother Cuthbert, that was considerate of you. We shall be very comfortable, I know. Would you assure Father Abbot that we shall be honoured to attend him before the bell for supper?'

'I shall come up myself to escort you, sir. Meanwhile, I shall order some water to be sent up and see to your baggage. Your attendant will be Master Henry.' The twinkling monk bowed his head in farewell, and closed the door quietly behind him.

Ginevra turned from the window, her heart now racing with an ever-growing realisation that she was to have no room of her own, that she was indeed being expected to share this one with Sir Jais for the night. While the notion was not entirely outrageous, for she knew that it was by no means unusual, she could not conceal her fear or her annoyance. Her first impulse was predictable. 'Where is *my* room, sir?' she whispered.

He leaned against the door, watching the narrowed angry eyes and the rigid posture of fear, knowing what to expect, almost sympathising with her. After an eventful day like this, full of new and startling experiences, and now this. . . He knew that she would be angry. '*These* are your rooms, *damoiselle*, and mine.' He folded his arms across his chest and waited for the onslaught.

'You deceived me! You *knew*. . .'

'I did not deceive you, Ginevra, and yes, I did know that we would have to share this room. . .'

'No! I can't share a room! I've *never* shared a room with a man. . .ever. . .' She pointed to the bed, wide-eyed, horrified, questioning. 'There's only one. . . where are *you* going to sleep?'

His reply was wordless, but crystal-clear for all that. His gaze went from her to the bed as though assessing its size and then slowly back to her with a smile playing about his lips and a twinkle in his eye.

'This is absurd! I shall go and speak with Brother Cuthbert. There must be another room somewhere!' She moved towards the door but he remained leaning against it.

She was like a caged animal, he thought, terrified of being alone with him, and though he loved to see her wild and angry like this, he knew that he would have to pacify her quickly before the luggage was brought up from the pack-horses. Unfolding his arms, he pushed himself away from the door. Ginevra, thinking he was going to allow her to pass, moved forward, but was caught hard against him instead. For a few moments she struggled to free herself, but his arms were too strong. 'Ginevra! Listen to me!' He held her until she stood quietly, panting with helpless fury. 'Listen, little bird. Let's solve one problem at a time, shall we?'

'No! I must get out of here. . .' She pushed against his restricting arms but to no avail. She did not want to hear him.

'All right! Easy now! We'll find a chance to speak with Brother Cuthbert after supper. But now we must prepare ourselves to meet the abbots and the other guests. You don't want to go down like this, do you?'

He would speak to Brother Cuthbert? Was that what he was saying? Ginevra stood quietly at last, taking in his words, longing to be reassured that he understood her consternation. Was he being serious? She raised her head to look just as he was lowering his, and found that their lips were only the distance of a kiss away. The steely-grey eyes held hers just long enough for her to see his intention and to feel his hand move across her back, pushing her arm upwards to his neck.

Obediently, as though in a dream, her hand found his shoulder as her eyelids closed, and she felt the pressure of his lips once again—warm, firm, experienced. All rebellious words were pushed away by the force of his mouth on hers. He teased her to respond while her anger still smouldered, daring her to prolong the fight without words.

She rose to his bait impulsively, allowing her anger and her newly awakened passion to join forces against him, blending, merging and finally fusing in total participation, searching his mouth, biting and tasting, giving expression to the frustrations of the day. At this moment, this was the culmination of her desire for revenge. Her anger, her fears, her frustrations and repressions, all now burst forth into an act of physical violence. It was the nearest she could hope to get, the nearest she knew or could think of to pay him back for his dominance of her. Conversely, a part of her knew that she was at the same time acknowledging her body's need of him. Since his first appearance into her life her barely aroused senses had leapt into activity like an erupting volcano and, though the experience so far had been too uncomfortable to come to terms with, its effect could be neither suppressed nor ignored. She allowed her fury to explode into her kisses, her body straining and quivering in his arms, her fingers digging deeply into the leather of his jerkin as though she were holding him to her by force.

Realising that his bait had been taken, he allowed

her the pretence of control, enjoying her arousal barely concealed as anger, amused and stirred by her passionate reprisal. Gradually he took command, only because he knew that time was running out. His ferocity now matched hers, as he had intended it should, and she was forced to a conclusion, breathless and shaking, clinging to him for support. Held in his arms, her body once more soft and compliant, she opened her eyes to find him regarding her with admiration, the distinct glint of approval now replacing the earlier cold steel of combat.

'Well done, little bird! I look forward to continuing that bout on another occasion. But now we must. . .' A knock sounded at the door and Ginevra immediately pulled away, both at the effect of his words and at her desire not to be seen standing close to him. But she was caught firmly before she could move away and tightly held within the circle of his arm. 'Stay where you are! It's only the baggage arriving.'

'Let me go, please!' she pleaded.

'No! Enter!' he shouted to the door. He directed the distribution of their luggage while his restraining arm held her to him in an outward display of gentle protection. Finally, with a few words to the servants and a nod of dismissal, they were alone again and she was released.

The kisses had acted like a powerful drug on Ginevra, and she was secretly glad to have had his support for a few moments before finding her legs again. Her confusion was still every bit as great as it had been previously, but now had an added ingredient of a physical passion that she had not known existed within her. She was dimly aware that it had been prompted by anger, but she was also somewhat mortified to discover that she had enjoyed it more than

anything else she could remember, and also that Jais
had appeared to enjoy it too, even though that had not
been her intention. She whirled round to face him
across the room. 'Why did you. . .?'

'Because you needed a few moments of support,
didn't you?' He grinned, anticipating her question and
aware of her embarrassment at the newness of her
reactions. She turned her back to him, knowing that he
was correct, but lost for a retort that would curb his
smugness. Nothing came, however, and she was
obliged to fume in silence. 'Didn't you?' His hands
were on her shoulders as he moved up quietly behind
her. 'It's all right, little bird, people kiss for all kinds
of reasons, and angry ones are just as good as any
others, on occasion.'

'You were not supposed to *enjoy* it!' she snapped
unreasonably.

'I know,' he laughed, sliding his hands down to
enclose her wrists. 'I know I was not, but I did! And
you did, too, didn't you?' He crossed her wrists over
her breasts and held her to him, waiting for her to
answer. But she would not, and he did not insist. 'Now,
our belongings are here and we have to hurry, or the
guest-master will arrive before we're ready. Come on,
now. We'll sort out territory problems later, but for
now we have to change. Come, I'll show you!' He took
her hand and showed her the small adjoining room,
where the garderobe was curtained off in one corner
and a table waited to receive water for washing.

Soon the water had been brought, bags unpacked
and clothes laid out ready—all conflicts put aside in the
mutual search for possessions. On purpose, Jais
undressed halfway between both rooms, refusing to
spare her the sight of his naked chest and back. The
sooner she got used to it, the easier it would be, he

thought, grinning to himself as he noted her curious sidelong glances.

Ginevra, however, washed and changed behind the closed door of the little room, enjoying the luxury of warm water and scented lye, the clean rough towels and the feel of the clean bliaud given to her by Johanna as a parting gift. At Jais's side she rummaged in her bag for the blue leather girdle to contain the roomy gown, and as she straightened she saw that he was holding her golden fillet at head-height, waiting for her to place herself beneath it.

'You may borrow it for this evening only,' he said.

'Thank you, sir. Are you quite sure you want it back?'

'I was never more sure of anything in my life, *damoiselle*. Let me tie your ring on.' She held out her hand with the ribbon dangling from it, and watched as he tied it in a bow round her wrist, catching the scent of him in her nostrils. His warm maleness and the touch of his fingers on her wrist sent her thoughts whirling into space and turned her knees to water.

Does he know? she wondered. Can he tell how he disturbs me?

Again there was a knock on the heavy studded door and they knew that it was time to go down.

It was with some relief that Jais noted that he and Ginevra were by no means the only noble guests staying there that night. He realised that this would help to deflect all but the most general questions about his affairs and family, which were sure to come his way via both Reverend Abbots. Naturally both of them knew the Prioress Claire, and were therefore delighted to meet and welcome Ginevra, the designer and brod-erer of that same frontlet which had been made for the church only a few years before. Father Gregory could scarcely believe how that young girl had now grown into this beautiful woman. But the abbots had other guests to entertain, some of whom were a part of the Fountains retinue and others who travelled in the summer months for convenience. And so the conversation was varied and general instead of particular, and Ginevra's natural grace warmed everyone's heart during the meal in the guest-house with the two abbots presiding.

Afterwards Brother Cuthbert delighted them by taking a party along to the church while the brothers were at supper to show off the altar-frontlet, chasuble and cope which Ginevra had last seen at the priory. He could still be heard talking of her prowess as he walked them back to the guest-hall, leaving her and Jais to walk on towards the mill-pond.

A breeze was beginning to ruffle the leaves, turning them up to show the pale undersides, and the sky held a solid bank of purple cloud over to the distant west. Above them, on the slopes of the crags and on the skyline, the trees were showing a greater disturbance, and the swifts swooped low overhead in the ominous green light of the evening.

Jais was glad to have a chance, at last, to talk quietly with Ginevra without the unsettling overtones of proposals and agreements hanging over them. He wanted to ease her mind about the future but was anxious that not too many questions be asked about his personal activities, which could easily bring her to the wrong conclusions. Her distrust of his motives and her resentment at his brutal haste were understandable, for she must have begun to wonder what each new day held in store for her. But beneath the storm of her confusion he could feel the warmth of newly kindled fires. Her struggles were not those of repulsion or disgust, but of fear of the unknown, which he knew that in time and with care he could overcome. Courage she had in good supply, but perhaps it was best not to put this to the test too soon, though it would take all his resolve to resist the temptation. He looked up at the darkening sky and wondered if there would be a chance to allay her fears before returning to their room for the night.

They reached the small stone bridge where mallards zig-zagged in the water beneath, looking for food. The pale green light now washed over the abbey, creating a strange feeling of oppression with the heavy sky. Ginevra was the first to broach the discussion of their future.

'Johanna tells me that you will take me to live with your sister until we. . .' She hesitated, unwilling to say the words.

'Until we are married.' Jais finished the sentence for her. 'Yes, Marianne lives only a few houses away from me in York. It will be best if you allow her to care for you until then. She and Richard, her husband, are wonderfully kind. I know you'll like them, Ginevra.'

'And then?'

'And then I shall take you to live with me in my home. . .'

'Where you have need of my skills?' The words burst out quietly, but with venom, and she regretted them immediately. Jais took hold of her arm and turned her to him.

'Ginevra! We have passed that hurdle. Let it lie. There will time enough for you to understand all that has happened. Until then, I ask you to trust me.' His voice was cutting, like a dagger.

She glanced up at him and saw his eyes glinting between narrowed lids, and she wondered what his worst anger would be like. Why does this man disturb me so? she asked herself. Why do I feel so unnerved by his nearness?

'Ginevra?' The voice was gentler now, and questioning. He took her shoulders, and they sat face to face on the low parapet of the bridge. She leaned towards him and placed her hand lightly on his sleeve.

'I beg your pardon for that. I think I am a little frayed by the events of the last few days. I'm not usually so prickly. And now. . .more faces to get used to. . .' Her voice was lost in a whisper, her head turned from him.

'You will be among friends, Ginevra, I promise you. Not adversaries. Marianne is never happier than when she has people to stay; she'll make you welcome. And I think you'll like my home too, but it needs a woman's. . .'

'. . .skills?' they said in unison, laughing together and shaking their heads at the scrapes words were getting them into.

'All right.' He laughed at her. 'We're allowed to say it together, but not separately. Agreed?'

'Agreed!'

They watched the mallards in silence for a while.

'Which one is Ginevra, I wonder?'

'The one over there, going round and round in circles.' She pointed to the little drab brown creature pursued by a glossy male with green and white flashes a-quiver.

A sudden gust of wind rippled the surface of the pond and bent the spiky sedges into a deep obeisance at the water's edge. At the same time a large splash fell hard on to Ginevra's hand, stinging her into action.

Jais pulled her up. 'We'd better talk indoors, I think. Come. Quickly.'

And with her hand in his she picked up the skirts of her gown and ran, reaching the steps of the guest-hall as the first rumble of thunder broke over the surrounding hills. It was quite clear, thought Ginevra, that there was going to be no chance to speak to Brother Cuthbert again that evening, for he was nowhere to be seen.

A fire had been lit in the stone fireplace, already filling the room with the scent of woodsmoke and casting a warm glow over the whitened stone walls. A small cresset, with tallow and wick ready for lighting, had been set on the stone wall-shelf, and a basket of logs had been placed to one side. Ginevra noted that items of clothing had been tidied away and the hurried signs of their departure erased as if by magic.

She removed her wet shoes and shook out her damp hair, warming her hands as she knelt by the fire. They were icy-cold and trembling; her body was suddenly shaking uncontrollably as the crashing storm now hurled itself at the horn window, combining with her own private storm within. She half turned and saw that Jais was removing his calf-length blue gown, just as a brilliant flash of lightning lit the room, bathing his body in a weird blue and white light. The crash that followed echoed round the valley as she leapt up with a cry and threw herself at the door—anything to get away from his presence, terrified of his nearness in the darkened room. Another tremendous and deafening crash shook the walls as she let out an involuntary scream of terror, her body now rigid with cold fear.

At that same moment she was swept up into his arms and carried across the floor. Her mouth opened to cry out in anguish but the cry never left her lips, for she felt herself being rolled gently across the bed, with the coverlet enclosing her as she went, constraining her arms and legs like a cocooned butterfly. Wrapped tightly, arms pinioned inside the fabric, she was scooped up to the middle of the bed as yet another flash illuminated the scene. She saw Jais above her, his face paled by the ghostly light and then dark again as she felt the hard pressure of his body on hers and his lips moving over her face, his deep voice soothing her.

'Easy, little bird, easy, now. There, now, little bird. Hush. Hush, now!' The low words continued as though she were a wild creature about to fly off in panic. 'It's only a storm. Easy, now, little bird. Easy, honey.' His voice spoke softly into her hair, stroking hands caressed her temples and warm lips nudged at her chin and cheeks as his body held hers to the bed. While the thunder crackled and crashed and the torrential rain beat at the window he lay on her, warming and stilling her trembling, his hands and gentle words drowning out the noise of the storm outside, and the one in her breast.

For all his hard frame and muscles the weight of his body was not uncomfortable. Lying under him, tightly bundled, being soothed like a baby, was a most delicious experience. The feel of his lips gentling her face, his warm breath and beard on her throat, sent shivers of ecstasy into her and a glow into her limbs. Gradually she stopped trembling, her fears now under control, her body content and relaxed. As his voice dropped to a whisper the thunder moved on down the valley and the lightning dwindled to an occasional glow in the night sky, and they lay for a long time without moving, listening to the rain and the wind rattling at them, to remind them of its presence.

'Are you asleep, little bird?' he whispered into her ear at last.

'I'm not sure. I don't think so. Just dreaming,' she murmured.

He smiled at her whimsy. A deep sense of wonder now replaced her earlier anxieties—wonder that she could now lie so close to someone who only yesterday had been a complete stranger to her. Could this be possible? Was she doing with this stranger what people did when they were married? Was this the consummation that Johanna had spoken of? Dared she ask him? In the darkness?

'Jais?'

'What, little bird?'

Her voice was no more than a whisper. 'Is this what. . .what. . .?' Her question tailed off to nothing. Perhaps she shouldn't have asked, after all.

'Is this *what*?' Jais raised his head and looked down into her eyes. He knew what she was asking.

'You know. Is this what we do when we're married?'

The face above her broke into a smile as he kissed the tip of her nose. How innocent this creature was, and how adorable. 'No. This is only a tiny part of what we do when we're married.'

'There's more than this, then?' She frowned.

'Much more!' He kissed her nose again, and chuckled.

Ginevra was glad that it was dark so that he could not see her face clearly. She could never have asked in the daylight. 'How much more?'

'I would be delighted to explain to you on another occasion, *damoiselle*, but perhaps not on this one.' He smiled again in the darkness above her. 'I think today has been eventful enough, don't you? And I think that now it's time for sleep.'

'Are you going?'

'No, I'm not going anywhere, I assure you.'

She watched as he left the bed and went to the fire, pushing the last log down on to the white embers and

sending up a new shower of sparks to light his face with
the new flames. With his back to her, he removed the
rest of his clothes, leaving his short white linen *braies*,
and then turned to her, his body rosy and tautly
muscular in the firelight.

'Now it's your turn, little bird. Come on!' He bent
to lift the edge of the coverlet, and pulling firmly rolled
her out of it, until she lay huddled against the wall, her
eyes now wide open.

'I can't get undressed with you there!'

'I think you probably can, if you try. Come!' His
quick grasp at her wrist eased her forward off the bed
to stand before him. 'Now, turn round.'

She turned, mute and obedient, while he assisted her
as far as her shift, but at that she balked. 'I can't take
my shift off, too,' she said to him over her shoulder. 'I
can't. Please, Jais. Please don't insist.'

He paused. 'Get into bed, little bird.' While she
dived under the warm sheets and coverlet, half wondering where he was going to sleep, he poured ale into
a beaker from the jug on the tray and held it out to
her. 'Drink.'

She obeyed, and handed it back to him, watching in
fascination the contours of his throat as he finished it
off. Then, without another word, he lifted the covers
and swung himself into bed beside her.

She heaved herself away in alarm. 'No, sir! Not in
my bed! No. . .!'

A strong arm pushed her backwards, sending her on
to the pillow with a thud. 'No, *damoiselle*, not in your
bed. In mine!'

'I cannot sleep with you, Jais. I am not used——' Her
mouth was stifled by his lips, and for a long moment
the pressure of his hard body on hers drove away all
words and all sense of outrage, leaving only the warm

and exciting movement of his mouth, and his hands on her shoulders.

This was what Johanna had said, she thought hazily. This is sleeping with him. Irrevocable. She cried out as he raised his head, but his voice soothed her again as it had done earlier.

'Gently now, little bird. Easy! There's nothing to be afraid of. One bed must do for both of us this night. Lie quiet, as you did before, and listen to the wind and the rain. Think how good it is to be safe.'

Safe? Was she safe? Her hands were now shyly touching him, feeling the warm masculine hardness of his shoulders under her palms, his massive arms bulging as he rested on his elbows above her. In the last dying flames of the fire her eyes roamed over him, taking in his powerful neck and the surprising hairiness of him, his beard, his dark-lashed searching eyes—those same eyes which had bored into her as she had backed through the door of the herbarium. She felt the weight of his thighs on her and a tremor ran through her breast and lay there, simmering inside in a strange ache.

It was just as well, he thought, to have a night like this, giving her time to see him, explore him a little. He smiled down at her, thinking of the day's events, of her attempts to anger him, thwart him, escape him, all to no avail. How she must have chafed at her lack of success.

'Jais.' Her eyes flickered up to his and held them sleepily. 'Jais. Did I make you very angry today?'

He tried to look solemn. 'Very. In fact, you came very close to being soundly beaten.'

'On the same day as our betrothal?' she asked, incredulous.

'Indeed, yes. Do betrothed ladies send letters to other men?'

She was silent for a moment. Then, 'Were you so angry at that?'

His laughter could not be contained, and he buried his face in her neck as the gales of merriment shook him. When he could speak he said, 'Not in the slightest, wench. Did you hope that I might be?' Taking her silence for assent, he shook his head at her feminine wiles. 'A lay-brother who can't read and who prefers men's company to a lovely woman's is not likely to make me angry. Nor was your little plan, *damoiselle*.' She caught the flash of white teeth in the darkness above her.

'How do you know all this, sir?'

'I know, *damoiselle*, because I make it my business to find out all the facts. Remember?'

She *did* remember. He lowered his mouth to hers and swept her into the circle of his arms, close against his body as he rolled over. His strong arms wrapped around her waist and neck left her no chance but to surrender to the firm warmth of his kisses once more. 'And now,' he said softly, 'it's time you slept, before I forget what it is I'm not going to tell you.' He turned her over with her back to his chest, and tucked one arm around her with his hand under her breast, feeling its perfect roundness. She gasped and pushed against him, twisting at the sudden rush of melting softness that shot through her thighs, but he held her tightly, whispering into her ear. 'All right, hush now, little bird. Time for sleep.' He felt her heart beating wildly, close to his hand, and knew that this was the first time she had ever been held so by a man. Much as he longed to explore further, he knew that she had had enough new experiences for one day and that now she needed rest.

Ginevra lay for some time before sleep came, listening to his even breathing and feeling the rhythm of his heart on her back. His warm male smell clung to her as she savoured the soft pressure of his hand on her breast, and as sleep overtook her she realised that she was as far from wreaking vengeance on him as she would ever be.

For all her tiredness, she awoke several times during the night, each time conscious of his body beside her and no space to move away from him. She had slept with Rowenna often; their bodies were soft and familiar to each other—the same size, same shape, comfortable. This one was hard and hugely angular, bumpy in strange places, alien, different. The weight of his arm on her body was disturbing but not uncomfortable; his large hand moved over her in his sleep, over her stomach, hips, thighs, breasts. How could she return to sleep when her body quivered under his touch, when his warm breath caught the back of her neck, when his legs were in the way of her feet?

Eventually she slid out of bed, moving down between his body and the wall to the bottom edge and away into the garderobe. Sitting there briefly, she listened to the rain on the window, wondering whether to return to the bed or whether to make a temporary couch in front of the fire for the rest of the night. But the fire was all but dead and she hugged her arms around her as she approached the bed once more, shivering a little, listening to his breathing, to the hoot of an owl, wondering what to do. She would have to climb back to his side on her hands and knees and somehow struggle into the sheets without waking him. Or climb over him.

It was as though the coolness of the room had allowed her animosity to surface once more, combining with her discomfort. Given a choice of whether to creep into bed with a man she barely knew or to stay and shiver here on the floor, which would she prefer to do? The question was hardly worth the effort of an answer. She padded softly over to the fireplace and sat before it, feeling the hard coolness of the stone floor through her thin shift. There was no chance of sleep but she was better here, she thought, than climbing all over the place in the dark just to be in his arms again.

His arms? His strong, warm arms, with hands that held and caressed. She moved her hands over her shoulders, remembering, savouring, and her eyes closed to capture the memory more clearly, though the blackness of the room was barely less intense. She *had* enjoyed lying next to him, she could not deny it, and at the time his kisses had melted her resentment. But she would not show him, even if it meant her discomfort, that she was willing for more of the same. Not even if she had to sit here all night.

A tiny sound from the bed brought her bolt upright. Was he awake? Had he noticed her absence? The slight change of temperature on her back coincided with the touch of his hands on her shoulders, sliding down beneath her arms. She was lifted to her feet, strongly and without argument. 'Do you really prefer the stone-cold floor to a warm bed, Ginevra?' His arms slid round her, across her waist and shoulders, the hands gently moving over her as he spoke. His lips were on her brow and she leaned back against him, her body already responding and contradicting all the wintry thoughts of the previous moments.

'I don't know.'

'Truly? You don't know?'

'No.' She shook her head, feeling his warm breath on her face.

His arms tightened gently. 'Shall I help you to make up your mind, *damoiselle*? I can be very persuasive,' he whispered in her ear. His words disconcerted her. She knew full well that she was no match for him if he should choose to persuade her, and which of them knew where that path might lead? Too far. Much too far. She was not prepared for that.

She turned in his arms and faced him in the darkness. 'No, Jais. I don't want you to persuade me.'

'You're afraid, Ginevra?'

'No, I'm not afraid,' she lied. 'I want to make my own mind up, when I'm ready. I must be allowed to make some decisions without anyone persuading me.'

She was perfectly right, he thought. Obstinate. Unreasonable, perhaps. But undeniably right. He must not override her every whim. At least it must not seem like that. 'Will your decision take long, Ginevra? My feet are getting cold.' His arms still held her and his hands gently caressed her long back over the fabric of her shift, seemingly innocent and yet knowing and arousing.

'I'm thinking.'

He grinned at her intransigence. 'Could you do your thinking in a warm bed, little bird? It would be more comfortable for you.'

'You'd try to persuade me. . .'

'No, I wouldn't.'

'Are you sure? Do you promise?'

'Yes. I promise not to try to persuade you.'

'Then I'll think in bed. . .'

She was led to the bedside, covers opened, nudged

inside by his hands and body over to the cool far side. Immediately she was turned to face him again, her head on his shoulder now tucked neatly beneath his chin. He grinned in the darkness. Her shift was ruckled around her hips, and as she sleepily snuggled to him for warmth her leg slipped over his and nestled comfortably on him. This was better than the cold floor. Better than it had been earlier, too, she thought.

'Are you still thinking, little bird?'

'Mmm, I think so. What was I supposed to be thinking?'

'You were deciding whether to stay on the cold floor or to get back into bed with your betrothed.'

'Mmm,' she yawned. 'Did I?'

'Did you what?' His hand continued its movements over her back.

'Did I decide which to do?' Her voice had become sleepy and soft as her questioning became confused.

'No. I think you're still making your mind up, little bird.'

She snuggled closer and nudged his bearded chin with her nose, smiling to herself. 'Good. That's all right, then. . .'

CHAPTER EIGHT

THE cavalcade assembled soon after dawn, and by the time Jais and Ginevra had bidden farewell to the Father Abbot, the guest-master and his staff the horses were waiting impatiently to be away. Ginevra's chestnut mare had been groomed to perfection, her mane and tail rebraided in a different design from that of the previous day. She looked at the handiwork with delight and then at the young groom holding the bridle. 'Did you do this?' she asked.

'Yes, mistress,' the lad said, keeping one eye on Jais as he spoke.

'She looks beautiful. Thank you.' The warm smile from her eyes was all the thanks he required and he responded with a respectful bow, full to the brim with admiration for the lovely young lady. Jais nodded to him, approval in his eyes.

He turned to lift her into the saddle. 'Perhaps, *damoiselle*,' he said, his mouth twitching at the corners and a twinkle in his grey eyes, 'perhaps, if you were to stay on the track instead of attempting to fly off across bogs and mires, your mare might still look like this for our journey through the city. Do you think so?'

She twinkled demurely back at him. 'I will certainly give it my serious consideration, sir,' she replied, and put her hands on the saddle, ready to mount.

'Yes, do so!'

She looked over her shoulder at the change in his voice, noting that the eyes were now narrowed, and she was reminded that it was not the letter to David which had brought her nearest to a beating yesterday.

The violent storm had swollen the river and left the track awash with deep puddles and mud, but there was a cooler, fresher taste to the air this morning. Though the sky was overcast and mists lay heavily over the dales, there was already a greenness to the grass which cast an extra wash of colour over the landscape. Marsh-grass waved like banners on the soft ground as the party picked its way across the moor, and more than once they found newly-formed rivulets of hill-water crossing their path on its way down to the bottoms. Curlew called in alarm at the trespass on their territory, and the men in the company laughingly mimicked the 'Go-back, go-back!' of the grouse as they clattered into the air with a suddenness which made the horses snort in alarm. Ginevra sensed an air of eagerness in the men now on the last short leg of the journey home, a subdued jollity and leg-pulling which she had not noticed yesterday.

During the crossing of the moorland Jais rode along-side her, but the thoughts of the previous evening were still so fresh in her mind that she found it difficult to continue seeing him as the same person she had known from yesterday.

Still, she found it impossible not to question how, and why, and should it be so? It was easier on the mind, she thought, more convenient to think of him as her adversary, one who should be flouted at every opportunity, just to prove that she was not the easy prey he obviously thought she was. Last night his tenderness, his warmth, while being what she had needed then, had made it difficult for her to remain aloof. Her newly awakened passions, her delight in his close contact, his caresses and gentling had now undone

much of the defence she had built around her. Should
she rebuild the walls, or allow them to remain in ruins?
And so she clung tenaciously to her dwindling reservoir
of resentment, fuelling it as best she might by harking
back to the uncomfortable circumstances of her new
role.

Descending to the plain, the party passed through
clutches of muddy hovels, many of them abandoned,
all of them showing signs of disrepair and decay. Grass
grew thickly on thatched roofs and crows flapped
noisily away as they approached. But now the moorland was being replaced by ploughed fields, and cows
grazed in the water-meadows. On the edges of the
woodland a herd of pigs snuffled under oak and beech,
and Ginevra noticed a thin wisp of smoke rising
through the tree-tops. The charcoal-burner, she
thought, and the image of her embroidery designs
appeared again in her mind as if by magic. She wondered if the charcoal she used for her drawings came
from here — or was this all used for smelting? It was
possible. Round the sectioned fields of ripening oats
wattle fences had been erected against the straying
cows and sheep, a temporary measure which would be
removed after harvesting. In view of what Johanna had
said about the labour problems, Ginevra wondered if
there was to be anything like a normal harvest.

As the hovels clustered more compactly along the
track yapping dogs appeared, and geese, hens, scruffy
children and scolding parents. Then Jais pointed to the
horizon, where white stone walls were just visible in
the pale new sunshine. Still some way out of town, a
tollgate was set across the road, where travellers ahead
of them were buying tokens to take them through the
city walls. Instantly Sir Jais's party was recognised by

the tollkeeper and waved through without stopping,
though the brawny youth stood watching long enough
to take a long look at the lovely lady on the chestnut
mare.

The white city walls of York were a graceful sight,
grand, massive and imposing. Ginevra was impressed
and couldn't help but show her delight, which was
instantly noticed, for Jais had been watching for signs
that her manner was softening somewhat.

'We're on Ploxwangate now.' He turned to her
kindly and caught her eye with his. 'And ahead of us
there is Micklegate Bar, where we enter the city.' He
pointed to the solid gate towers through which people
were now passing, handing over their tokens as they
went. 'The bar is up to let us through, but it comes
down at sunset every night,' he explained. 'Excited?'

Ginevra smiled in answer, and nodded. The colours
were the first to catch her attention. The gay clothes of
the more prosperous townspeople and merchants, the
colourful statues and signs hanging from ale-houses
and dark little shops, the white limestone and red tiles,
and flashes of metalwork, all contrasting with patterns
of wood on white plaster. The neutral tones of the
work-clothes and the filthy streets awash with water
and refuse did not entirely appal her; her hungry eyes
merely saw them as food for the artist in her. Textures,
light and shade, contrasts. She turned from side to side
in her saddle in an attempt to catch glimpses of all that
was going on; as a country girl she found it strange to
be suddenly involved in such a concentrated bustle of
activity, to be assailed by unidentifiable smells and to
hear unaccustomed noises.

The cavalcade eased its way slowly through the
crowded streets, slowing down and halting frequently,
and there was almost a feeling of anticlimax when they

reached the area near the minster which, although busy, was somewhat calmer and less congested. Jais noticed how her eyes lit up at the sight of the carved tracery windows and the ornate west doorway, still teeming with workmen and wheelbarrows dodging round piles of rubble.

'Plenty of time to look later,' he assured her, 'and then I'll show you where our Edward and Phillipa were married twenty-two years ago.' Ginevra had not realised that the King and Queen had been married here and felt a sudden glow of pride to be in a town of such importance, especially riding at the side of this man on the black stallion to whom people looked with deference. Here and there he greeted an acquaintance with a smile and a raised hand, but did not halt to talk on this occasion. Soon all except Ginevra's pack-horse and groom were turned off towards another street, and they were left to continue along Petergate and into a narrow cobbled lane between buildings just beyond the west door of the minster.

Sounds were suddenly extinguished as though a door had been closed behind them, except for the clatter and echo of hooves on stone. Then they were out into an open courtyard bordered by lawn, trees, flowerbeds and shrubs. On the far side stood an attractive two-storeyed house of stone and timber with an impressive flight of stone steps leading up to an ornately carved door. Ginevra was instantly reminded of a picture she had seen in a Book of Hours which she had sometimes been allowed to borrow at the priory, a picture of neat courtyards and a garden, with swans floating gracefully past on the river. Was there a river here? The glimpse beyond the trees showed her that the minster loomed like a huge white giant within a stone's throw of them.

'This is where my sister and brother-in-law live,' said

Jais, dismounting and patting Negre's neck. Handing him over to the groom, he turned to lift Ginevra down. As on all other occasions during their journey he held her waist with strong hands which lingered as he set her down, even though he knew that she was perfectly capable of managing alone. This time he did not release her, for he could guess some of the thoughts that must at this moment be going through her mind, and hoped that his hand lightly resting on her waist would reassure her. Ginevra appreciated his closeness as her eyes noted the grey-white stone of the lower walls topped by timber and plaster. This was different from the entirely stone or timber houses of the dales; the mixture was interesting and decorative. The mossy stone-flagged roof swept down like a hood over a twinkling lined face. Leaning against Jais briefly, she felt his hand tighten on her waist, and as they moved towards the door at the top of the steps she noticed a tiny bunch of heartsease growing in the stonework. The sight of the delicate, heart-shaped flowers was like a cooling balm to her mind, a symbol of comfort, a message of hope.

Ginevra did not have quite the same qualms about meeting Marianne as she had about meeting Johanna. Not only was she trying hard not to prejudge new acquaintances in her usual impetuous manner, but Jais had already assured her that they would be welcome, and he was proved correct.

Though Marianne couldn't help but be surprised to see her brother with a young lady, bags, baggage and all, her reaction was not in the least unfavourable and her delightful smile was truly genuine as she held out her arms. She was younger than her brother by some six years, and every bit as attractive. A feminine

version of him, if that were possible. Slender and
petite, with twinkling grey eyes under delicately arched
brows, black-haired and very pretty, she swept towards
them both in a fashionable surcoat of fine mauve shot-
silk, her hair braided into cauls of gold wire at each
side of her head.

The two were obviously glad to see each other. Jais's
courteous formal kiss to her hand was followed by a
warmer one to each cheek, a sight so very attractive
that Ginevra was entranced as she stood to one side
against the richly carved wooden panelling. Her
thoughts were leaping ahead, waiting to discover how
Marianne would react to the idea of having an
unknown guest foisted upon her without notice. But
Jais had said that she loved having people to stay, and
this would certainly put his assurances to the test.

Her greetings to Ginevra were kind and warm, her
eyes showing only the merest hint of the amazement
she must have felt on learning that this was her
brother's wife-to-be.

'Betrothed? But how wonderful. My felicitations to
you both. You make a very handsome couple.' And
she laughed merrily, showing beautifully white teeth
against her olive skin. There was no sign of hesitation
as she assured them both that she would be only too
happy to have Ginevra stay with her and Richard. He
was due back home on the morrow from a buying trip
to Venice and Genoa.

'Excellent!' said Jais. 'Let's hope he got some bar-
gains.' Marianne eventually excused herself to give
orders for a room to be prepared, leaving Jais and
Ginevra to say their farewells.

'What does Master Richard buy in Italy?' asked
Ginevra. She knew that this was to be a temporary
parting of the ways and wished to appear neither too

sad nor too relieved for, in truth, she did not know which she was after the eventful journey of the last two days.

'Well, the family name is Mercer, so I leave you to guess,' he said, taking her arm and walking her across to the big window of the solar overlooking the garden. 'They've been mercers for many generations, and what Richard doesn't know about fabrics is hardly worth knowing. His shop is not attached to the house; he keeps it separate in town.' His face turned serious as he took her shoulders and turned her to face him. 'Ginevra, you won't try to fly, will you?'

She turned her anxious face to his, fleetingly, and her eyes then swept over the lovely room, the costly tapestries, the carved panels and tables. All at once she felt like a street urchin in a king's palace. 'I'm so out of place here,' she said desperately, spreading her hands. 'Look at me!' She pulled at the dull grey-blue gown she had worn last night, awaiting the expected reaction of horror from him. But instead his hands shook her shoulders gently and he smiled down at her, bending his dark head to look into her eyes.

'I know what you're saying, little bird, and I know it won't help to tell you that it doesn't matter what you're wearing when clearly, to you, it does. But, since it worries you, you should know that you couldn't have come to a better place to solve that problem. The Mercers have more fabrics for dresses than you could ever have dreamed of. And, what's more, Marianne's always had a passion for dressing up, ever since she was a child. Believe me, the first thing she'll want to do is to re-dress you from top to bottom. You'll have a wonderful time together, I know.'

Ginevra placed a hand lightly on his chest to show that she understood what he was telling her. He let go of her shoulders and placed his hand over hers and she felt the beat of his heart under his tunic, strong and steady. She felt the hard edge of her gold fillet there, too.

He continued to reassure her. 'Don't be concerned about not having the things you need, little bird. All this was discussed between Alan and myself.' He noted the pained look of anger that passed like a dark cloud over a sunlit landscape and held her hand tightly against him as she attempted to pull it away. 'No, hear me, Ginevra! It's no use not wanting to hear. You *must* hear what concerns you. I told you that once before, don't you remember?'

She remembered clearly. Then, as now, she was being held by one hand, though this time the grasp was more intimate. 'I think I still have the bruises,' she said, with a reproachful glance.

He grinned briefly, and went on. 'The question of money *was* discussed, and he agreed with me that all your needs would be my responsibility. . .'

'He was not in a position to do otherwise, was he?' she retorted, suddenly angry at her brother's illegal usage of her dowry. 'He left me nothing of my own, not even my room! Just my mare, that's all! Why do you think I had such pleasure riding away across the moors on her yesterday?' She was blazing now, in full spate, with hurt pride unleashing the flood of bitterness, pulling at her hand, but still unable to release it from its prison under his. 'I'll tell you! Because the mare, and the miserable clothes I stand up in, and the moorland, are the only things I can call my own. He even begrudged the food I was about to eat! And then *you* came along and made him an offer! Well, he couldn't resist *that*, could he? Especially when you——'

'Ginevra! That's enough!' Her shoulders were seized roughly and she found her rigid, furious body being pulled tightly against him inside strong arms. He rocked her like an infant, his hand holding her head on to his wide chest. A moment later his mouth covered hers, gently pushing away the thoughts of ill-usage and insecurity which had dominated her thoughts for days. His kiss and his tenderness softened her, though her words trickled forth now like the last remaining raindrops after a storm.

'And then you had to come after me and spoil it all,' she mumbled against his tunic while his finger stroked her cheek gently, 'and round me up as though I were a silly sheep!' Her disordered images made him smile, knowing that the flight across the moors was still vividly in her mind. He put her away from him, gently, and lifted her face to his with one long finger.

'A sheep, Ginevra? A *sheep*? Oh, no, I think not! Negre and I don't herd sheep. We may go hunting a doe now and again, but I assure you that yesterday we were *hawking*! And I don't let my most precious birds get too far away, especially while they're still young and. . .'

This was too much for Ginevra. Her laugh of disbelief at his absurdity overcame her self-pity and she caught his hand, holding it against her cheek tenderly. 'Don't say another word,' she laughed softly, 'or I might be tempted to believe you!' She moved away from him to the window and looked out on to the sunlit garden. 'Jais, do you intend to leave me here for some time?'

'No, I don't, little bird. But I have some details to arrange and business to attend to after my northern visits. And I'm still waiting for your assurance that you won't try to escape me!'

She was glad that her back was towards him for she could not find an immediate answer. Obviously he needed her assurance for his own peace of mind, though she could not see why it was so necessary. The conditions she had left behind were such that there was no point in her turning back unless there was some emergency. 'I won't try to fly, I promise,' she said flatly, looking across at the white bulk of the minster glowing in the sun. She turned to him at last. 'I would not be discourteous to Marianne.'

Jais nodded, relieved at her acceptance of the situation. 'Then I shall leave you for the moment and return tomorrow, later on. You're tired, and you need some rest and peace.' His handsome face showed concern for her, and she was suddenly struck by the thought that she did not want him to go. In spite of their clashing of wills his presence indicated security and reliability, two factors which had seemed only a short time ago to be disappearing from her life. So far, he had done everything he had said he would do, even disagreeable things. He had been rough with her, and tender too. Fierce as well as kind.

'I shall take your mare with me and stable her—well out of sight of my Negre, of course.'

She smiled at that, as he had hoped she would. 'Will you ask that young groom to take care of her for me, please? Special request?'

He took her hands. 'I shall see that he gets your message this very day. You've made conquests of the whole lot of them. Did you know that?'

She could not help wondering if that included him too, but had to admit, rather sadly, that there were no signs that this was so. Clearly he was a man of some experience, who must have had many women in his arms, and Ginevra saw no reason why she was to be any different except that she had some skills which he admired. And she was young. He had said so.

CHAPTER NINE

LEFT alone in her room, Ginevra looked around her with mixed feelings at the differences between this lovely house and the one she had left. This was lower-ceilinged and more intimate than northern hill-houses like Scepeton Manor. This was cosy by comparison, she thought, looking more closely at the tapestry on the wall. She gazed at the scene of peasants snaring rabbits and unleashing hounds on to pale deer, their leaps frozen in space. Ladies in richly figured gowns with emblems embroidered on sideless surcoats glanced coyly up at their menfolk in adoration. She gave a wry smile.

The rest of the room was panelled in wood, beautifully carved and decorated with open tracery along the top edges where it overlapped the plastered walls. Above this painted patterns had been executed in gay colours, making the room bright and splendidly radiant. There were several stools and chairs, and a table of carved oak on which rested a bowl of dried flower-heads, petals and leaves. Ginevra bent closer to look, aware that it was giving off a delicious smell of roses and a hint of spices. Lavender too, and coriander. She stood back and took a deep breath, allowing the perfume to transport her back over the moors to the priory herbarium where she saw the tall, dark guest again, looking into her eyes with amusement. Her eyes closed and she felt again the weight of his body, as she had done so many times since last night, felt his mouth

moving over her face while the thunder and lightning
wreaked havoc around them.

It was like this that Marianne saw her as she quietly
re-entered the room. For a moment she stood and
gazed at this exquisite elfin creature, eyes closed and
head held back, the slim body and pale copper hair.
She was going to have such fun dressing her and
showing her things, even though Jais had indicated that
there was little time. If they were in love, she thought,
they were certainly not going to let anyone know it.
And yet it was difficult to believe that they were not.
The handsome brother who had been sought-after for
as long as she could remember had remained utterly
free until now. Such a beautiful couple they would
make.

'Ginevra?'

'Oh!' She came back to the present with a shudder.
'I'm so sorry, Mistress Mercer. I was somewhere else,
I think. Your bowl of perfumed petals. . .'

There were still two maids in the upper room as
Marianne entered with Ginevra. This house was
obviously large enough to take many guests without
the lack of privacy one was forced to endure at home,
and Ginevra thought of how difficult it had been to
distribute an extended family among so few rooms.
Why, this room was for her alone, and was as big as
Alan and Johanna's solar. This was a far cry from the
linen-room. The large bed, and white bedcover bordered with gold and white fringing, looked soft and
inviting.

The windows overlooked the back of the house, and
she could just see the large lawn and orchard in the
distance. Wooden shutters were folded back on to the
white plastered walls, which reflected the light back
again on to a long, polished steel mirror hanging on

the opposite wall. For a moment Ginevra was puzzled. It looked as though someone else was in the room until she moved and understood, and walked slowly towards herself, filled with curiosity. The other three women watched, enchanted, as the two images peered even closer, scrutinising every detail, turning sideways and then sideways again. Hands touched the bodies, stroked and smoothed, found marks on the fabric of the gown and then turned away from each other in despair.

'Oh, what a sight I look!'

'I don't believe you could look anything but beautiful,' Marianne said warmly. 'Even if you. . .' She had been about to say, even if you were in rags, but stopped just in time. 'Even if you had travelled a thousand miles.'

'I feel as though I have!' Ginevra flopped into a well-cushioned chair.

'Of course. And you must need some refreshment. Now, let's see. . .'

And while Ginevra watched from the comfort of the chair a bath of hot water was prepared, with small bowls of scented lye-soap and clean, sweet-smelling towels, and a heap of fresh undergarments, gowns and kirtles, bliauds and surcoats was found. Her eyes stared in astonishment at the array now piled on the bed, table and chairs, and before long she had been stripped of all her old worn things and placed in the steaming bath, smelling sweetly of herbs and lathered with soap-wort—which was laughingly called Foam Dock. Gentle hands bathed her from head to toe and soon merry laughter could be heard echoing down the passageways and through the open windows.

Ginevra's clean and glowing body made Marianne gasp with admiration—such a slender and supple back,

long neck and limbs. Surely Jais must be deeply in love
with her? With the glowing copper hair flowing about
her this girl was well set, she thought, to provide him
with some competition. Maybe that was what he'd
been looking for all this time, but she wished she knew
what the urgency was all about.

Slowly the transformation took place, layer by layer.
Ginevra was dressed in a tight-fitting tunic and skirt of
pale green silk and a loose, open-sided surcoat of green
velvet trimmed with gold, and the borrowed gowns
were adjusted to show the gold girdle of the tunic at
each side. Her hair was combed, braided and arranged
skilfully in a gold net behind her head, and topped by
a deep silk-covered fillet over the linen barbette which
enclosed her face—a style Ginevra had not seen before.
There were gasps of pleasure as she stood for them to
see the result of their efforts.

'Look in the mirror again now, Ginevra.'

She turned, and as one of the maids rubbed away
the steam with a towel the reflection of the new
Ginevra appeared, as graceful as ever, but now with an
air of refinement and sophistication. She and the
reflection surveyed each other seriously and in silence,
their eyes moving downwards and up again to the bare
neck, the new headdress and the swirl of green silk and
velvet around her feet. I've changed, she thought. Is
this really me? She lifted her arms to see the effect of
the long, streaming tippets extending from her sleeves
at the elbow. They were lined with pale pink silk,
echoing the pink of her complexion and slender hands
and the embroidery of pink and gold on the green
leather shoes. The women glanced at each other and
raised eyebrows, smiling with pleasure at the sight
before them.

Though Ginevra had known Marianne only a short

time, she was overwhelmed by her kindness already, and her generosity. She turned and hugged her, finding it impossible to put into words what her heart was feeling.

'They look much better on you than on me,' said Marianne, touched by Ginevra's spontaneous reaction and delighted by the result of their efforts. 'What a good thing we're almost the same size.'

'Oh, mistress, just you wait,' laughed one of the maids, pushing her stomach forward and cupping her hands beneath it suggestively. 'You'll be wanting a whole new wardrobe soon!'

'Hush, you two!' said Marianne, laughing. 'Let's have these things put into safe-keeping. Ginevra can have them until *she* doesn't need them any more, either.' And the three fell into gales of laughter, leaving the young guest to turn scarlet with confusion. She realised that they were assuming motherhood was not far from her mind, having seen the betrothal ring tied to her finger.

'Are you indeed expecting?' she asked.

'Yes, my dear. Though if these two blabbermouths had not said anything no one would have been the wiser for a few more weeks.' She laughed in mock-annoyance. The two giggling maids scurried off to tidy the room leaving Ginevra, once again, to stare at her reflection, silently asking it how much it knew about the getting of infants. The blank expression told her that it knew nothing.

'The truth is,' she agreed with it when her companions had left her, 'the truth is that I don't *know* what happens.' She stood at the window, looking into the garden, then turned away and sat on the edge of the soft feather bed. Her hand smoothed the white cool cover, her mind projecting pictures on to its

surface, seeing the dark outline of Jais's face as he had
lain above her during the storm last night. Much more,
he had said. *How* much more? She remembered his
hands on her shift as he had held her in his arms, and
slowly her hand crept up to hold the breast which he
had cradled. It had no effect on her. And yet, she
thought, why did his hand feel different? Why had she
reacted so immediately and with such intensity?

She had seen dogs and oxen mounting each other
from behind and had assumed, from the hastily withdrawn eyes of her priory companions, that this was
some mystic and bestial function which some instinct
prompted them to do. She supposed that if her mother
had not departed this life quite so suddenly she would
by now have found the chance to explain something of
the mysteries of getting a woman with child. But then,
she thought sadly, no one had expected anything quite
like the awful sickness which had swept through the
country. Even Jais and Marianne had lost their father
at that time, too. The nuns had never discussed child-
bearing with their pupils, nor had anyone ever dared
to suggest that they should.

'Best if you didn't have too long to think about it,'
Alan had said. Think about getting married? Going off
with a complete stranger? What? She had seen the cat
giving birth, cows dropping their calves, sheep their
lambs. But never people. So what happened? Was it
too awful even to talk about? She wished Rowenna
were here to talk to and laugh with, though as far as
hard facts were concerned it was just as much a puzzle
to her, too. She had once offered the information that
'it' happened in bed, at night. Exactly *what*, though,
Rowenna couldn't say with any certainty, and so they
had both remained baffled. All the same, the recollection of being in bed with Jais all night made her

stomach feel weak and her legs tremble. He had said, in the guest-house last night, that he would be delighted to tell her on another occasion, so she would simply have to wait on his pleasure. But she could not help wondering what Johanna would have explained to her if they had not been interrupted. What was it that she would have said if there had been time?

Time! Damn the man and his unreasonable haste. She looked again at the reflection and knew that what she saw was yet one more manifestation of this same haste towards the unknown, towards a future which she seemed helpless to control. I *will* make you pay, she said to the new Ginevra facing her. But, to her consternation, it looked back at her blankly.

That evening Marianne and Ginevra ate quietly together in the privacy of a cosy chamber filled with the perfume of freshly picked flowers, one of Marianne's weaknesses. She forbore to ask Ginevra questions about herself, realising that the girl would require answers to some of her own first, and anyway Jais had said not to ask for information at this stage, unless Ginevra should offer any. It was all very mysterious, but she had no doubt that her brother had his reasons. He always did. She could see that rest was needed too, and time for reflection, space and peace. As an attentive hostess, she saw to it that Ginevra had a plentiful supply of these.

The day that followed was an unforgettable one of exciting discoveries and new sights. The first thing, Marianne said, was to find some fabrics and have a wardrobe made, something fitting for the Lady Ginevra de la Roche. Ginevra looked startled at the sound of the new title and Marianne saw at a glance that she had not given it any previous thought. So, no aspirations in that direction, it seemed.

But the choosing of fabrics was something after Ginevra's own heart, and when Marianne opened up a closet in one of the upper rooms, full of bolts of the most exquisite cloth that Ginevra had ever seen, her face lit up like a thousand beacons. Ah, thought Marianne, now this seems to have set a fire to the brand. She watched as Ginevra fingered the bolts, naming many of them as they were recognised. 'Sendal, brocade, damask, sarsenet, shot-silk, velvets, moiré-patterned taffetas, half-silk. . . Oh, Marianne, this is unbelievable! Is this what Master Mercer brings back from Italy?'

'Some of it,' said Marianne. 'The rest is in the shop in the city. These pieces are for our own use. But how is it that you know all these types? Are your people in the business, too?'

'No, not at all. I was taught to do ecclesiastical embroidery at the priory of Our Lady of Aire, so I'm familiar with many of these fabrics, though there are lots here I've never seen before.'

'A broderer?' So, thought Marianne, so that's the way the wind blows. And from the priory, too. Now why did Jais not want me to mention the workshop, I wonder? Is he up to some trickery, or is there some perfectly simple answer?

Ginevra was clearly in her element, the rest of the morning being spent with the maids and the family dressmaker measuring, calculating, flinging ells of billowing, sparkling fabrics into the air and draping them round Ginevra's lovely form to see how they fell in folds and caught the light. Soft, lightweight linens and silks for shifts to wear under her gowns, heavier ones for nightwear, figured velvet for a surcoat trimmed with marten fur, sarsenet to line the sleeves—all were tried, accepted or rejected, until her mind was giddy with the choices. 'The cost, Marianne! Think of what this is going to cost.'

'I've been informed that the cost is something we are not to think about.'

'You mean, it really doesn't matter how much?'

'It really does *not* matter at all.' Marianne looked at Ginevra's disbelief and added kindly, 'Jais wants you to have everything you desire. No, he didn't say everything you *need*, he said *desire*.' And that was all she would say on the matter. So, in spite of the cost to her betrothed, Ginevra dispensed with all feelings of guilt and allowed herself to be persuaded that she would need a wardrobe that would have made Rowenna green with envy.

'Now, the next thing you need is a maid,' Marianne insisted. 'One of your very own. I've got just the girl for you. She's my Martha's sister, Oswinna.'

Ginevra was again overcome by such kindness, feeling that there must be some small thing she could do in return. Her enquiry about the situation of the herb-garden caused Marianne some surprise but in a little while, after a brief excursion to the garden and through the kitchen, Ginevra came to her with an infusion of pounded rose-petals, rosemary, wild strawberries and honey, stirring it gently in a goblet. 'Please rest a little now and sip this,' she said to the delighted Marianne with a smile.

'What talents! What is it for?'

'It's to prevent a miscarriage,' Ginevra said gravely, having looked it up in her mother's ancient recipe book. 'At this moment it's all I can do to repay your kindness to me.'

'I think that Jais is a very lucky man. I hope he

realises what a treasure he'll be getting.' Marianne's
nose was deep in the goblet, savouring the sweetness.

'I think he means to make use of my skills in every
way he can,' Ginevra answered quietly, absently watching two butterflies chase each other outside the
window. Something in the voice, a certain sadness,
made Marianne look up at her.

'That's rather an odd thing to say, Ginevra,' she
remarked quietly. 'Is something wrong?'

There was no answer, and she would not pry. Jais
had explicitly told her not to ask any questions, but the
girl quite clearly was unhappy. She was sure that things
had been moving too fast for her, and that as a result
Ginevra was feeling threatened and unsure of herself.
She could well imagine that this young convent-girl
would be no match for Jais's forceful ways.

Marianne rose and went to put her arms around her.
'Let's go into town and find the shoemaker. And we
need a girdle or two, and some purses, too. I'll show
you the shop while we're there—would you like that?'
Ginevra nodded. 'And you mustn't mind my brother's
ways,' continued Marianne. 'Men who know what they
want are infinitely preferable to those who don't.'

'Even at the expense of other people?' Ginevra could
not help saying, aware that she was making herself
difficult to understand. But Marianne, like her brother,
was perceptive, especially of people, and she could see
the direction of her question.

'His expectations of people are high. But he only
cares about those people he feels are worth caring
about. And that *must* include you, Ginevra, for I can't
see him wanting to marry anyone for any other reason.
He's been avoiding mothers with marriageable daughters for many years.'

The thought of Jais being the hunted one instead of

the hunter seemed, for a fleeting moment, so totally absurd to Ginevra that her tension was suddenly released into a burst of laughter.

'It's true!' said Marianne, catching the infectious laugh.

'Yes, I'm sure. It's not the impossibility I'm laughing at, just the picture of Jais being pursued by hordes of screaming mothers and daughters!' They collapsed into helpless giggles, the scene vivid in their minds.

Marianne dabbed at her eyes. 'Let's make a list,' she said.

Changed into plain woollen gowns and leather shoes, they ventured into the town accompanied by several servants and their maids. The larger the party, Marianne said, the less likelihood there was of being robbed by pickpockets. As before, when Ginevra had turned into the seclusion of the close, the noise was the first thing she noticed. Now as they turned on to Petergate the hum of activity swelled, though she was assured that this area was relatively quiet, being mostly occupied by bookbinders and mercers.

'I'll take you to the shop first, as we're nearly there anyway,' said Marianne, turning into an open doorway under a deeply jettied overhang. Ginevra had noticed that the buildings here appeared to lean towards each other as they rose upwards from the ground, the upper storeys projecting like brows over the eyes of the windows. The Mercers' shop, open to the front of the street, was elegant and colourful, stacked on all three sides with bolts of fabric, some hanging in twisted bundles from rods strung across the ceiling. For some moments Ginevra stood speechless as the colours, patterns and textures made their impact on her. In a smaller back room, the Mercers sold mirrors, threads, needles and pins, and all the tools required for sewing and even some for embroidery.

'Do you think I could buy some threads and a small piece of linen, just to embroider on? I haven't done any for well over a week, and I'd love to do some again now. And I'll need a small frame too.'

In view of Marianne's agreement with Jais not to speak of the workshop, she could only yield to the perfectly natural request, though she found it difficult to keep silent while knowing that he already had in abundance all that Ginevra was purchasing.

These delicious acquisitions safely packed up, it was difficult for Marianne to keep her young guest's mind on anything else as they turned into Stonegate. But one thing *would* catch her attention. 'Look, Ginevra! The big house in there, beyond those gates. Do you see the top of it?'

Ginevra looked beyond the stout wooden gates set halfway up an archway at the imposing stone building, larger than any other she had seen so far. It occupied the entire corner of Petergate and Stonegate, not far from the Mercers' shop, standing solid and secure. 'It's very grand,' she remarked. 'Is that where the Lord Mayor lives?'

Marianne smiled. 'Not yet,' she said, laughing. 'It's where Jais lives.' She watched Ginevra's wide-eyed look of disbelief as the golden-brown eyes were turned to her in wonderment, and then back to the house.

'Are you teasing me, Marianne?' she asked, frowning.

'No, Ginevra. I'm not teasing. That's Jais's house. That's where you'll live when you're married. Come! We have no time to call just now, and I expect he'll be doing business anyway. We mustn't disturb him.'

'Business, Marianne? What business?' She was suddenly curious, but Marianne's attention had been caught elsewhere by two figures, who at one moment had been walking towards them, deep in conversation, and who had then whipped smartly round and hurried back along Stonegate. It was clear to Marianne that she had been the cause of their hasty change of direction.

'That's odd,' she said, looking puzzled. 'What's *he* doing round here, I wonder?'

'Who was it, Marianne?'

'That,' she said emphatically, 'was Master Patrickson. Not one of our favourite people. Don't know who the other man was. But he looked very uncomfortable to see us. His shop is down at the other end of town, so I don't know what he'd be doing up here. No matter!' She took Ginevra's arm. 'Let's go and find the shoemaker, shall we? And there's a stained-glassmaker's place on Blake Street.'

They dodged the puddles and a wooden barrow piled high with bales of wool, Ginevra exclaiming with delight at the display of wares along the shopfronts, the smell of newly baked pies and the colourful song-birds in wicker cages. Except for one thing, all else was driven from Ginevra's mind as they picked their way through the narrow streets, gaping at the shops, their noses invaded by smells as a woman carried a basket of fish past them.

'That reminds me,' said Marianne, stopping in her tracks so abruptly that the young maid behind can-noned into her. 'Jais will be with us this evening for supper. It's Friday, isn't it? And I've forgotten his favourite oysters! Ralph and Jem, go down to the fish-landing by the bridge. . .' And she gave them money for the purchase.

Jais would be with them for supper! The words

sounded like music in Ginevra's ears. The glimpse of
his house had given her much to think about; she had
had no inkling that it would be as fine as that or that
she would be expected to be mistress of such a large
household. She frowned a little to herself as they
walked back home, deep in contemplation. What was
it that Marianne had said to her that morning? 'His
expectations of people are high.' Well, his expectations
of her must easily exceed her own if he thought that
she could manage a place of that size, for she had
already acquainted him with her skills and he had
appeared to be well-satisfied with them. Any others
would have to be picked up along the way, but she
remained mystified as to why he should think she was
particularly suitable.

CHAPTER TEN

THE news that Jais was expected for supper that evening in the great hall made Ginevra's heart beat abnormally fast. The thought of seeing him again soon, in spite of her carefully nurtured indifference, was enough to reawaken the thoughts and fears which had been allowed to rest in semi-slumber while her material world was being refurbished. Now, suddenly, this indifference appeared to be wearing thin as she sought the most attractive of the gowns Marianne had lent her, though she would not admit to herself why this was so important.

It had already occurred to young Oswinna that life was going to be hectic if her new mistress was going to be as demanding as this every day.

'No, not that one, Oswinna. I should try the russet, perhaps, d'you think?'

'Yes, mistress, better than the forest-green?'

'Oh, Oswinna, I don't know. But I must decide soon. Yes, the russet. Take these away, will you? Then I shall not see them.' So the armfuls of gowns were removed and then hands laced, adjusted and braided to Ginevra's nervous satisfaction. What would he think of the new elegance? The hair coiled and netted, with no wimple to cover her neck? Would he approve? Did she care about his approval?

She stood back to view the image of the new Ginevra, now dressed in a russet bliaud girdled with a new leather belt. The surcoat of deep brown velvet created an effect of rich copper tones with her hair.

She nodded to the image in the mirror. Well, my girl, the outer covers may have changed, but what about the merchandise inside?

The thought that this, too, had changed over the past few days had already flitted through her mind on more than one occasion, only to be pushed rudely out again as being too uncomfortable to entertain. It was strange, though, how the new clothes had brought with them a sense of confidence. Even though events were still not under her personal control, the knowledge that she no longer looked like a wild country-girl helped to assuage her anger at the enforced changes to her life.

Yes, she would be cool. She would display this new Ginevra in an outer shell of self-assurance. Reserved, distanced, poised. She would adopt a new suit of armour; indifference must be cultivated and worn for him to see along with the silken gowns, the new shoes, the. . .

A knock on the door startled her out of her new composure and sent her hand flying to her breast to quell the sudden lurch of her heart. Was that all it took to undo her new intentions? His hand on the door? Just that and no more?

He was wearing a soft blue calf-length bliaud which accentuated the greyness of his eyes. Wide bands of silver embroidery decorated the neck, hem and sleeves while the tight-fitting sleeves of the chainse beneath picked up the glossy blackness of his hair. Ginevra noticed the exquisitely chased design on the silver belt sitting low on his hips and her eyes moved up to see the welcome light of a smile in his eyes. How could one be indifferent to this? she wondered, her expression of aloofness melting as ice before the sun. Her happiness burst out like spring flowers and she smiled.

Reserve, she thought. Be reserved, then, if not indifferent. Poised, distant, cool.

'Ginevra.' His voice was deep and husky, making her name sound like a caress. He held out his arms and she moved towards him, ignoring the inner voices. They shouted to her from deep inside the newly polished armour but he was there, and she heard them only as on a faint breeze. 'Ginevra. I believe you're pleased to see me. Am I right?'

Woman, they screamed, for pity's sake hold back!

Something penetrated her dream, just rippling the surface. Her lips would not form the words he wanted to hear. At least *they* were under control. 'No, sir. You are mistaken. . .' And she walked into his arms. 'I am not pleased. . .to see you. . .' Her hands stole upwards to his shoulders, and beyond. She felt his hands on her back, moving, smoothing, and her fingers encased his head, found their way into his hair and drew his mouth down to hers. Before her eyes closed she caught the glint of astonishment and then amusement in his eyes. Then her body arched into his and her lips told him what he wanted to know, and more. The voices melted away, pushed deep into the pool of her senses where they could not surface. Jais took full advantage of her body's betrayal. The first kiss was hers to control. The next ones were his.

Ginevra's head moved sideways on to his shoulder and her fingers followed the line of his square jaw, eventually managing to hold back his lips so that she could breathe. Her gasp of air came like a sob and she buried her face into the crook of his arm, hiding from his eyes. Holy Virgin, she thought, was there no armour strong enough to protect her? Did it take only a word from him to overcome all her carefully planned resistance? Now he must be even more sure of his ground.

Trembling, she held on to his shoulders for support, her eyes searching beyond him for visual affirmation that she was back in the real world again. With her cheek against his arm, she came face to face with the mirror, and the image of two lovers standing together as one. Above hers, Jais turned his head and saw them too.

'Who is that woman, Ginevra?' he asked in a whisper, as though the sound of a voice might disturb the vision.

Ginevra looked at her thoughtfully, seeing an elegant, wanton creature, red-lipped and languid with desire, pressed tightly against a black-haired courtier.

'We're not well-acquainted, sir. But I believe her name is Juniper.'

He smiled, keeping his arms tightly about her. 'Juniper? Tell me more of her.'

'She's a prickly shrub who bears aromatic black berries and thrives on limestone soil. In Italy, she's known as Ginevra.' She felt the laughter vibrating in his chest and saw, in the mirror, his teeth part as the silent mirth escaped through his lips.

Shaking his head in amazement at her imaginative recognition of her other self, he asked, 'What does she do best, this Lady Juniper?'

'She flavours red meat dishes, sir, mostly.'

The aptness of her description brought a burst of musical laughter from his chest, and throwing back his handsome head he cradled her to him in delight. As his laughter subsided he found his voice again, and placed his hand beneath her chin to turn her face to his.

'Then I am doubly fortunate, *damoiselle*, to have two such beautiful and fascinating ladies in my arms. I think this might be the perfect time to give you both something.' His eyes were full of laughter, but Ginevra could not guess what he might mean. He released her and deftly untied the betrothal ring from her hand and then, slipping something from a small pouch, placed another smaller ring on her finger. 'I promised you another one that fits,' he said.

'It's beautiful,' Ginevra whispered, looking closely at the glowing topaz set between two tiny golden hands. 'And it fits perfectly, too. Thank you, Jais.'

'I shall put it on your other hand tomorrow, Ginevra.'

At first his words did not register with her as she admired the ring on her hand. It was only when they sounded again in her head that she understood the full implication of what he was saying. She looked hard into his eyes in disbelief, searching them for signs of a joke, light-heartedness, even. But they looked back into hers without wavering and she knew that he meant what he had said. All the old angers crowded at once into her mind as she turned away from him.

She shook her head, her hands forming into tight fists. 'No, sir. That's impossible! Quite impossible!' Was there to be no choice about *anything*? Not even a choice of days?

'Ginevra!' He had not moved, but his voice arrested her. 'It has been arranged for tomorrow. Richard has just this moment arrived from Italy, and both he and Marianne will be our witnesses.' His voice softened a little. 'You cannot escape it, little bird. It was an agreement we made together.'

She whirled to face him, pleading, her body tense with apprehension. 'Not yet! Please, can't it wait a little longer? Jais. . . I'm not ready. . . I can't. . . I. . .' Her hands spread out before her, indicating the total helplessness she was feeling as once again she was swept along into his scheme of things. 'Best if you didn't have too long to think about it. . .' The words re-echoed in her head. So soon!

'Listen to me, Ginevra!'

'No! I don't want to listen to you. . .' She threw up an arm to ward off his words, but he caught her wrist and held it tightly. 'No! Let me go! I don't want to hear. . .you're unreasonable. . . I don't want to marry you tomorrow. . .or any other day. . .' She pounded against him and struggled in fury as he caught her other wrist and held her to him. But his grip was like steel and she was helpless. Impotent. 'More time. . . please. . . I need more time. . .please, not yet. . .' Her voice became hoarse with incoherence, fading to a whisper as she pushed her face against his chest. You're still a stranger to me. I'm afraid. These words stayed unspoken in her head. It was no use. He would never understand.

'Ginevra, listen to me, little bird. . .' And as though he had heard her inner words, he soothed her panic with his soft voice, though he was secretly amused that this could be the same woman who had greeted him with such passion only a few moments before. 'Listen! Stop beating and listen.'

She stood, exhausted and shaking against him, her face hidden in his chest. He took her wrists and held them behind her back. Pinioned like this, she had no choice but to hear him. 'You know that the longer the marriage is delayed, the longer Alan and Johanna will have to wait for help. You can't have forgotten that.'

'That's just an excuse! You're using that as an excuse for your unchivalrous haste!' She squirmed to free herself but to no avail, and he waited for the outburst to subside.

'Chivalry has nothing to do with it, Ginevra. There are people on the estate living without proper food and shelter. Are you refusing to help because of some whim?'

'It's *not* a whim, you inconsiderate brute!' she hissed, writhing in his arms.

'Does a bargain come into effect only when it suits your convenience?' There was no answer. 'Answer me!'

Knowing that his reasoning was on a surer footing than hers, she could not answer him. Her reasons were, to him, no reasons at all. But she did not want to hear of those who were depending on her. She had not asked for it to be this way. Why had these responsibilities suddenly been heaped at her door? 'I will direct your life, *damoiselle*, whether you allow me to or no.' Those had been his words and she had accepted them at the time, though for what reason she had no clear idea. Once again she had to concede that he had the upper hand, for the time being. She would have to go through with it. She lifted her head and threw him a look of resentful anger. She could see the V-shape of his black-bearded jawline and the set of his firm mouth. Arrogant. Determined. Immovable. Jet of the Rock. The name suited him perfectly. Jais de la Roche.

He bent his head to look at her, gently letting go of her wrists as he felt her body relax against him. Taking her face in his hands, he replaced the stray wisps of hair and smoothed her eyebrows with a finger. 'Whatever happened to the Lady Juniper?' he asked softly.

Ginevra shook her head. 'I don't know anyone by that name, sir,' she said in a quiet voice, not looking at him.

He smiled and kissed her gently on the lips. 'Let's go

down to supper, little bird. Richard is anxious to meet you.'

The return of Marianne's husband from Italy helped to ease the tension between Ginevra and Jais, for the two men were extremely good friends of long standing. From the easy banter which was projected into the conversation Ginevra gathered that Jais had been responsible for bringing his sister to Richard's attention. Apart from their height, the two men were physically unalike. Richard was a thick-set, fair-haired barrel of a man, with a trim beard and twinkling blue eyes, but his easy pace and gentle manner belied a razor-sharp intelligence and a formidable business ability. His good-looking affable face and open affections made Ginevra respond to him immediately, making her forget her anger for the time being. She could not hold out without great discourtesy against the warmth of these wonderful people, against the intelligent conversation, of which she had had but little over the past years, and the easy companionship.

They were fascinated by the news of Richard's travels, the two men exchanging experiences which made Ginevra aware for the first time how well-travelled Jais was—how well-read, too. It was a side of him she had not had a chance to see before, and as she listened to the conversation of these quick-witted and highly literate men, laughing and courteous, or serious as the occasion demanded, she had to acknowledge to herself that this was a circle of warmth she would like to enjoy forever.

Although academically not on the same level, she was included into the conversation without a hint of condescension. Richard and Marianne wished to know more about her knowledge of herbs, and her quiet confidence as she explained the efficacy of various concoctions and how they were prepared made them sit back in amazement.

'You're far too good to be married to this lout here,' said Richard, indicating Jais with his head and laughing.

Jais leaned forward, looking worried, but with a smile behind the eyes, his hand closing quickly over Ginevra's. 'You're not doing my cause any good, brother-in-law. Kindly keep your opinions to yourself until I have her safe!'

There was much laughter all round, and even Ginevra had to join in, though the talk about Jais's good fortune made her blush with embarrassment. But she kept her hand under his, feeling its warm strength, and out of the corner of her eye she looked at the long, sun-bronzed fingers and the covering of fine black hair along the length of them. Jais gave hers a conspiratorial squeeze as he saw her colouring up, relieved that her anger had not extended further than the door of her room.

Marianne had noted with approval Ginevra's choice of gown, the perfect matching of colours and accessories. Ginevra showed her the new ring. 'It's to be tomorrow, then, Ginevra.' It was a statement, not a question.

Ginevra looked at her new friend, whose kindness had meant so much to her over the past two days. 'I didn't think it would be so soon, Marianne, but Jais insists. . .'

Marianne caught the hint of anxiety in her voice. 'Richard and I will be with you, too. Would you like Oswinna to be there, just to help?'

'I *would* like it, Marianne, and do you think your

two maids could be there, the ones who helped to remould me?'

'Of course. They will want to, I know. But you are not remoulded, Ginevra. You're the same lovely person you were when you came. Richard is very taken with you. I shall have to beware or I might lose my standing with him!' They laughed, and the men's heads turned to see what fun they were missing. And Ginevra felt, as she had never felt before, that she was honoured to be included in this family.

As they left the high table Marianne looked at her young guest sideways, noting her flat stomach. It couldn't be that she was. . .? No, surely Jais would not be so easily caught; that was unthinkable. But for the life of her she could think of no other reason why the marriage vows should be said in such unseemly haste. Even before the poor girl had had time for new gowns to be made. Marianne shook her head, puzzled. Perhaps Jais had told Richard something. In which case, she thought to herself with a smile, I shall have to wheedle it out of him. She smoothed the creases from the back of her rose-red surcoat and turned the smile to her guests. 'Now, you go up to the solar and I will join you presently.'

'Marianne tells me that you are an accomplished broderer too, Ginevra,' Richard said as he escorted her to the solar.

Ginevra looked at him, trying to assess how much his statement stemmed from politeness and how much from genuine interest. She judged that being a mercer he would most likely know something of the craft, and his open face, bent towards her, prompted her to try him out. 'I don't think I would claim to be accomplished, sir, but it's true that I've spent many years with the Prioress Claire, in Airedale. Have you heard of her? She's the best there is.'

'Indeed I have heard of her, *damoiselle*, and I know of her fame. If *she* taught you, then Marianne was correct, you must be accomplished. And Jais has told me of the vestments you made for Beesholme Abbey, too. Do you hope to continue after your marriage?'

Ginevra's heart missed a beat. This was dangerous ground which she would rather not tread lest she rake up a source of conflict between herself and Jais which should remain hidden to others. She saw Jais watching her from where he stood at the table, pouring wine into fine crystal goblets. He came to them, holding one in each hand, keeping them back until she had made her reply. 'That would be my dearest wish, sir, but unfortunately one cannot do *that* kind of embroidery outside workshop conditions, except as a pastime. And I don't wish to spend my days embroidering on horses' caparisons or monograms on gowns.' She felt she had said enough. Too much perhaps, but the temptation to say it out loud, without fear of a reprimand, had been too great to resist.

Fortunately Richard found her answer much to his liking, and nodded agreement. 'There you are, my fine peacock.' He looked at Jais in amusement. 'If you had that in mind for Ginevra, you may as well forget about it. You'll have to find someone else to do that for you.' He accepted the goblets and gave one to Ginevra, laughing as he did so.

Jais entered the lists, shaking his head. 'Then it looks as though I shall have to take you back to Airedale, *damoiselle*. Would you wish me to?'

She was unhorsed, and they both knew it. For all his laughing words, she knew that the steely eyes had her at bay. Whichever way she moved, she was his. Richard looked at her, sensing that here was something more than the sum of its parts, then he looked at Jais, and waited.

Yet again Ginevra allowed her impulses to lead. Her free hand sought out Jais's and held it tightly, like a lover. She looked up at him and noted that the former challenge in his eyes had softened to an expression of surprise, even bafflement. 'No, Jais,' she said softly, as though Richard had not been present. 'No, I would not wish to go back to Airedale. I would stay here with you.'

There was no verbal reply, only a look which said everything that words could not. Richard broke the silence. 'Ginevra, you may not be aware of it, but that is probably the one and only time that Jais will allow you to have the last word.' Their laughter broke the spell.

'What am I missing?' said Marianne, entering the room at that moment.

Jais took her hand and kissed it gallantly. 'Dear one, thank you for my oysters. You remembered!'

She kept her hand in his and returned the kiss with a smile. 'It's funny you should have mentioned the oysters. Ralph and Jem told me just now that they'd seen Master Patrickson on the fish-landing when they went to see if they could buy some.' There she paused for effect.

Jais and Richard looked at each other and then at Marianne, bemused. 'She'll tell us if we wait long enough, Jais. Just be patient,' said her husband, quickly dodging a playful swipe at his head.

'I was just about to tell you!' In exasperation, Marianne looked to Ginevra for support, rolling her huge dark eyes to the ceiling.

'I can see it's high time I returned home,' said

Richard, shaking his head at Jais. 'It looks as though you've let things get out of hand here!'

'I've got my hands full, thank you, brother-in-law,' Jais replied, deliberately looking sideways at Ginevra, and grinning mischievously.

'Marianne, I believe we should leave these two. It's quite clear we're not going to get a word in edgeways, are we?' Ginevra pretended disdain and they turned simultaneously, catching each other's eyes in a mutual understanding. But the two men moved in unison, too, and both women found themselves being led to the wide cushioned window-seat and plonked firmly down.

'Dearest heart,' said Richard, with great solemnity, his eyes belying the expression, 'pray tell me. What *was* Master Patrickson doing?'

'I can't remember!' Marianne and Ginevra kept stony faces while Richard groaned and looked to Jais for help.

'Isn't he the one we saw earlier, in town?' Ginevra said quietly, knowing full well what the reaction would be. She saw the two men stiffen.

'Mmm, that's right.' Marianne nodded, equally quiet.

'You saw him twice in one day?' Jais sounded surprised.

'No, we saw him once. Ralph and Jem saw him twice; that's why they thought it interesting enough to mention to me. But if it's of no concern. . .' Marianne looked up and saw that Jais and Richard were reading each other's faces, and the lightness in her voice trailed away as their disquiet became apparent.

'Tell me, sweetheart——' Richard was more serious now '—where were you, where was *he* when you saw him?'

'He and another man were walking towards us at the

top of Stonegate when he saw us on the corner, and so they quickly turned round and hurried away. In the same direction they came from.'

'They were near Stonegate House?' asked Jais softly.

'They were outside it. Why?'

'Who was the other man? D'you know?'

'No idea. He looked as if he might have been a sea-captain, though—you know. . .'

'You mean foreign-looking, bearded? How, exactly?'

'Jais, I can't really tell you. It was only a look, an impression, that's all. He was tall, I remember that. Taller than Patrickson, and yes, he did have a black beard. Bigger than yours.'

'I thought *that* one was this Master Patrickson you've been talking about,' said Ginevra, now quite mystified by the drift of the conversation. 'Who is he?'

'He's the smaller one of the two,' said Jais to her, 'and he's bad news. It looks as though he's been let out of prison, Richard. Perhaps we'd better watch out!'

'Prison?' Ginevra exclaimed horrified. 'Whatever for?'

'He's lucky to get out, but I suppose his money helped,' said Richard. 'He was imprisoned for illegally exporting woollen fabrics without a licence. Two years, I think. Wasn't it, Jais?'

'Yes. He's a mercer, Ginevra, and both Richard and I discovered what was going on, so we alerted the King's officers—the customs men—and he was caught. Now I suppose he's going to carry on from where he left off, by the look of things. And if he's hanging around the Staithe, near the foreign boats, he's obviously looking for someone to work with. I wish I knew what the tall friend looked like.'

'He had a huge beaked nose and very deep-set dark

eyes, with bushy eyebrows and a black pointed beard.
He was holding his head down to hear what the other
man was saying, so I saw his hair, parted down——'
Ginevra paused and held out her left hand in a chop-
ping motion '—*that* side!' She continued in a steady
stream of words, her eyes looking far away into a space
at the top of the wall as the other three stared at her in
amazement. 'He had a large hood round his neck, up
to his ears, and it had a decorated border of a square
key-pattern in silver round the edge. Deep gold. . .that
was the colour. . .deep gold, with a shady black figur-
ing. The border was round the edge of his tunic, too.
Quite fitted, it was, with shining silver buttons all the
way down.' Her hands depicted the garments as she
described him in detail from the top of his head to his
fashionably pointed shoes. 'Does that help?' she asked,
bringing her eyes back to Jais's incredulous face.

'Does that help, indeed!' He bent and took her
hands, pulling her up to stand before him. 'Do you
mean to tell me that you noted all that in the time it
took them to turn and walk away?'

She nodded. 'Yes. D'you want to know what the
other one was wearing, too?'

'Go on.' He kept hold of her hands while she
described Master Patrickson in vivid detail—his ruddy
jowls hanging over the collar of his shabby grey gown,
the wide dagged sleeves lined with scarlet, the sparse
sandy hair and little piggy eyes which flickered with
alarm as he saw Marianne. Every detail. Richard
hooted and looked at Marianne, both of them
dumbfounded.

'Oh, and I should think he was probably left-handed,
too,' she added as an afterthought, absently.

'Left-handed? Who? Patrickson?'

'No, the other one. A right-handed man wouldn't

part his hair down that side——' she touched her head
with a finger '—would he?'

'You are amazing, wench! D'you know that?'

'Do you recognise the description?'

'No, do you, Richard?' He slipped an arm around
her waist and pulled her in to his side, protectively.

Richard went to sit by Marianne. 'No, I don't,' he
said, 'but that's a marvellous bit of observation if ever
I heard it, *damoiselle*. Don't you think so, sweetheart?'
Marianne nodded, equally impressed. 'It'll certainly
help us to recognise him next time we see him, though.'

Ginevra felt the hardness of Jais's thigh as she stood
against him, and a warmth flowed down her legs as she
remembered that this was to be her last evening as an
unmarried woman. Out of sight of Richard and
Marianne, her hand stole across his back from one
shoulder-blade to the other and back again, then rested
on his waist. Her gesture was returned by a tightening
of his arm, though his voice gave no sign that anything
had passed between them. All the same, he was as
acutely aware of her nearness as she was of his. Her
softness in the curve of his arm, the tentative hand
questing the contours of his back challenged his concentration, defying him to continue speaking without
hesitation when his one desire was to sweep her up into
his arms and carry her into the darkness of the night.
For him, tomorrow could not come soon enough.

CHAPTER ELEVEN

THE gentle patter of Oswinna's feet on the polished wooden boards slowly worked its way into Ginevra's sleepy reverie halfway to wakefulness. She watched the clothes being shaken and folded, the water brought in for bathing, her clothes for the morning being laid ready for wear, and thought of all that lay in store for her. Was it really possible for anyone to fall in love with a person they had disliked so intensely less than a week ago? Johanna had said that she was in love, but was this really what it felt like? She sprang out of bed. What use were questions now, she asked herself, with no one to provide the answers?

'Have you decided what to wear for the wedding, mistress?'

'Yes, Oswinna. Mistress Mercer and I found something last evening; it's in her solar. Wait. I'll go along and get it, then we can see what needs to be done.' She would have a chat with Marianne while she was about it.

Barefooted, she slipped along the passageway. The solar door was ajar, and as she neared it voices floated towards her. Not wanting to interrupt a private conversation, she hesitated, ready to turn back. But two voices, clearly Richard's and Marianne's, held her attention, and in that fraction of time between going on and turning back her ears caught snatches of sentences.

'Workshop. . .lost two of the best broderers. . .need

a new one. . .with her experience. . . Claire?. . .is
she. . .?'

Ginevra felt her pulse through her bare feet on the
cold floor of the passage, unable to move but not
wanting to hear any more. It must be about me, she
thought. They're talking about me. Claire? Broderers?
What is going on? An iron band tightened round her
chest as she tiptoed back to her room and sat heavily
on the bed.

Oswinna looked closely at her. 'Are you all right,
mistress? Did you get the dress?'

'Er, no. . .yes. I'm all right. Er. . .no, I'll get the
dress later. . .'

'Poor love, you're sufferin' from nerves, aren't yer?
Canna get yer anythin'?' she asked kindly. 'A posset'll
do yer good.'

Ginevra felt sick. A posset? Yes, a posset would be
nice. What did they mean? 'Need a new one.' 'Workshop.' Whose workshop? Did Marianne have one, or
Jais, perhaps? What *was* going on? Should she ask
Oswinna? No, that would look very strange. Marianne,
then? No, she would surely have told her. The questions would not go away, and she sat for some time
with a frown hovering between her brows, concerned
that time would not now allow her to investigate her
newly aroused suspicions. Pensively she began her
preparations for the day ahead, her silence and air of
abstraction puzzling the young maid, who could not
understand how anyone could be other than brimming
over with joy at the thought of marrying Sir Jais.

But as Ginevra had feared, there was no time to
make any further discoveries before the wedding, for
Marianne saw to it that she was fully occupied. She was
allowed no time to brood, for Jais's sudden decision to
hold the wedding so soon had taken everyone by

surprise; it was as though he had been awaiting Richard's return.

To Jais, the small formal ceremony meant more than Alan's had to him, for he realised that until it was consummated there was always a small chance that she might halt the proceedings. Although he had had a chance to bed her already, he knew that during their night together at the abbey he had gone as far as he could without sending her flying back, irretrievably, to the burrow from which he had so summarily prised her. There was a limit, he had to admit as he lingered over the memory of her soft body lying against his.

Naturally she had challenged his seemingly indecent haste, as had Marianne and Richard, and happily he had found that the same reasons had done for both of them—though he wondered how far they were deceived into thinking that Alan and the future of Scepeton Manor were his prime concern.

Consequently there had been no time to make grand preparations nor to invite guests, a side-effect he was not unhappy with, for the only people he wanted around him at a time like this were his family, though it was a pity that Ginevra's could not be with them, too. He made a mental note to forbid the usual public bedding ceremony, too. That was something they could both do well without. Now, as he prepared himself for the event, he could only pray that the impetuous lady had not changed her mind.

His prayers were answered. She arrived, with his brother-in-law and sister and maids of honour, at the porch of the little St Michael-le-Belfrey on Petergate, the wooden church hiding in the shadow of the minster, only a few moments after his own arrival.

Ginevra could not mistake the glow of admiration in his eyes as he held out a hand to receive her at his side. The sight of her unbound glowing curls topped by a simple garland of pink roses was breathtaking. The cream silk bliaud and pink-figured brocade surcoat perfectly complemented the deep rose-coloured gown she had chosen to wear. She smiled at him shyly, but with apprehension clearly written on her face, all questions of importance unanswered, unanswerable. Like a bell tolling inside her head the only sound she heard rang out loud and clear: 'too late, too late. . .'

In spite of her dream-like state, she missed none of the details, finding comfort in his masculine elegance, seeing him fully attired with sword and richly jewelled belt around his slim hips, his wide shoulders accentuated by the crimson velvet cloak carelessly thrown to one side. Her heart gave a lurch of pride hearing the whispers of admiration from the three maids behind her and she couldn't help but agree with them that he *did* look magnificent.

'You look beautiful, little bird,' he whispered in her ear as he squeezed her hand comfortingly, though she was sure that he would feel its trembling in the coolness of the porch, in spite of the warm, late May noon. She was relieved to know that Marianne and Richard were with her, even though her own folk were not. They had been so kind and tender towards her that morning, sensing her nervousness, her air of distraction.

The short ceremony was over almost as soon as it had begun—brief vows and the exchange of rings, the benediction beneath the white care-cloth and then the kiss. Ginevra's mind was blank, almost numb as she received his embrace and she held on to him tightly to prevent herself from stumbling. His arms were strong and supportive, his mouth tender. The brief mass before the high altar somehow augmented the feeling that this was part of some strange fantasy which would vanish as suddenly as it had appeared.

Afterwards Richard and Marianne embraced her with hearty kisses and the little maids threw handfuls of wheat which caught in their hair like tiny seed-pearls. Laughing, they shook themselves and each other free of the bits and Jais popped a few of them into his mouth and into Ginevra's as they walked hand in hand up the pathway towards home.

It was the first time that Ginevra had been inside Stonegate House, directly opposite the church where they had just been married, though Marianne had pointed it out to her on the previous day. It occupied a large area, stonebuilt on the site of a previous Norman house with stone flags on the roof which were the envy of many of the other less well-to-do merchants whose houses were thatched. Jais was well-pleased with Ginevra's reaction, her exclamations of delight at the large windows, some with tiny pieces of coloured glass let in, and the pale oak panelling along the passage-ways. Her smiles were, he thought, sure to be a good omen, an indication that her earlier reluctance was now fading a little.

He swung her hand gently to gain her attention. 'Well, Lady Ginevra de la Roche? Will this do for you?'

Ginevra smiled at him, aware that he was seeking her approval. 'Sir Jais, it would indeed be a hard woman who would be unhappy with such a lovely house.'

'It is only lovely now that you are its mistress.' He swept a gallant bow, raising her hand to his lips as he did so. The others laughed and applauded this display of chivalry as he led her into the great hall.

Despite the air of intimacy during the feast, the laughter and goodwill, Ginevra's thoughts were far away on another plane. Jais had made every effort to provide an atmosphere of conviviality on a subdued scale so as not to intimidate her. The company in the hall was curious but not intrusive, friendly but not oppressive, and she had responded with graciousness to their good wishes. But she realised that this was only a prelude, and while she wished desperately to be alone with her thoughts she also wished to be magically transported into the middle of tomorrow, knowing but not having to experience.

She was both relieved and tense when the time came for Richard and Marianne to leave, having promised her that they had no intention of escorting her to her chamber as was the usual custom. Once they had bid a tender and rather tearful farewell, Ginevra was allowed the privacy of the beautiful solar upstairs. Jais had taken it upon himself to show her the chests where she could keep her clothes, the window-seats from where she could see into the extensive gardens, the close-cupboard where drink and tiny biscuits had been placed for the evening, and then, considerately, he had left her alone with Oswinna.

They explored with zest, poking into every nook and cranny and exclaiming with delight at the fresh colours of the tapestries on the walls, the cool white bed-hangings and dull pink bedcovers. There were embroidered pillow-beres, exquisitely carved bedposts, chairs and stools, tables and chests, and both of them were quite certain that the room, with its north-and west-facing windows, was the loveliest that anyone could imagine. Ginevra stood by the big oriel window overlooking the garden and allowed waves of peace to wash over her, absorbing the greenness of the lawns and trees and the gleam of the minster over to the right, through the orchard.

A high stone wall at the nearest end to the house caught the light from the low evening sun, glowing pink. That could be the wall of the herb-garden, she mused. Yes, if the kitchen is over there, then that's where the herbs will be. Without waiting for another thought to distract her, she opened the door in the corner of the room and slipped down a flight of stone stairs into a covered passage which ran parallel to the north side of the great hall. Sure enough, there was a heavy oak door on the garden side.

In the herb-garden, beyond the kitchen buildings, Ginevra found the peace which she had longed for throughout the day. At last, here was quiet and solitude, a chance to redirect her thoughts towards more familiar channels, to well-known plants growing in neat sections of bordered plots. The intricate system of geometric pathways reminded her, once again, of the Book of Hours.

A stone fountain in the centre of the garden jetted water high into the air to be caught by a naked stone infant holding a scallop shell, its base encircled by clumps of lavender and marigolds. She breathed in the evocative perfume and turned to explore further, noting pots of new seedlings and signs of recent planting-out.

Wandering up the central path, she passed under the archway in the wall and into the kitchen-garden, now finding herself amid a sea of lettuces, cabbages and onions in much better condition than those at Scepeton Manor. At the far end there was a covered walkway with stone pillars supporting a thatched roof, which she presumed led to the kitchens, or to the buttery perhaps,

and a large window showed above a bank of bay trees
with a door at one side. Thinking that this might
somehow lead to the inner house, she tried the handle
and, finding the door unlocked, entered.

A dark foyer led to another door at an angle, and
this, too, was unlocked. Her curiosity was now
aroused, for there were no kitchen noises to verify
her assumptions. She entered, then stopped on the
threshold, speechless with disbelief while a thousand
thoughts raced through her mind. What was she
seeing?

The room was well-lit with natural light from the
north-facing garden window and also—Ginevra looked
upwards—from a panel of glass pieces let into the
thatch of the roof. Even at this late hour the white-
painted walls reflected light all around on to several
huge wooden embroidery frames shrouded with white
cloths, and some smaller ones on tables. Her heart
beating furiously, and trembling with excitement, she
lifted the white cover off the nearest frame, recognising
immediately the unmistakable semi-circular shape of a
bishop's cope, one side of which was rolled along the
longest edge of the frame. The design was similar to
ones she had worked at the priory—arcades and roun-
dels, saints and kings, biblical scenes in gold threads
and glowing coloured silks. She moved on, seeing the
flat pattern-shape of a mitre, back and front pieces side
by side. Here was a stole, partly worked in or-nué, the
gold threads shimmering under the coloured silks. The
effect was breathtaking. She moved on through the
rows of frames, hardly able to control the trembling in
her limbs, recognising the scrolling borders, the strap-
work bands, the leafy intersections. Ends of thick gold
threads lay neatly bunched under the last gold stitches,
waiting for work to be resumed. Her eyes were drawn

to a white curtain hanging across the entire wall of the room, from floor to roof. She gingerly drew it aside, and her eyes widened again as rows of shelves were revealed, covered with the materials of embroidery and bolts of fabric of every kind, many which were new to her. Linens, canvases, soft paddings, satins, velvets, silks, rich Italian brocades. . . She moved on to where boxes were neatly arranged, each one labelled: gold, passing, purl, spangles, pearls, cords, needles, bodkins. . . She dropped the curtain, shaking her head, stupefied.

The pink of the sky was now flooding in through the window, casting a rich glow over the room and its contents. Ginevra sat on one of the stools and looked about her, shaken and bewildered. What does it mean? she thought. A slow anger began to gather momentum, beginning in her stomach and moving upwards into her throat and head.

'I know what it means,' she said out loud through her teeth. 'I *know* what it means!'

Words fell over themselves inside her. It means that what I overheard this morning is all true! He *does* have a workshop, and he *does* need me to replace somebody. And by the look of all this he needs somebody good, and urgently. This lot will have been commissioned for a certain occasion, if I'm not mistaken. And I suppose he thinks that once I'm safely married to him, I'll be stuck. I'll have to pick up from where somebody left off and get on with it. One of the family! That's what he said in the orchard at home, 'This keeps things in the family!' He had *this* in mind, didn't he? Once I'm in the family I'll have to stay, or the help for Alan and Johanna will stop. Very clever! This will tie me down perfectly! Well, we'll see!

Trembling with outrage, she let herself out of the

room and hurried along the covered walkway, hoping that the door ahead would lead her into the house. It did, to the same passage alongside the hall which led to the solar staircase. Back in her room, she saw that the sheets on the bed had been turned down and that Oswinna had left.

In a pile of discarded garments, Ginevra stood in her shift, rummaging frantically in the chest for her old cream bliaud. They can have everything back! She voiced the words soundlessly, tears stinging the back of her eyes, making it even more difficult for her to see in the darkening room. I don't want anything of his. I don't care if I have to walk all the way, but I'll get there, somehow. Curse him if he takes me for a simple fool. Damn him! Has need of my skills, does he?

Her hair now in dissaray, the garland of roses on the floor, she shook with rage, hurt and humiliation. She heard no sound of Jais entering, only the pounding in her breast.

He stood in the fading light of the sun's last rays, trying to make sense of what was happening. 'Ginevra?'

She whirled to face him. 'Viper! You. . .you toad!'

'Ginevra! What on earth is the matter?'

'The matter? You ask of me what the matter is? When you've been hiding the fact that you need me to replace two of your workers? You. . .you *bartered* with me! That's what the matter is!'

'Will you please tell me what you're talking about? Replacing workers? What workers?' He had not moved from the door, but stood watching her frantic rummaging.

'The workroom!' she spat, pointing to the oriel window and to the garden beyond. 'Out there. Deny that you hatched this plot just to get me here to work for you! You used the Airedale estate as a ruse to get me here!'

Jais made a move towards her, his face showing both incredulity and amusement at her rage. He glanced towards the window. 'So, you found the workroom. Pity, I was going to show it to you tomorrow as a surprise. . .' But before he could take another step, a garment from the chest came hurtling through the air towards him. He caught it in one hand and threw it to one side. 'Ginevra! Will you be calm for a moment while I explain. . .?'

'Explain?' She was backing away from him, but her eyes were flashing and bright with hot tears, her voice hoarse and choking. 'Surprise? You deceiving toad. . . Don't tell me anything. . . I don't want to know. I've seen all I want to see.' Another garment came hurtling towards him, but he saw it coming and dodged to one side.

He stood still and watched her, his eyes like two black lines, his mouth grim, deliberate. 'This discovery of yours, *damoiselle*. Are you sure this is the real reason for your outburst? It seems to me that maybe your anger is borne on the wings of fear.'

She dived for a pillow from the bed and hurled it with both hands at his head. But again he caught it. 'I'm going! I won't be kept here. You're all in it together. And you thought I was fool enough not to discover the real reason. . .' Her hair tumbled across her face, her breasts heaving with sobs of anger as she moved to the chest to claim the gown she had been searching for. 'I will *not* be bargained for! Or bought. Or sold. I'm free!'

For an answer Jais turned to the door, calmly locked it, and put the key high up on top of the close-cupboard. Then, without another word, he began to remove his clothes, keeping his eyes on Ginevra all the time.

Horrified, she watched from the other side of the room while he stripped to his brief white linen *braies*. 'What are you doing. . .?' she whispered, a red-hot ball of fear rising in her throat.

'I think it's time I clipped your wings, my lovely bird.'

She clung tightly to the curtain at the end of the bed, for her legs had suddenly turned to water. Standing with his back to the window, he watched her like a hunter, totally relaxed and still. He was so big. The black fur on his chest spread across to his wide shoulders and tapered to a narrow line down his stomach. His legs were muscular and long. She could see the muscles of his thighs in sharp relief under the bronzed skin as he moved slowly towards her.

No, not the bed, she thought. I must get away from the bed. Blind panic rose hot in her chest as she made a dive across the room, but with a lightning reaction he reached out sideways and scooped her up against his body. With wildly flailing arms she twisted sideways, found his upper arm with her teeth and bit hard. His arms slackened as he felt the sharp pain, just enough for her to push and free herself. 'No!' she gasped. 'Get out! Go away! I don't want to know.'

He laughed softly and his eyes gleamed, hands ready at his sides for her next move. 'Easy, little bird. You will have to learn some time. It may as well be now. All this anger is really panic, isn't it?' His voice was soft and deep, and Ginevra could only stand, transfixed, as he moved towards her again.

With a howl of blind fury, she hurled herself bodily at him; no other course of action seemed possible. He laughed, low down in his throat, as her soft body, light and lithe, hit his hard chest, and as her fists beat at him he blocked every move with his arms, watching her eyes to see where the next onslaught would come from. She knew he was toying with her, knew that fear was to be her undoing, that sooner or later she would tire.

The shift that covered her nakedness was slipping off one shoulder with her efforts, and she knew that it was in danger of exposing her. But the hem was now well down under her feet, and as she turned to pull the fabric free Jais's hands shot out and ripped the garment from neck to hem. With a cry she stepped backwards, fell over the pillow on the floor and went down with a crash amid a tangle of linen. In an instant he had pulled it away and was upon her; pinned under his body she could only twist and kick wildly. Screams rose in her throat but could find no voice. The darkening room swirled about her as she felt her wrists being grasped and held wide apart on to the floor above her head.

'No, no, please!' She could only just gasp out the words, but he remained motionless above her, sitting gently astride her hips to still the writhing panic-stricken body, his eyes scanning her slowly. As she watched mortified, his gaze travelled over her, taking in every detail of the soft rounded curves and the skin glowing from exertion. She clenched her teeth, trembling in silent terror under his scrutiny, her breath bursting from between her teeth in torrents as she squirmed and twisted to escape him.

At last Jais nodded in quiet satisfaction, and smiled as though well-pleased, then brought her wrists together behind her back and lifted her off the floor. 'Come, my lovely one. There are better places than this, are there not?' His hands hurt her wrists as she felt herself being carried easily across to the bed. She stiffened and kicked, but the breath was knocked out of her as she hit the bed and felt the weight of his hard chest and, before she could recover another lungful, his mouth was on hers, insistent, dominating.

She pushed frantically against his shoulders but he was unrelenting, and finally she ceased to struggle and lay limp and breathless, moaning with the shock of his assault. Now his body was hard on hers, not as it had been at the abbey with her shift between them, but alive, warm and vibrant, his hard muscles shocking her sensitive skin into awareness.

His lips were against her mouth as she lay panting and trembling. 'Stop fighting now, little bird. There's no need to fight. Hold still. Easy now.' As he spoke into her mouth she felt him untying the drawstring of his *braies* and sliding them away, then his hand came back to take her pushing fist. He held it above her on the pillow, lowering his mouth to hers again in a long kiss which sent a fire through her veins, melting her resistance, shrouding her thoughts in a swirling mist of sensation. But his nakedness was new and terrifying.

She moaned softly. 'Jais, please stop. I don't want to know, I don't want. . .' But her words fell on deaf ears as she felt his kiss again silencing her protests and closing the door to all except sensations. His hand was on her shoulder, caressing, stroking, moving down to her breasts, and she arched her back and struggled again as she felt the brush of his palm across her nipples. In spite of all her efforts, her cries of fear mingled with cries of ecstasy as the kisses and caresses continued unabated, and finally she lay under his hand, panting and weak with an inexplicable ache in her thighs and belly.

Jais watched as his hand moved over her, and then he released her wrist, but she had stopped fighting. In the fading light of the room she saw the shadowy movements of his arm as his strong fingers explored her, boldly caressing, teasing and stroking, making her aware for the first time of her body's responses, its exquisite sensitivity on every surface. The sensations were almost too much to bear. As her eyes opened again she saw his dark head moving down to her breast cupped in his hand, saw his mouth close over the erect nipple, sucking, nibbling and teasing with his teeth and lips. The effect on her was instant. With a cry and a gasp, she twisted towards his shoulder and bit softly, keeping the hard flesh clamped between her teeth until he had taken his pleasure. She heard him chuckle, low down.

'That's better, little bird. Two can play at that game, eh?'

Ginevra pleaded, a thread of fear once more surfacing. 'Jais, stop now. . .please. . .'

'No, Ginevra. I'm not going to stop.'

'No more. Please, no more. There is no more, is there?' She knew that there was more to come, for she could feel a hardness pressing on her stomach between them and a growing heat of longing inside her, aching, wanting, waiting for possession. She knew something more was to come.

'Don't fight me, Ginevra. I won't hurt you. I promise I won't hurt you. Trust me. . .'

'Jais, no. . .' She trembled under him, but his lips silenced her yet again, and soon his hands moved over her, caressing the inside of her thighs. The melting sweetness of his touch brought new delights which she could never have foreseen, never have imagined. Moving, searching, exploring her most intimate parts, he sent waves of sensation trembling through her as, moaning with pleasure, she felt him gently ease her thighs apart with his hand and knee, felt his hard warmth push against her, into her, felt them fuse and become one. He lay still on her as she gasped with surprise, and as he began to move saw her half-open eyes flicker and close, felt her shudder under him. Her lips parted, whimpering, as their bodies moved together, slowly and rhythmically, while the sensations built up like a fire inside her, the exquisite excitement mounting as her fears were replaced by ecstasy.

Jais moved harder, deeper into her, his loins unrelenting, until she felt that her whole body was being stormed, blissfully ravaged, vanquished. Faster and faster, the fire raged into a roaring furnace, her body now responding to his movements. Then she felt him throbbing inside her like a pulse, and heard him groan as his release came. Limp with exhaustion, and quivering with the impact of her new experience, she lay under him, panting and floating in a sea of langour, struggling to recapture the reasons for her fear, and failing utterly.

Her fingers caressed the curve of his shoulder which lay against her mouth, feeling its hard smoothness. So, this was it. This was the irrevocable thing. The consummation. Her legs still enclosed him and as she lay, still panting, she felt his warmth fitting closely against her, as though they had been specially designed to dovetail one into the other, neatly, without discomfort. This was amazing. . . She had had no idea. . .

He raised his head and looked deeply into her eyes, searching hers for signs of distress. 'No tears, little bird?'

She shook her head. 'Jais. . . I didn't know. . .'

'No, you didn't know, did you?'

'Is that what you said you would be delighted to show me?'

He smiled and kissed the tip of her nose. 'Yes, little bird. That was it.'

'*Were* you, Jais?'

'Was I delighted?' He grinned down at her concerned face, laughing softly, his chest heaving on hers. 'I have never been more delighted in my whole life, little bird. Truly. You are all that I knew you would be, and more.' He kissed her, tenderly, moving his lips over hers in a delicious exchange of sweetness. 'And now we'll rest for a while. That was quite a rough encounter for you, wasn't it? It's not always like that. We'll try it again soon, shall we? Gently.'

CHAPTER TWELVE

WRAPPED in her torn shift, Ginevra stood by the north window of the solar, looking away to the right where the new rays of light were just appearing over the horizon. In her hands she held the limp garland of pink roses which only yesterday had adorned her head, reminding her that time had now flown, that things had changed, that Ginevra was now more complete.

No sense of awe or wonder engulfed her, only a sense of inevitability and the satisfaction of knowing. Jais had been right; he had not hurt her. He had told her that women who rode often had less of a problem on their wedding-nights than others, though she was not too sure exactly where the connection lay. But he had taken her again later, slowly and gently. This time, while still feeling that he had much to answer for, she found herself responding less tensely, eagerly and without fear. And afterwards he had laughingly teased her about having both the Ladies Ginevra and Juniper in his bed, making her blush in the darkness while he rocked her in his arms, her lips against his throat. In truth, she said to herself, glancing down at the roses and easing them away from their binding, in truth it had been the most exciting experience of her entire seventeen years.

But her indecision about her role in the scheme of things had hardly been helped by events. The net that had surrounded her before had now been drawn tight, emotionally and physically. In spite of her terrible anger at the discovery of the workshop, and her accompanying thoughts of duplicity, there was the knowledge that if she would only loose her pride from its cage she could be involved in the occupation dearest to her heart, and on a high level, too. As the sun had gone down last evening she had screamed that she would return home. Now it had reappeared and she knew that she could not. Jais had effectively clipped her wings with a physical bond as strong as any falconer's jess.

Without a glance at the bed where he lay sprawled, she crossed on silent feet to the west window, gazing into the far distant sky beyond the town, beyond anything.

Jais was not asleep. He had watched her silent pacing, her glance towards the key on the top of the cupboard, her long communication with the western sky and the absentminded plucking of the garland, and he had guessed some of the thoughts which must be passing through her mind. He had seen through the turbulence on the surface to the deeper fears beneath. In revealing to her the raptures of which her body was capable, he had also given her another reason to reassess the situation. His head-on assault was not what he had planned but, he thought with a wry smile, some drastic action had been necessary. He wondered if there were any bruises as a result.

'Come here, little bird.'

Ginevra was jolted back into the world by the sound of his voice; she had thought he was asleep. Instantly her hands drew the torn edges of the shift across her breasts, though she did not turn to him.

His voice was low, but insistent. 'Obey me, Ginevra.'

She made a tiny movement of her hips and he could see the struggle between body and will, so he waited, knowing she would come. Slowly and reluctantly she moved towards the bed, holding the shift in place. She stopped at the side as Jais leaned forward and took her wrist, pulling her on to him and forcing her to let go of the fabric. The touch of his fingers on her breast shot like a flame through her, and she snatched at the bedcovers to hide her nakedness from the light of day. But he held the hand away firmly, laughing gently at her embarrassment as she turned her head from him.

'No, Jais, please. . .it's daylight. . .'

'Ginevra, there are some things one can do at any time of the day or night, and making love is one of them. I want you to see what happens. It's just as good when you can see!'

'Jais, let me go. Let me get dressed. I'm cold. . .'

'Then I will warm you like this.' And he held her across his legs as he looked for bruises on her body, obliging her to watch as his hands explored her thoroughly, handling her purposefully, intimately, knowingly.

This time her eyes were wide open as she was swept into the current once more, moaning with pleasure, faster and faster. She saw him as he entered her, saw his handsome face and the grey eyes above hers, fierce and possessive, saw the muscles of his body rippling in the early light, and then she knew that night and day were no different, only variations on the same theme.

Later, as she lay against him back to front, warmed and passive, she pulled gently at the hairs on his forearms with her teeth and heard him growl behind her.

'Wench! Beware!'

'Jais,' she said, taking another nibble at the hairs, 'you realise that I'm still angry, don't you?'

'Yes, little bird,' he chuckled, tightening his arm about her neck and nuzzling into her hair.

'And that. . .this. . .doesn't change anything.'

'No, of course not. You're still the same Ginevra you were yesterday.' He snuggled deeper into her neck, laughing. '*Just* the same.'

'Yes, don't think you've won.' She pulled hard with her teeth, making him wince and try to remove his arm from under her head. But she held it fast.

His head shot up to watch her taking her revenge. 'No?'

'No!'

'We have more fighting to do?' Something in his voice warned her that this conversation was not proceeding in quite the same way she had planned. He was sounding far from contrite and she knew that the narrowed eyes were watching her with interest, even amusement.

She pushed his arm up suddenly, and made a leap off the bed before he could stop her. Picking up the pillow left on the floor from last night, she hurled it with all her might at his laughing face, knocking him back on to the bed. 'I'm not entirely without weapons, sir!'

He lay flattened, arms outstretched, heaving with laughter. 'Then I shall have the pleasure of disarming you, m'lady, before you claim victory!' And he tucked the pillow behind his head, thinking how he would enjoy the combat.

That morning he took Ginevra to see the workshop.

Her amazement at learning of his business was considerable. Having at first assumed that he was merely a landowner, she now learned that he had for many years been the owner of a highly successful workshop of ecclesiastical embroiderers. Experience had taught her that work of this kind was in such great demand that there were never enough highly skilled people to provide it and that no other country could match it in excellence. The work she had done at the priory had often found its way to Italy, France, Spain and the Low Countries via the flattering hands of wealthy donors, anxious to buy for themselves places in heaven when their time came. The plethora of newly founded churches, cathedrals and abbeys had also, she knew, made the demand for beautiful vestments grow to such proportions that it was difficult to keep pace with the commissions. At the priory the only factor which had slowed things down had been the difficulty in buying the expensive threads and fabrics needed in a place so off the beaten track as Airedale. But here she understood that Richard was in a perfect position to obtain the rare and costly fabrics on which the craft depended and which had made Jais's reputation. For while some vestments were constructed entirely on linen, there was now a growing demand for more sumptuous cloths, particularly for rich altar-cloths.

Ginevra had learned that Marianne, too, was a broderer, and had been involved with the workshop as its organiser and overseer, taking decisions about designs, patterns and techniques. But the workforce was now in serious trouble. Since her announced pregnancy and the death of two of the best workers in the recent sickness, it was clear that deadlines would not be met.

While she had eaten a hearty breakfast of fine white bread and butter with a dish of dates and boiled plover's eggs Jais had explained to Ginevra that he had just taken on a new apprentice, but that so far they were not sure how well he was going to serve. He had been with them only a short time, though he seemed willing enough.

'And you were visiting the priory on embroidery business last week?' Ginevra had asked, her mouth still full of food. Jais laughed at her hunger.

'Making love has given you an appetite, little bird. It occurred to me once before, I remember, that *that* might do the trick!' He had ignored her withering glance. 'The prioress is an old friend of ours. I took her some threads while I was seeing the estates.'

'And you told her that you needed another worker. And she, no doubt, thought that I would be useful to you, since she couldn't afford to keep me anyway. . .' Her words had been stopped by his look, warning her of danger.

'Ginevra! That's enough! We will not go into all that again, since it serves no useful purpose. No one will force you to embroider if you don't want to, but I'm going over there in a moment and you are welcome to come too, if you wish. I would be happy to show you round as an honoured guest.'

She could not help but smile at his wiles, transparent as the crystal goblet in her hand. Her eyes had held his across the table. 'Sir, I do not know whether to applaud your deviousness or to damn you for it!'

'Part of the art of warfare, little bird, is to know when to make a head-on assault or when to go via another route.'

'And were we talking about warfare, sir?' she had asked softly.

Jais had stretched a hand across the table and covered her smaller one with his. 'Would you like me to demonstrate my meaning, my lady?'

She had jumped up, pulling her hand sharply from under his. 'I would like to visit your workshop, if I may, sir.' Anything, she had thought, to take his mind off the other thing for a few moments. He had laughed, almost silently, and she had realised that once again she had been goaded along his chosen route.

This time, although it was Sunday, the room was alive with activity, and, instead of the white emptiness of the previous evening, covers were off and work was already in full progress under three pairs of hands. As Sir Jais and his new lady entered the two broderers and one apprentice stood respectfully to greet them and wait to be introduced, their eyes curious but friendly. They had been told about Sir Jais's intended marriage only two days ago.

Meg Brewster and Alice Metcalf were both well-established broderers who had been with Jais ever since he had taken over the business nine years ago. There was little about the craft which they did not know, whereas Tom Fuller was an eighteen-year-old apprentice of only some seven weeks. While the two women worked on the cope and mitre Tom prepared pounce from French chalk in the pestle and mortar, ready to mark a design on some waiting fabric.

'This is part of a complete set, Alice?' asked Ginevra, at once feeling totally in her element here. It was impossible not to feel the thrill of involvement, seeing the rich sheen of goldwork and perfectly executed stitchery growing beneath skilful hands. She looked at the huge cope on the frame, partly rolled at one side.

'Yes, m'lady,' said Alice, the elder of the two, a woman of about forty years whose bosom rested gently on the edge of the frame. 'Chasuble's bin done, an' t 'maniple. Stole's nearly finished, and Meg's got ter finish t'mitre, an' then it'll atter be med up. An that sh'd tek us abart a week, A sh'd think.'

'But then there's quite a lot of this one still to be

done,' Ginevra noted, looking at the roll of unworked fabric on the opposite side of the frame.

'Aye, well, m'lady, this'll tek a bit longer. That's why we've come in on a Sunday. We daren't miss a day just now! When Meg's finished she'll atter get underneath to 'elp me get ter t'middle.' Ginevra looked at Jais with a grin, and then at Meg and Alice. It was just as well that Meg was relatively petite. They all knew from experience that the only way to reach the central portion of the design on the frame was for one person to lie underneath and pass the needle from the underside back up to the worker on top, as the worked part of the design could not be rolled up once it was covered with embroidery.

'It looks as though it's nearly three ells, Alice.'

'Aye, m'lady, it is!' Alice said emphatically. 'We'll both atter work on this'n. Trouble is, we shan't 'ave time to teach 'im owt!' And she flung her head in Tom's direction.

Jais was watching Ginevra in quiet admiration, feeling a pride in her obvious knowledge and also pleasure at her instant rapport with the workers. If he did not press her, but let things happen by themselves, he felt that there might be a chance she would succumb and take an active part. He hoped so. Not for his own sake, but for hers.

Ginevra was delighted when they were joined shortly by Marianne and Richard, and she returned their embraces with warmth. Their presence somehow added a completeness to the situation.

'So, this is your first visit to the York Broderers,' said Richard, releasing her from a bear-hug. She exchanged a fleeting glance of amusement with Jais, and while Marianne continued to escort her round the workroom, showing her the patterns, fabrics and

already worked pieces from the set of vestments, Jais
and Richard looked over the bolts of new Italian fabrics
sent in earlier from the recent expedition. They were
piled high at the end of the room.

'Come along, young Tom, you can make yourself
useful here.' Richard nudged the lad in the shoulder,
'Help me check this list.'

Tom was an attractive youth, with curling brown hair
and dark blue eyes, a ready grin and a willingness to
be of service. He had missed little of Ginevra's easy,
informed chatter. The preparation of the pounce had
taken slightly longer than it need have done so that he
could observe her, and admire. She was even lovelier
than when he had seen her last evening in the garden.
He handled the fabrics willingly, noting their beauty
and richness with a keen eye.

There was a noticeable glow surrounding Ginevra
this morning, and Marianne wondered if she was now
more reconciled and content than when they had last
spoken. She noticed her animated air here in the
workroom, surrounded by embroidery. But was it only
the embroidery? she wondered. Or did Jais have
something to do with it?

As they waited for the men to finish Ginevra took
the opportunity to solve a puzzle in her mind. 'Why
did you not tell me that you and Jais and Richard were
in the embroidery business?'

Marianne smiled. 'We had instructions not to say a
word. And even I dare not disobey my brother.'

'But why didn't he want me to know?' she persisted.

A raised eyebrow and an enigmatic smile was the
only answer she received.

She put the same question to Jais as they sat together
over the mid-morning meal. 'Because, wench, I wanted
it to be a surprise. No. . .not what you think!' He

silenced the ready retort with a fierce glance. 'I wanted it to be a pleasant surprise, for your delight.'

Ginevra was contrite. She could see that he had genuinely wanted her to be pleased, though there were still many things that she didn't understand about it. 'And I spoiled your surprise by seeing it last night. I'm sorry, Jais.' She lay her hand over his and he instantly picked it up and kissed it lightly.

'Well, only from the outside. No real harm done.'

'No, from the inside. I'm afraid I went in.'

'You went in? How did you find the keys?'

'I didn't need any keys. I was looking at the herb-garden when I walked up the path towards the house. I saw the window and door and thought it would lead me back. I wasn't prying. I just walked in.

Jais looked concerned. 'Were the keys in the doors?'

'I don't know. I was so angry when I went out. . . I didn't bother to notice. But are you saying that it should have been locked?'

Jais was silent for a moment, his eyes holding a remote look. 'I locked it myself before I went to the church. . .' His expression was now stony, the grey eyes puzzled.

'Then who. . .?'

Jais looked at her hard, trying to find an answer in his head. 'There's sure to be a good reason. I'll find out. Don't concern yourself, little bird.' He smiled. 'Now, I think I shall take you on an inspection of your new home. It's about time you became familiar with your new nest.'

Or cage, thought Ginevra. But the glum thoughts which threatened to surface were dispelled as the handsome house was revealed to her. It was even larger than it appeared from the front, for she was introduced to a complex of kitchens, buttery, dairy and bakehouse

which would have sufficed for a whole village in the
dales, Ginevra thought. The house-steward and the
head officers were presented to her and the function of
their duties explained, for here was a more involved
system of management than she had encountered
before. She visited the stables and was able to make
much of her chestnut mare at last, and to admire the
other occupants, all beautiful and costly creatures.

But most of all she discovered more about her new
husband as head of the household; the way that this
had been organised reflected his appreciation of detail.

His perfectly trained servants fulfilled every role with
superb efficiency and loyalty, were well-mannered,
clean and discreet. They accepted her into the huge
house as though she had been there for years, and her
presence at table was an extra incentive to the cooks to
produce the daintiest morsels and delights imaginable.
There was no doubt that there was general relief and
approval of Sir Jais's choice of lady, for she made her
orders sound like requests, and her knowledge of how
things should be done surprised even herself. She won
all hearts as soon as they saw her.

But have I won Jais's heart? she asked herself. Though
the days and nights had passed, not a word of love had
been spoken. She did not dismiss her own feelings
about him any longer, for now she had to acknowledge
that this ache to see him, hear him, could not be
anything other than love. And yet, while he obviously
enjoyed her company at all times, he had said nothing
of loving her, and while this state of affairs existed she
could only assume that she was needed for his convenience, in the workshop and in bed. For her skills,
in fact.

And yet to feel his touch, his kisses and embraces,

were longings which stayed with her throughout the
day, though she pretended a reluctance that she hoped
would deceive him into thinking that if he cared not for
her, then she cared for him even less. So came the
jousting each night, when both would do their utmost
to gain the upper hand, knowing who would win but
knowing also that the loser had never really lost at all.

Sometimes Ginevra shed real tears of anger that she
was never in a position to hold out against him, partly
because of his greater strength and partly because her
body seemed to have a will of its own. She had already
begun to wonder how long two people could go on
living and making love together when one of them had
to maintain this pretence in order to save face,
especially when only a short time ago she had made
her dislike of him all too obvious. How was she going
to make him pay except by hurting herself in the
process? Had she even begun? How could she tell him
of her desperate love for him and admit, once and for
all, that her pride had dissolved in its well-protected
fortress, that her vow, which at one time had been all
she could cling to, had now lost its meaning? Worth-
less. Empty.

Her struggles spilled over into the daytime when, in
her attempts to fan the flame of her weakening resentment, she did her utmost to provoke him.

One noon she returned her mare to the stables to
find that her young groom had been soundly berated
by Jais for allowing her to go out into the town
unaccompanied, though she had told the lad that this
was not necessary.

'I am used to going out alone,' she replied to Jais's
interrogation in the privacy of their solar, 'I don't need
people around me forever, as some people appear to
do!' She glared at him.

'The city of York is not Airedale; it is highly unsafe. The grooms have my orders to accompany you at all times! It is a duty they will not take lightly if they value their position!'

'I was only seeing the pagonds being prepared for the Corpus Christi plays.' She sounded exasperated as she flung off her headdress and began a seductive wriggle out of her surcoat. 'I can see better from horseback, and I can outride anybody. Even you!'

He let that pass. They both knew that it was a wild challenge without foundation. 'You will not go out alone in future, if you please, my lady!' In spite of his voice holding a hint of menace, which she was fully able to recognise and appreciate, she chose to defy him without a hint of diplomacy.

'Or you will dismiss my groom? Is that it?' She paused and turned to him, casually undoing the neck of her shift and attempting to sound scornful, but aware that her heart was beating unbelievably loud in her chest. 'It sounds, sir, as though you can't wait to do it! Are you unhappy about his regard for me, perhaps?'

Her clean shift was on the bed beyond him, but her attempt to pass him was forestalled. He was not angry at her pinpricks, merely amused that she found this a weapon worth using against him. But perhaps he should teach her a lesson, and now was as good a time as any. He slipped his hand beneath her shoulder as she passed and held her back. 'I'm jealous, am I?' He smiled. 'Of a *groom*?'

'No, sir, not of the groom. Of his regard for me!'

'Ah!' He raised his eyebrows in mock surprise, his eyes glittering dangerously into hers. 'Ah, his *regard*? Then I ought to have some means of comparing our regards, should I not, wench? Come, show me!'

She knew she had gone too far. Knew, but was

helpless to stop herself. The hard inflexion of his last words warned her of trouble ahead and she pulled away from him, her heart racing out of control. 'No.'

'Yes, Ginevra. I insist!' With the merest bend of his black head he picked her up like a toy, carried her over to the bed and lightly tossed her on to the covers. Before she could roll off on the other side, her body was straddled, her hands caught and held under her back as she fought against the restriction of his thighs. She would not plead, nor cry out, for she knew she had brought this on herself and must not give him the satisfaction of seeing her regret. Her eyes blazed at him, challenging, taunting, locked with his in a fierce battle for dominance. 'Now, wench! Where does this regard begin? Is it here?' His large hand eased the shift down off her shoulders to a place below her elbows, where it acted as a bond to keep her hands imprisoned by her sides. She closed her eyes and waited as his hand withdrew from her wrists, fully aware that her chances of revenge had now all but gone.

His kisses were long and slow, now tender, now fierce, leaving her no time to recover from one before the next followed without mercy. At last her stifled cry was recognised as a plea and he gave her space to gasp for air, to look at him and see his implacable expression. His hands were now playing a languorous game over her stomach and hips, avoiding her breasts, smoothing a pathway upwards to shoulders and throat. 'Well, Ginevra? Are you not going to tell me?'

'There is no answer to your question, sir. You know well my meaning.' She pulled hard to free her hands from the tangle of her shift while he watched her efforts, amused. Finally she freed one hand and braced it against his wide shoulder. 'You know, too, that this is no way to revenge yourself on me!'

'Revenge, Ginevra? I thought that was the game *you* had chosen to play just now.' He waited, watching her as his words were weighed in her mind, and she knew that she was laid bare to him, mentally as well as physically. His hands continued to move over her, teasingly outlining the circle of each breast, but she grabbed at his wrist and, pulling his hand up to her mouth, bit sharply into the base of his thumb.

His grin deepened as he waited for her to release it, then he caught her hand lightly and held it to one side. 'You are still fierce, little bird. And resentful. And bent on revenge, too, are you not?'

Ginevra turned her face away into the covers. 'I swore I would,' she whispered, half to herself, 'and yet I can't find a way. Damn you! Damn you!' She blazed angrily at him once more, making contact with his grey eyes, now dark with desire. A fine veil of black hair had fallen over his brow like a dark mane, and in spite of her fury and her helplessness she felt an ache growing inside her for the full weight of his body, for the heat and the hardness of him.

'No, you can't find a way because your heart isn't in it, Ginevra. So the only thing you can do now is to let it go. The bargain is sealed, and I have you fast. And letting loose your barbs on me will make no difference to that. Nor to this. . .' As he spoke his fingers traced a spiral around her breast, moving upwards towards its peak. Her cry was a wail of ecstasy, despair, submission. It was what he had been waiting for, controlling the timing of it to perfection when he knew that her petulance and her desire had fought each other to a standstill. And now, as he removed her shift and released her hands, Ginevra yielded to his mastery once again.

CHAPTER THIRTEEN

THE next day her spirits were revived somewhat by the arrival of her new gowns, and she was happy to spend some time trying on the new bliauds and tunics, surcoats and the newest cote-hardies. There was time to try out the newest-style caul, too, a litle basket of gold network fastened to each side of her head to hold her coiled hair. She stood in her silk shift before the polished steel mirror, wrestling with the intricacies of the caul and the coiled braids, not wishing to call for Oswinna's help. The loop of wayward copper hair fell out again for the third time, knocking the fillet and caul askew. With arms aching from the effort and now thoroughly frustrated, she yanked the thing off her head and hurled it across the room. It fell into the corner with a clatter, rolled and lay still.

Anger suddenly overwhelmed her and she found that she was sweating and hot, tears close to the surface. She threw herself face downwards onto the bed, tense and fighting back a sudden rage. A soft step sounded outside the door and she knew that her unreasonable behaviour might be taken for waspishness again. Her heart thudded on the soft covers. Was she to feign sleep? Or dress and leave him alone? Or wait for whatever came? The choice made itself, as often happened.

'Asleep, my lady?'

She chose not to answer; neither was any answer needed, for Jais had heard the clatter of the caul as it hit the wall and he could see the tenseness of her body.

Checking that the caul was not damaged, he replaced it on the chest and looked at Ginevra's rigid form, sword-straight, face deeply buried in hands and bed-cover. Her hair, half loose, told him clearly what had been the ostensible cause of her outburst but, as usual, he guessed that this was only a manifestation of something deeper.

He sat on the bed alongside her feet and gently lifted one slender foot onto his knee. Ginevra felt the firmness of his warm strong hands on the sole of her foot, massaging each toe in turn, stroking the instep, the heel and the top. Gently, and without saying a word, he continued to caress her foot as she lay there unmoving, feeling the tension flow away and the calmness return to her breast. Then he picked up the other foot. The effect on her anger was like a warm, luxurious bath, soothing and sensuously relaxing. He massaged her feet lovingly until calmness returned and no ill-feelings remained, only the warm touch of his hands and a feeling of peace.

She turned and sat up, sleepily moving towards his back. Laying her cheek against his broad shoulders, she slipped her arms about his waist, feeling him take her wrists and hold them gently on his lap.

He did not turn his head but said, smiling at her change of mood, 'If, m'lady, you would care to don one of your new gowns, I would like to take you somewhere. I have something to show you.'

'What is it?' she mumbled, her mouth against his broad back. He smelt spicy and fresh. His hair was just above her nose and she saw how it curled over the top of his gown, black and glossy. How she loved him!

'I have great difficulty remembering with your mouth hot on my shoulderblades, m'lady.'

Ginevra giggled and nipped at his back with her

teeth, only getting his gown in her mouth, little else, but enough to make him tense the muscles of his body. His hands tightened too, and his voice was suddenly dark and expressive. 'Did m'lady have something else in mind?'

With a yelp, she realised the potential danger of her position—legs each side of his body on the edge of the bed. . . She pulled with her arms, but he held her fast. Her heart now beat wildly. 'No, sir!' she squealed. 'I would like to go with you and. . .whatever it was! Please let me go and dress.' And she pulled frantically while he remained motionless. Her chin stuck into his back. She was laughing helplessly, hysteria mounting.

'Are you sure. . .?' He chuckled deep down in his throat.

'Yes, yes. I'm quite sure. Let me go, you brute!'

He kept hold of her wrists and stood up to face her, keeping her legs apart with his. He looked down at her with mock severity on his face and, leaning over, pushed her back on to the bed until he stood above her. Teasingly he smiled at her laughter and heaving breasts, making one last bid to prolong her doubts about his intentions. 'Would m'lady like to change her mind? I can be very accommodating.'

By now she was almost speechless with laughter and mounting excitement and could barely gasp the words, 'Jais. . . Please. . .'

He released her hands and helped her to her feet, laughing with her while holding her close to his chest. 'You must learn, little bird, not to send the wrong signals to the adversary. He may become confused, you see! And that can be dangerous.' He kissed her softly. 'Now, go and put some clothes on, if you please.'

* * *

They entered the great minster of York through the west doorway. Ginevra's first thought was that it was the biggest building she had ever entered. Jais watched her face as her eyes opened wide in astonishment. The clusters of columns marched down the naves like bunched stems of white stone angelica, their arches meeting in points of perfect symmetry. On top of these were balanced more windows, flooding the interior with white light. She was speechless.

Dodging in between the throngs of pilgrims, builders and sightseers, Jais turned her round to face the door and pointed upwards. She gasped as the light from outside flooded through arched windows of coloured glass above the doorway, the delicate tracery within the top curves balanced on narrow lancets like finest lace. 'Do you see the shape, in the centre?' he said above the clatter.

'It's a heart!' she answered, smiling in delight.

Scaffolding was still scattered in patches along the nave and piles of stone slabs and carved wooden roof-bosses, coils of ropes, pulleys and blocks littered the central area, where people anxiously pushed past to reach the shrine of St William.

'The roof will be glorious when it's finished,' she remarked, noting the fine ribs springing from the corbels at the tops of the vertical columns. Some of the bosses were aleady in position over the intersections.

'I wanted you to see this,' said Jais as he led her to a more peaceful area at one side, 'because it is here that the vestments we're making will eventually be seen.'

'You mean, *here*, in the minster?' Ginevra was amazed.

'Yes. John Thoresby will be the new archbishop in two years' time. They're for his enthronement. Special commission. I thought you should see the setting to give you an idea of what it's all about. It helps, doesn't it?'

Ginevra nodded, her face now alight with interest. 'It always helps to know where they'll be seen. The colours. The direction of the light. The sheer scale of the place. . .' She waved a hand. 'It's much, *much* bigger than I realised. You know, Meg ought to put more spangles on that mitre if it's going to be seen from such a distance.' Her eyes flickered from one end of the nave to the transepts at the far end. 'And the colours. I wonder. . . We really need to bring the fabrics in here. . .' She shook her head. 'Too pale!' Jais could almost see her mind working furiously, visualising the impact of the partly worked vestments within the setting of the vast building. She grabbed his hand. 'I need to see further up here. Come!'

They set off, weaving in and out of the throng, to the transepts which ran along the top end of the nave from north to south. Holding her surcoat out of the dust, she dodged around the obstacles until they stood beneath the squat tower. Her eyes lit up once more as she gasped in wonder at the soft grey-greens of the five lancet windows on the north side. She took hold of Jais's arm urgently. 'Look, Jais, look there! No, you'll have to half-close your eyes.' He did as he was bidden. 'Now, do you see the outlines of those rounded patterns all the way down? With red centres?' She pointed.

'Yes, I see them. They're different in each window.'

'Exactly! Well, wouldn't it have made sense to use these same patterns on the vestments somewhere? Pick up the green and red, too, but make them brighter, really vibrant. That would be seen from one end of the building to the other, wouldn't it?'

'My lady,' Jais said, smiling down at her, 'I think you

ought to have been responsible for the designs. Where were you?'

She smiled back ruefully, shaking her head. 'This is breathtaking. But the pieces being done in the workshop bear no relationship to anything here. We ought to have vestments specially designed for the man *and* the place.'

'But it's in two years. Do we have enough time to start again? With another set?'

Her thoughts raced ahead, hardly noticing their use of the word 'we' instead of 'I'. She knew full well that there would be enough time if she joined in, too. And if she could have Rowenna's help, and maybe some of the others, then there would be enough time! These were questions which could not be resolved here and now. 'Let's give it some thought,' she said.

I swore to make him pay, Ginevra reminded herself, watching Oswinna's deft hands arranging her thick copper hair into the golden cauls. How I have changed. The reflection stared back, detailing in silent agreement the newly acquired bloom of womanhood, the knowingness, the sleek air of completeness. The eyes flickered a secret smile to her, showing her a poised and beautiful woman in a new bliaud of violet silk shot with pink, a brocade surcoat of violet and gold worn over the top. Gold buttons decorated the narrow front panel, picking up the glint of gold enclosing her hair and the gold of her soft leather shoes. How things have changed, she agreed.

But has *he*? What is all this about, I wonder? This lure to entice me into the workroom, knowing that I want it above all else. As he lures me into his heart, knowing that I want that, too. Even though I resist, even though I try to make it hard for him, why does he always win every bout? I swore to make him pay for robbing me of my right to make my own decisions. But did he? Wasn't I the one to decide?

She touched the golden band on her forehead, remembering the moment of decision in the orchard, the moment of inexplicable madness which had sealed her fate. Her hands, watched by the reflection, wandered downwards over the curve of her breasts under the surcoat, reminding herself of his conquest. But is this love he feels, like me, or simply the love of conquest. He has my body, he may suspect he has my love, too; now he wants my involvement in the work. How *am* I going to make him pay? Do I really want to? Will I not be holding out against myself in the end?

The image and reflection eyed each other, both knowing the answer. Then why am I the one who has to give way? Damn him! She closed her eyes. Perhaps the inner voices would give her some answer. But they had given up, long ago, and now were silenced, drowned and swept away on the flood of her new-found passion.

Her eyes opened slowly to see Jais's face behind hers in the mirror, and for a moment she thought it was a part of her daydream. But the feeling of his hands caressing her bare neck declared his reality. As though her skin were the plumage of a half-tamed bird on his wrist, his fingers continued to stroke while their eyes remained locked together in the mirror. Robbed of her will to move away, she watched his hands moving down over her shoulders beneath the surcoat, cupping her breasts, and as her eyes closed his head was moving down to her throat. Damn. . . Damn. . .

With Marianne and Richard's company at supper that evening, the meal was taken later than usual in the large family solar downstairs instead of in the great hall. Few houses could boast a room for this purpose, but Jais had wanted to follow recent trends for a more intimate setting, once in a while, with family or business guests. And so it was that the four were able to talk while eating tiny pieces of battered fish, roast chicken pieces dipped in honey and pounded herbs, and stewed oysters.

Jais told them of Ginevra's remarks in the minster earlier that afternoon, and explained her ideas on designs linked to the five narrow windows.

'But isn't there a problem of timing?' asked Richard as he prised an oyster open with his knife. 'Two years is hardly long enough for just Alice and Meg. And designs not even begun.'

Ginevra was anxious not to sound too enthusiastic, nor too involved. She hoped she had not implied that she wanted to take it upon herself to organise this. After all, Marianne was still in charge here. Or was she, in view of the fact that she would soon have to abdicate her responsibilities? But if she let them take her idea to one of the professional designers, a monk perhaps, it would all be out of her hands again. On the other hand, if she committed herself to designing the vestments and organising the work, she would be totally involved up to her ears. If she let it go, and work continued as before on the present set, she would have missed the chance of a lifetime. To design and be responsible for the new Archbishop of York's vestments would be an honour no broderer would let slip.

And yet. . . She looked at Jais. He was sitting back, letting the action unfold before him, watching Ginevra's struggles in the dilemma of her own conflicting needs. 'Yes,' he said, 'it's true that two years is barely long enough, even under Alice and Meg's hands.

Tom is really only good enough for the preparation and even then he needs to be shown everything. Nobody has time for that, either.'

'What we really need is several more pairs of hands,' said Marianne, 'and now I shall only be around for a few more months before. . .'

Richard closed his hand on her arm and smiled at her. 'If you had not seduced me, wench, this would not have happened. And now I'm to be a father and I'm not sure that I can cope with it!'

Marianne pretended exasperation at his coyness and rapped his knuckles with a spoon. 'You big oaf! Seduced *you*, indeed. . .' But her shoulders were encased in a hug of appeasement as all four laughed together. At that moment Ginevra thought that her heart would burst from love of them all.

Richard returned to the problem. 'Don't we know anyone who could be brought in to help? Someone with some real experience?'

'The only other workshops of any size are in London,' Jais interrupted, 'and I expect they're suffering as badly as we are after the pestilence. I hear they're already cutting corners by using the same designs over and over again to economise on time and money.'

'The work's bound to suffer, surely?' exclaimed Richard. 'We don't want to follow that example!'

'Wait!' Ginevra twisted a tiny, star-shaped sugared biscuit round on the table before her, watching it glint in the light. 'Wait a moment. When I travelled from the priory with Mother Breda recently——' her eyes caught Jais's and she continued, talking to the biscuit '—she told me that. . .some of the other girls would be leaving soon. . .' She was choosing her words with care, for she was still not sure how much Richard and

Marianne knew of her circumstances. 'They're skilled embroiderers, too. Some are nearly as old as me. They're not indentured apprentices, but they've had as much experience as most and there's no law against using workers that someone else has trained. In fact, I'd trust them to do anything from a cope downwards.'

'Aunt. . . Prioress Claire's pupils!' Marianne looked across at Jais, hoping that her quick slip of the tongue had not been picked up, but Ginevra was already thinking ahead.

'My special friend, Rowenna, was exceptionally good, and some of the girls live in York anyway. I wonder. . .' She looked at Jais out of the corner of her eye and saw that he was stroking the stem of his wine-gass with the back of his finger, just as he had stroked her neck earlier. Their eyes met and, in that instant, they read each other's minds. Ginevra looked away, confused. 'Please, will you excuse me for a moment? I will rejoin you shortly.' She slipped quickly away from the table, her face flushed, her mind holding the image of his hand luring the bird with irresistible titbits, stroking and caressing, tightening the jesses. . .

The cool air of the passageway was refreshing as, with clenched fists, she stood trembling and unsettled. I am getting drawn into this too deeply, she thought. How could I be so stupid as to plunge into yet another dilemma when I'm still stuck in the previous one? I've only to begin discussing it like one of the team, and then he's won! I can't play his game. His hand is too skilful!

And yet, in spite of her mental barriers being brought into action yet again they were not closed completely, for she found her feet were taking her not to her solar but towards the covered walk to the workshop. The keys were missing from their usual place on the wall and Ginevra assumed that Jais had not yet locked the room, though this was not usual at this time of day. With a glance up at the full moon in the now darkened sky, she knew that there would be enough light to show her the whereabouts of the rolls of parchment, and the charcoal. Strange, she thought as she pushed open the unlocked doors, this is most careless of Jais to leave it unlocked, especially after his unease last time it happened.

Standing in the moonlit room with the lambent light filtering through the skylight on to the ghostly shrouded frames, Ginevra was reminded of the first time she had entered — her feelings of anger and astonishment. Now she felt that it was more of a familiar haven, a place where all her creative needs could be expressed. She had begun to love the place.

Suddenly an inner sense warned her that all was not well, not as it should be. The hairs on her arms and head bristled, and she held her breath while she savoured the air inside her nostrils. There was a faint aroma, something in the room. Slowly she turned to look across at the curtain over the shelves where the new Italian fabrics had been placed only recently, and saw that it was drawn aside to show a gaping black space where they had been. At first she could not understand what she was seeing. Then she realised.

A tiny rustling sound at her shoulder made her turn, and her mouth opened as a surge of tangible fear flooded into her chest and legs, heightening her senses to a screaming awareness of danger so imminent that it was already too late. Her body reacted before her reason, and she whirled as something black and stifling engulfed her head, pulling her backwards and off-balance over something hard and painful in the small of her back. She went crashing to the ground, writhing

and kicking with the strength of ten Ginevras, hardly
feeling the grasp around her body and knees, hardly
hearing the crashes of the wooden frames around her
as she fought into the blackness.

'Bitch! Tom! For God's sake, keep her still, can't
you?'

'God's wounds! I'm trying. . .'

'Here, hold this!'

A sharp pain across her temples was all she felt.
Nothing more.

'What did we say to make her leave us like that?' asked
Marianne. She looked at her brother across the table.
'Have you been teasing her, Jais? You can go too far
sometimes, you know.'

Jais looked at her without speaking. She had put into
words precisely what he himself was thinking, though
he was trying hard to appear unconcerned.

'She said she'd rejoin us,' Richard ventured, idly
poking at a soft date with the point of his knife. 'She's
not unwell, is she, Jais?' His meaning was understood,
but dismissed with a quick frown.

Jais kept his eyes on Marianne's, imposing on her
face the image of Ginevra as she had watched him
stroking the stem of his wine-glass, her look of confusion, her quickly averted eyes. Oh, God, no! he
thought, a blanket of fear sweeping over him. I've
pushed her too far this time. Clumsy brute! Oh, God,
what a clumsy brute! He pushed away from the table
and stood, in one quick movement. 'Excuse me, please.
Don't go. I'll be back in a moment!'

He moved like lightning, bounding up the stairs to
the solar, three at a time. One glance confirmed that
she was not there. In the passageway he noted that the
keys were gone. She was there, then. She had to be

there. The doors to the workroom were unlocked and swinging freely in the evening breeze. By the dim light of the moon he could see the signs of disturbance, frames and covers lying in disarray on the floor, silks and spangles scattered, the gaping spaces on the curtained shelf, and no sign of Ginevra. Slamming the doors behind him, Jais ran through the vegetable-garden and into the herb-garden beyond. If she was anywhere else at home, this was where she would be. He walked peering to right and left at the still foliage, shining grey in the pale silver light as though to accentuate the terrible darkness crowding into his mind and the fearful pounding in his chest. Never before had he felt this way and, please God, never again. As he reached the outer garden door leading on to the narrow lane at the back of the house he saw that it was slightly ajar. The lock had been smashed as though by a hammer. No other signs, except for some well-trampled edging plants. A deadly silence hung under the moon.

His entry into the great hall that evening was one which would be repeated in the servants' story-tellings for many a long year. The appearance of their master's white face at the screens-passage alerted the occupants even before he had spoken, and they were already halfway to their feet when his voice cut through them like a sword.

'Toby, Willem, Rufus, Ned! Horses. . .quickly! Saddle Negre and one for Master Mercer. . .a fast one! Courtyard! Now! Ben, we shall need ropes. Dickon—two swords, daggers. You come, too. . .'

Richard emerged at the other end of the hall having heard the shouts, and seeing Jais's white face and fierce expression ran to him. 'What is it?'

'I'll need you, Richard. Do you come with me?' He

turned and started out of the hall. 'They've taken her, Richard. The swine have taken her!'

'Of course I'll come! But what's happened, Jais, for God's sake?'

Jais stopped abruptly by the door and turned to his brother-in-law and friend. Richard had never seen his face look so terrible, so tortured. 'Those bastards! Swine! She must have gone to the workroom, Richard. It was something I did. . . Christ's wounds, but I'm a *fool*!' His hands clenched into fists as he looked at Richard in despair. 'She must have entered at the very moment they were taking. . .'

'Patrickson!'

'Yes, I believe so. I believe he's behind this!' He buckled on the sword handed to him by Dickon, signalling Richard to do the same.

'Do you know where to look?'

'All I know right now is that she's *mine*, and I intend to get her back!' the voice was chilling, icy, murderous.

As they prepared to mount the approaching horses Richard thought that he was glad to be on Jais's side.

CHAPTER FOURTEEN

GINEVRA moved her head to escape the coarseness under her cheek, puzzled why the sheets should be rough and foul-smelling. She must ask the servants. . . Dim shadows swirled about her, faces formed, then blackness swamped them. Then more faces. A hand shook her shoulder, not gently but insistently. What did Jais want?

She opened her eyes at last, but was punished by a pain which shot through her temples. The hand was not Jais's but Tom's. What was the young apprentice doing in her room?

'Wake up! Wake up, m'lady! Come on, wake up!' The shaking continued until her head rolled back and she could force her eyes to stay open, frowning at the pain.

'Tom?' This makes no sense, she thought.

'Aye, it's me. Don't scream!'

Slowly her eyes began to focus on the small dingy room, and memories floated like ghostly shadows into her consciousness—the workroom, struggles, blackness. What had happened? What was this awful smell? 'Tom?' she repeated.

'Come on. Sit up.' He took her by the shoulders and heaved her up against the wall, pulling her legs out straight. She felt sick and her head throbbed with every movement. She tried to touch it, to give it some comfort, but found that her hands were tightly bound behind her, though her ankles were free. Tom's shadowy figure moved away and clattered down the wooden staircase. Voices sounded dimly below her, then more footsteps on the stairs and a man's high voice, reedy and strangely unattractive.

'Now then, m'lady! What an unexpected pleasure!'

From her position low down on the floor all she could see of the man was a gown of grey and the ends of his long dagged sleeves showing linings of scarlet between the folds. A wave of a sickly body-stench swept over her, causing her to turn her head away, but a hand took her chin firmly and yanked her head back to a face now level with hers. Her nose wrinkled at the touch, smell and sight of him even before she could force her eyes to open once more, knowing that they would be offended. Two pale and prominent eyes stared closely into hers, bulging through puffy lids, the cheeks and mouth flabby and moist, nose squat and bristling with sandy hairs. The sight brought another wave of nausea into her mouth and she gasped for air.

'The Lady Ginevra de la Roche! The raving beauty they've been telling me about. Well, well. Dainty little thing, ain't yer, m'lady?' He laughed, a high-pitched giggle, the slack folds of his face creasing up to reveal yellowing teeth. She pulled her chin away to escape the sight, but he kept it firmly within the grasp of his fat little hand, his fingers bruising her jaw as he turned her head this way and that. 'Well, now I can see for myself. What a bonus, eh, lads?' He stood up at last and turned to Tom. There was another lad of about the same age and size whom she did not recognise. 'Got the stuff *and* the lady, too. Very good. Very good. That'll give 'em something to think about.' And he giggled again. 'While we're up here we'll have a look, then. Bring 'em out!'

As they moved about the room Ginevra's befuddled mind began to clear, though her pounding temples made it difficult for her to think. But think she must. Unmistakably this man was Master Patrickson, the man they had seen in town that day before her wedding. He had been wearing the same shabby gown then and, though it was easy for her to recognise him, she had been standing among a group of young people, maids and servants, so it was only Marianne that he had noticed. Consequently he was not to know that Ginevra knew him. That might be to her advantage, she thought.

The pale light of dawn was just visible through the opaque yellowy-greyness of the horn window, allowing her to make out the confines of the room where the three stood just out of reach of her feet. The light from the open staircase cast a dull gleam on the low wooden beams, barely clearing the heads bent over the bundles on the table by the window. There were piles of some twenty or so bolts of fabric stacked to one side of the table, the threads of the topmost piece glimmering where the early morning light caught it at an angle. But they did not turn to the fabrics as she thought they would. Instead Tom brought forward a large, untidy bundle of linen, which he laid out on the table and slowly unfolded before them.

'Couldn't bring the stole,' Tom was saying. 'If you could've waited another day or two somebody might've finished it. . .'

'I told you it had to be today!' Patrickson snapped testily. 'We need the holiday crowds around to cover our movements. You know that!'

Holiday crowds, thought Ginevra. What could he be referring to?

'Yes, well,' Tom went on. 'I thought *she* might have had a go at it, but she didn't seem to want to get cracking for some reason!'

'You mean, *she* does it, too?' He turned round sharply to look at her intently once more, and Ginevra closed her eyes quickly.

'Aye, she's not just 'is wife. She's one of 'is workers, too. Mistress Mercer and 'im needed her to work for 'em, you know.'

So, she thought, even young Tom could see how the land lay. Now another kind of pain added itself to the one already throbbing in her head but, in spite of this, her eyes opened wide in horror as he exposed the contents of the bundle. For a fragment of time she could hardly reconcile what she was seeing with those who were handling it. In the man's hands was the glowing mitre which Meg had just finished assembling, glittering richly even in the poor light of dawn. She gasped in astonishment. 'You can't have that!'

Pain shot through her again at the effort the words had caused her, but they took no notice of her cry and continued to unwrap the other pieces in the same set of vestments—the maniple, and then the large chasuble with the richly embroidered orphreys meeting in a y-shape on front and back. Ginevra was horrified, but Patrickson was giggling with delight, his fat little hands patting at the precious things and twirling the mitre around between his grubby fingers.

'Well, not a complete set, but never mind. These'll fetch quite a bit—together *or* separate.' As he spoke he set the mitre on top of his own balding head, the wisps of greasy sandy hair sticking out like old straw beneath the decorated border. Ginevra groaned, wondering what Meg and Alice would say if they could see what was happening to their months of skilful work on the head of this obnoxious jester.

Tom turned towards her and shot her a furtive look over his shoulder, catching her eye for a fleeting moment. He did not join in the laughter and she felt that there was a look of concern in his eyes for the lack of care over the embroideries.

'Pity you couldn't've got the cope, too,' Patrickson said as he replaced the mitre on the table. 'But we've got *her*, and we can find a little extra use for her before we strike a bargain, eh, lads?' His giggle was suddenly ominous rather than pathetic, sending a shiver of cold fear from the nape of her neck to the base of her spine. Again Tom turned to look at her, concern now clearly showing in his eyes, but the other lad broke in.

'Hey! It was my idea to bring her along, remember? Maybe I should have first go!'

Master Patrickson's hand shot out to grab the lad by the neck of his tunic. 'Don't you dare, you little runt! She's mine, until I say otherwise. Understand?' He glared, red-faced and menacing.

'Hush!' hissed Tom, leaning towards the window. 'Hush, you two! Listen. What's all that clattering?'

The argument ceased as abruptly as it had begun and the two craned forward to hear, rigid with concentration. Their words had shocked Ginevra, leaving a trembling ball of fear deep inside her while she weighed the implications of their disagreement. Surely Jais would look for her. Surely he would not want to lose her so soon, before she had had a chance to reveal more of her skills. Holy Mother, she prayed, please get me out of here before. . . She would not think about it in any more detail.

'It's the pagonds, I expect,' said Patrickson. 'They set off just after dawn from Toft Green.' He opened the creaking window a little way to get a view of the street below, letting in the sharp clatter and rumble of hooves and wheels and the chattering of voices. 'Yes, it's the pagonds. They're off across the bridge now.'

Suddenly it made sense to Ginevra. The pagonds. The same ones she had seen being prepared the day before, or had it been the day before that, when Jais had been so angry at her venturing out alone? Her mental efforts to shed some light on the events outside were halted for a time as she recalled his concern for her safety on that day, and a warm sense of relief stole into her breast with the thought that, yes, he might well come to find her.

But of course, today must be the feast of Corpus Christi—a holiday, and the day when the plays were performed on wagons, or pagonds, by members of all the guilds. The procession of forty-eight wagons would stop at twelve different venues all round the centre of the city, performing every play at each one—from the Story of the Creation to the Last Judgement. According to Oswinna the last one might be as late as midnight tonight. That was what Master Patrickson must have meant when he had spoken of the theft having to be done on this day only, so that the crowds of people would make it more difficult for a search party or the hue and cry to operate. Clever, nasty little man, she thought, watching him close the window. Her hopes plummeted again like a stone into a well. How could anyone find her with holiday crowds and the guild mystery-plays to block the way?

'Anything else?'

'Yes. This is what I was trying to get hold of last time when m'lady came in——' Tom nodded in Ginevra's direction '—and I had to hide. I thought she'd bring t'master back, 'cos the doors were open, so I 'opped it.'

She watched as Tom pulled out a large roll of parchment from beneath the chasuble. 'There you are! That's what you wanted, isn't it?'

'The patterns! Well done, lad. I've got somebody who'll give their right arm for those. De la Roche's lot'll be stuck without 'em!' And his chuckles were almost uncontrollable at the thought of his own good fortune. 'Now, you two, get this lot packed again. How many bolts are there here? Twenty, is it?' He nodded in satisfaction as the lads agreed. 'Straight from Florence, eh? That'll fetch a tidy penny or two.'

'What are you going to do with *her*?' asked the other lad as Patrickson turned to pass her. They looked at her, coiled up on the filthy sacking, noting her graceful figure and lovely pale face with a red bruise now clearly showing on her forehead.

'Hmm.' The man smiled. 'Bit of sport first, perhaps. Then I think I know who'll be glad to part with a fair price for her. Broderer, too! Hmm!' He smoothed his hands over the grey rounded belly. 'Leave her here for now while I make a few enquiries. No hurry. Come!' He turned to go.

'Please!' Ginevra's plea made him pause. 'Please, will you untie my hands? I need to use the bucket, and I can't do it like this. Please?'

'I'll do it!' Tom stepped forward before the other two could respond. 'It's all right, I'll tie her again when she's done. No. . .' He laughed at the warning look on Patrickson's face. 'I won't get up to any tricks.'

As they disappeared down the staircase Tom took her shoulders and helped her to stand on shaking legs against the wall. 'Turn round, m'lady, can you?' he whispered.

'Yes. Tom, please help me! Don't let them. . .' she could not say to him what she thought they might do, but looked at him over her shoulder. Had she detected sympathy in his glance earlier?

'Stand still. There!' The bonds were loosed and she

wriggled her numb fingers and rubbed her sore wrists. 'Now, listen to me m'lady, while you're doing that. I'm sorry, but they'll be up here again if I don't make haste. Just get on with it, and listen!'

She understood his urgency. It was true, there was no time to be squeamish and ladylike now. She staggered over to the filthy bucket in the corner, the stench almost making her retch, but she had no option but to make use of it. Meanwhile Tom whispered to her, averting his eyes as much as he was able.

'I didn't want this to happen, believe me. Not for you to be harmed. It was John. . .he clobbered you. . . and there wasn't time to argue. But I don't know how I can help just yet. I'll do what I can, but if they suspect I'll be in. . . Quick!'

The high-pitched voice shouted from below. 'Come on, you rascal! What are you up to?'

'Coming, sir. Just fixing the bonds!' His voice dropped to a whisper again, unease clearly showing in his eyes. 'I'll try to stay around to protect you. Here, hold your hands behind. . .'

'No, Tom! Please. . .'

'It's all right. I won't. Just pretend. Keep pretending.' At that, he wrapped the strip of linen loosely around her wrists, turned, and almost fell down the stairs in his efforts to appear normal.

Ginevra leaned against the wall once more, her heart pounding inside her ribs as though it would burst. So, he was on her side. Holy Virgin, she prayed again, thank you! There was one, at least, who wished her no harm. Her head still splitting with pain, she took deep lungfuls of air, foul though it was, in an effort to gather her thoughts. And as the voices continued below she flexed her aching legs, back, hips and neck to bring her body once more under control, biting her lips to hold back the sobs of pain and fear.

It was clear to her from what Master Patrickson had said earlier that she was being housed somewhere inside the city walls, within sight of the Ouse Bridge across which the procession of pagonds still flowed in a stream which would take hours before the last one could act out its first performance. The clamour of bells floated across the city as though competing for attention. Could Jais hear them, too? she wondered. She allowed the noise to wash over her like waves of comfort, a link between herself and others that she hoped would be listening. Would he really search for her like any other bird he had lost? She felt that he probably would, if only to reclaim his own property. She had to believe that; there was little else for her to believe in.

It also became clear to her that she was not going to be allowed to starve, for Tom brought her a hunk of dark bread and a mug of ale some time later. Until she had begun to eat she hadn't realised how even the remotest parts of her face were involved in the process as she winced and held a free hand to her head. There was no time for Tom to linger, as she would have liked. Only his hastily whispered, 'Courage!' was a salve to her anxiety as the food was to her hunger.

The light now filtered more strongly through the window, allowing her to observe more closely the dirty, wattle-filled walls between the dark wooden uprights, the one table piled with stolen fabrics and embroideries, and the bucket in one corner. Apart from the sacking she sat on, nothing else was to be seen. The tiny room had no door, however, and she was able to hear the voices below, keeping her in touch with their movements, though their precise words were drowned

by the clatter which still continued outside. Apparently
the pagonds were still moving forward, except for the
many times when everything seemed to come to a
standstill.

Ginevra made a valiant effort to keep her senses
alert to all that was happening, so when the light from
the staircase was suddenly blocked off her heart thudded in fear as she sensed someone's approach. Instantly
she recognised the pale head of Master Patrickson. She
struggled to her feet and in one stride she was by the
side of the table, facing him as he entered the room
alone.

He was grinning in anticipation, his little hands
plucking at the grubby gown as he approached. 'Now,
my pretty one. You and I must have a little talk
together.'

If only she could keep him talking, maybe she could
distract him. Anything. . .'Did you say that you knew
someone who needs a broderer, sire?'

Piers Patrickson liked the sound of that. Sire, she
called him, as though he were someone of great
importance. Yes, he liked that. He moved closer. 'I
have contact with broderers everywhere, my dear,' he
said pompously. 'Such skills are in short supply at this
time.'

'So I've discovered, sire.' Her head was hurting with
the effort of speaking. 'Do you know of workshops in
London, too?' He was now up against her, allowing
her no room to evade him. The awful sickly reek of
him passed over her in waves, and his face, beaded
with sweat, was so close that she could see the red
veins in his eyes. His hands now encircled her waist
inside the wide side-openings of her surcoat. She
thought she was going to be sick, but fought the feeling

down as she remembered Tom's earlier words. 'Just pretend, keep pretending.' That was it. Pretend.

'London? Yes, London, too. But I have something further afield in mind for you. Flanders, perhaps. Or the Rhinelands, or. . . Italy?' As he spoke, almost caressingly, his hands moved upwards to her breasts. 'Meanwhile I have to know what kind of a bargain I'm offering, don't I? Now, my lady, let's see what we've got here. . .' And he squeezed.

His hands, though small, were strong and painful, making her cry out at his wilful brutality. But instead of leaning away, she summoned up every ounce of courage she could muster and slumped heavily against his filthy gown, closing her eyes and letting out an audible gasp as she allowed her knees to buckle beneath her.

The sudden redistribution of her weight threw him off-balance, pushing his arms away and forcing him to take a step backwards. She hit the floor with a realistic thud, sending a lightning stab of pain once more into her head. But to all intents and purposes she had fainted, still with hands tied behind her, though the linen strip had almost come adrift.

'What the. . .? God's *wounds*! Stupid bitch!' Ginevra felt his foot push viciously at her buttocks, then her chin was seized and pushed away again in savage frustration. She forced herself to remain limp and totally passive as the floorboards wavered beneath her cheek, his departure making little sound except for the creak of the wooden stairs. His high voice rose in anger at the two lads below, almost reaching screaming pitch, making it easier for her to hear the words. '. . .Staithe. . .do what you like with her. . .stay here!' The door clicked open and slammed, bounced back off the latch and was slammed again.

Slowly she sat up, and leaned against the leg of the table, trembling and aching, waiting for the hot surges of fear to pass away. He had gone. But for how long? Would he try again? Would she have the courage or the strength to fight him off? Gently massaging her arms, she winced at the lingering pressure of his brutal fingers as they had mauled her. God forbid that he should get a second chance. She must get away. She must!

The sound of the lads' low voices could be heard beneath her, rising and falling as though in heated argument. Was it about her? she wondered. How could all this be happening? Surely it was a bad dream, a nightmare. With eyes wide open, she brought her mind into sharp focus, concentrating on Jais, seeing his eyes, boring into his spirit, holding his attention with her own. She called him with her inner voices, Jais, Jais, my dearest, my love. I'm here! Come for me. Please, come for me. Jais, I love you. You know I love you. Jais. . . Jais. . .

Her eyes blinked back the tears and she bit her lips to still the trembling. 'Hear me, Jais. Please, hear me,' she said in a whisper.

Never before had there been such a commotion in the usually peaceful and well-ordered household of Sir Jais de la Roche. From the moment of Ginevra's disappearance, hardly a soul had so much as laid a head on a pallet. It was rumoured that the master had a good idea who had taken her but that the man had moved premises and was nowhere to be found in the city. Come light, things might be easier, but with everyone crowding in to see the mystery plays, and a holiday, too, there were added complications they could have done well without. The man had chosen his day perfectly.

At intervals throughout the night, one of the search-party would return to exchange news, gobble down some food and then go again. But the master appeared only once, looking, they said, as fearsome as the devil himself, white and silent, except to bark out more orders. All that could be done at Stonegate House was to prepare for her safe return home and pray that she would be unharmed. No one had the slightest doubt that the master would turn York, or even the world, inside out to find her.

Jais had posted two extra men on the Staithe with instructions to watch people coming on and off the boats. Ginevra's descriptions of the tall man and Master Patrickson were passed on to them in great detail, and they were to report immediately on any sighting of the two. But the extra activity everywhere was going to make this, they agreed, very difficult, for the pagonds were by now moving towards them up the Micklegate towards the Priory Church of the Holy Trinity for the first performance, and the same crowds which were now pushing past them on the bridge would soon be escorting the great carts and all their attendants back this way into the city.

'I'm going to need my eyes in my backside for this job,' one of the men remarked, grinning ruefully.

'Well, lad,' said the other, 'I reckon they'd be more use today if you stuck 'em on t'back of yer 'ed. Come on, keep yer eyes peeled, back an' front!' They needed no encouragement, for they felt the outrage of Ginevra's abduction as keenly as did everyone else in the household.

* * *

The voices stopped, and somewhere on the other side of the building a door creaked open and slammed shut. Had they gone? Ginevra heaved herself to her feet and across to the stairway, straining her ears to catch a give-away sound, but it was not necessary. The top of a head appeared, turning the corner of the first step. It was John, and he was coming up to her!

She whirled across to the table, terror now surging back into her body and lending her an extra strength as she watched his tall figure emerge into the room, carrying a mug of ale. 'Well, well! It doesn't look as though you need this to revive you, does it, my lady?' The emphasis on the last two words left her in no doubt of his attitude towards her. Placing the mug down on the floor by his side, he moved slowly towards her.

Tom! she screamed inside herself. Tom, for pity's sake, help me! 'Come on, now,' he was saying, watching her eyes fill with fear. He was young and well-built and had already hit her once in the workroom. She was sure he would do it again, if need be. 'Come on, I can be rough or gentle, whichever you choose. But don't take too long about it. . .'

His hand shot out to grab her, holding her now against the table with his body, and in a blind panic she screamed, 'Tom! Tom! Help me!' She realised later that he must already have been there as she called, for John's grip of her slackened immediately as he was grabbed from behind and swung round with great force. Clinging to the table for support, she saw Tom's fist make contact with the lad's jaw, sending him hurtling across the room into the wall at the far side to land with a sickening crash. The soft wattle in-fill crumbled under the impact, showering him with grey dust and bits of flaked plaster. Tom went and stood over him.

'Now, get out! Get out! This is *mine*, I tell you!' He jerked his head towards Ginevra.

The lad, holding his bleeding mouth, glowered at Tom and then at Ginevra. 'You liar!' he said, mumbling through the pain. 'You bleeding liar! You're not going to touch her. She's your master's. You wouldn't dare!'

'Get downstairs, before I knock you down 'em!' Tom replied, and stood rigidly watching as the lad slunk away, holding on to the wall for support. He waited, and then turned into the little room.

Ginevra, shaking with relief, held out a hand to him and was about to speak when he took her wrist firmly in his, urgency clearly showing in his eyes. 'Scream!' he mouthed to her silently.

Her eyes opened wide in astonishment, and a frown indicated her total failure to understand what he wanted her to do. Why would she scream, now that she was safe?

'Scream!' he hissed, bringing his face closer and moving her backwards on to the pile of sacking.

'No, Tom! No, please! What is it?'

'Louder, m'lady! Oh, for God's sake. . .!' She felt his arm go round her and his lithe body pressing her down to the floor as her legs crumpled under his weight. Before she could believe what was happening, she felt his hand on her thigh beneath her gown, moving upwards, and all at once her reserve burst through in a piercing scream. Scream after harrowing scream filled the room, mingling with the merry noise outside. The tight rein on her composure now snapped under the strain, letting her terror run free in a violence of flailing arms and clawing hands: her body convulsed, gasps and cries exploding between her yells like demons out of hell.

Tom fought to control her, let her scream hysterically for a few moments then, failing any other means to silence her, kissed her. Deliberately covering her nose and mouth, his kiss had the intended effect, and her body slumped, drained and exhausted. 'Hush. Hush, m'lady! I won't hurt you. You're safe from me, I promise,' he whispered. 'I'm not going to rape you. We're pretending!'

The words found their way into her dazed mind and at last she lay still, listening to the whispered words as his mouth was held against her ear. What was he saying? What did he mean? Pretending? Hot surges of relief flooded into her, hot tears spilled out and racking sobs replaced the former anguished cries of fear. Now she wept uncontrollably, howling like a child for all that had happened and not happened, for all that she had wanted and thought that she lacked, for the one that she loved in whose arms she was not being held.

Tom lay on her gently, holding her firmly beneath him, and allowed her to cry, knowing that it was having a double effect and was serving two purposes. So he waited, without attempting to halt its flow, satisfied that it could be heard downstairs and would be misconstrued exactly as he had intended.

At last, with dried-out sobs erupting between her swollen lips, she lay limp, totally spent. Tom pushed back the hair from her forehead and wiped the last tears away, making streaks on her flushed cheeks which dried quickly with the heat. He looked beyond her head to the stairway then smiled at her, his eyes warm with admiration and concern.

'Tom?' she whispered.

'It's all right. Just keep still,' he whispered in her ear. 'We're pretending, remember? It's got to look as if we're. . .you know!'

Yes, she did know now. At last, the picture had become clearer inside this muddled framework of people, theft, abduction, attempted rape. . . What next was she to encounter? she wondered. Through eyes still sore and damp with tears she looked at Tom's face above her, and wondered how and why he had become mixed up with people as vile as his two accomplices.

'What's going to happen, Tom?'

He looked at her still, lying so soft and defenceless, and thought of the countless times since he had first seen her on the eve of her marriage when he had longed in his dreams to hold her like this. 'Keep your voice low, m'lady, unless you can make it sound angry, or pleading. I don't know what's going to happen, except that he's gone to find his friend, the Italian captain. He's the one who'll want the embroideries. It'll take him some time to get through the crowds, though, and even then he might not find him.'

'But you're in terrible trouble, Tom, aren't you?'

'I am now,' he agreed, and a frown passed like a cloud over his eyes. 'If that fool hadn't called me by my name in the workroom, you wouldn't have known I was involved, would you?'

She shook her head in agreement. She would never have suspected this pleasant young man, who had always been so willing and courteous.

'Well, once you knew it was me, we had to bring you along. But I didn't want him to harm you. Oh, God's wounds! What a mess!' He shook his head and looked away briefly, then at her wide, lustrous eyes. 'This is the only good thing I've got out of it, so far.' His face was serious, and Ginevra felt that she must deflect his attention quickly before the situation got truly out of hand.

'Will you have to run away, Tom? Leave York?'

He nodded. 'Oh, yes. But I'll have to find a way of getting you to safety first. Don't know how, but remember, I'm on your side. Just go along with what I do. . .pretend to be upset—that'll please him. He's a vicious little pig. Oh, *no*!' His head lifted as the sound of the latch was heard quite clearly, his body now tense and alert. 'It's him!' he hissed.

Ginevra coiled, ready to leap to her feet, her shoulders already off the dirty sacking, pushing at Tom with a sideways roll.

'No! Get *down*! He's got to see us. . .' She was shoved violently back with a thud as Tom held her down again, pulling up the skirt of her gown on the side nearest the stairs. At that same moment the high-pitched voice called up.

'Get down here, young Fuller! You've had long enough!' His steps were heard softly on the wooden stairs, acting like a signal to the two above. Instinctively fighting Tom's exploring hand, Ginevra was torn between pretence and reality, accepting the need for one while dreading the extent to which the other would force her.

Tom's hand halted on her bare thigh as Patrickson's head appeared, their eyes now almost level with each other above the floor. 'I'll be with you in one moment, sir!' Tom grinned at him. 'That's all I need!'

'Hah!' the man laughed, turning while looking over his shoulder. 'That's all you need, eh? You've had time enough for ten men, you young rascal! Hurry up. *I* need you!' The footsteps receded.

'Yes, sir.'

Ginevra was trembling uncontrollably, her eyes again wide and dark, reflecting the total defenceless-ness of her position against this young man who promised not to harm her. How could she believe what he said? Did she have a choice? She was given no space to reflect, for his hand was now moving beyond her thigh while he watched her eyes for the reaction he knew would come. The scream, like the ones before, echoed round the room and caught the ears of the two downstairs. Then it stopped abruptly.

Tom's kiss, not a gag this time, lasted all of the moment he had requested and some more, while he kept his warm hand on the smooth skin of her hip. This, he was determined, would be his reward for aiding her escape, as he had every intention of doing. No matter what befell him afterwards, no matter that he would never see her again, this would be something to remember. Just a kiss, no more than that.

She realised by the feel of his lips that this was what he must be thinking, and although the kiss was not given freely she did not entirely resent it, either. He was not brutal, only deliberate, and obviously intent on using his last moments with her to the full. As his hand moved over her hip she tore her mouth away at last and pushed him into awareness. 'Tom! No, please don't! Tom! No more!' she yelled, purposefully loud, with an added edge of panic for all to hear. And they did. All of them.

With a rueful smile like a farewell, he stood up, kissed the end of his finger and touched the tip of her nose. The smile was still there as he bounced down the stairs, casually pretending to tie up his points to his belt and running his fingers through his curly hair.

'Took yer time, lad, didn't yer,' Patrickson said.

The other lad sat with swollen lip, silent and subdued, a red bruise surfacing under his cheekbone. That's in return for the one you gave to my lady, thought Tom, without looking at him.

CHAPTER FIFTEEN

THE clamour had died away some time ago and the
vesper bells from the nearest churches and priories
were sounding across the darkening city as Ginevra's
sleep of exhaustion continued, in spite of the busy to-
ing and fro-ing within the room. Since Master
Patrickson's return the two lads had been kept busy up
and down stairs, wrapping the bolts of precious Italian
brocades, velvets and glittering gold-threaded veils into
anonymous-looking bundles. They had taken these to
various parts of the city in exchange for the ready
money of wealthy patrons, mercers and merchants,
who pointedly refused to ask about their provenance.
It was as the money began to pile up under Piers
Patrickson's grasping little fingers on the table downstairs that at last he began to feel that he was getting
even with one of the men responsible for his imprison-
ment. He intended to get even with the other one as
soon as the captain arrived, after dark.

He had seen the two de la Roche men at the top of
the steps of the Staithe at the far side of the bridge,
and as a result had been forced to make a lengthy
detour to approach the captain's boat from the other
end. In case the lads' many trips across the bridge
should be noted and remarked upon, they would have
to pull their hoods well down and keep behind others
to avoid detection. It was an added risk which he had
not foreseen, but there was no other way across, and it
was no good waiting until after dark or keeping the
fabrics here longer than was strictly necessary.

234

Anyway, he had agreed to deliver on this day. He did not want *them* to start a search for him, too.

Meanwhile the lads were busily making their errands among the hordes of sightseers and holidaymakers, revellers and pilgrims flocking around the pagonds, the ale-houses and the various stalls of the fair. Tom's only fear was that he should be seen by those who knew him, whereas John was not known well in York. Now they were on their last return, tired and thankful that the day was almost done. The leading wagon, belonging to the tanners, which showed the Story of the Creation, had now long since completed the circuit and was leading the way back across the Ouse Bridge and down Micklegate as Tom followed in its wake. The crowds were dense, and hurrying was well-nigh impossible, for there were other pagonds following close behind, blocking the narrow road and causing a pile-up of gaily-coloured awnings and bedecked horses.

As Tom moved nearer to the steps leading down from the bridge to the Staithe, where the foreign boats were anchored, he again noted the black and green liveries of his master's household among the crowds. Instantly he moved across to the other side of the road and looked away, his hand to his face. But the eyes in the back of the head had served their purpose for one of the de la Roche men as he noted the young man's return only a little time after seeing him going in the opposite direction with a bundle under his arm and, while there was nothing too alarming in this alone, he felt it strange that Tom should have bolted across to the other side of the road to avoid being seen rather than greeting them as he would normally have done. After a quick conference with his partner, he hurried through the crowds to Stonegate House.

* * *

'Jais, dearest,' cried Marianne. He swept into the hall as the vesper bells clamoured from the minster, through the courtyard and past the silent servants, busy about their duties but longing for the latest news. 'Jais, have you heard anything?'

His face was haggard, the mouth set in a thin line. He was tense and desperately unhappy, and Marianne could see the muscles of his cheeks working as he fought to reply to her query, steadily and without emotion. His voice was husky with fatigue. 'One of them's seen Tom, the apprentice,' he said, 'twice, on the Ouse Bridge. Obviously trying not to be seen. Carrying a bundle into town.'

'That's significant?'

'Yes, it's significant, but one of them came to tell me here, and the other one was ordered to stay, so we don't know where he was heading. All I can think of is that if. . . Ginevra. . .' here he paused to control his breath '. . .If Ginevra is with the stolen goods. . .they may well be at that end of town. It's the only lead we've had so far, and we've searched all day.'

Marianne put her arms round her brother in an attempt to comfort him. At last she knew his true feelings. 'Where's Richard?' she asked softly.

'He's gone across to the other side of the bridge to see what he can see. But I'll send him back if you. . .'

'No! No, you must keep him with you. He wouldn't come back without you and Ginevra, anyway. It's only a matter of time, dearest. I know you'll find her.'

'Oh, Marianne! My God! I never thought I could feel this way. I've got to find her. She's my life!' He hugged his sister in a bear-like embrace, rocking gently.

She had never heard Jais speak like this before.

'Now, I'm going. If there hadn't been so many damned people about we'd have found her by now.

The little swine had it all well-planned, didn't he? If
he's hurt her, I'll. . .' He put her away from him almost
roughly.

'Dearest, don't torture yourself! God speed!'

He went, taking more men and horses to exchange
with the ones who had been in the saddle all day. But
himself and Negre he did not spare.

It was quite dark by the time Tom roused Ginevra with
more food and ale. He had bought the little pasty from
one of the market stalls and smuggled it to her from
inside his jerkin, knowing that there was little else
provided for her. There was no time for words, only a
brief smile as she formed a quick 'thank you' with her
lips, and then he was gone. She ate her pasty raven-
ously, feeling calmer after her deep sleep, in spite of
the rancid odour of her rough bedding. Deftly unbraid-
ing her disordered hair, she made it into a tidy plait
behind her head and smoothed down her crumpled
gown, brushing off the accumulated bits of debris from
the floor.

The room was now too dim to see anything clearly
except by a faint glow of light percolating through the
thick horn window. Without making a sound on the
floor, she crept across and opened it, easing it slowly
on rusty iron hinges. Craning her neck through the
gap, she could just make out the line of the river,
sparkling sluggishly with the reflection of torches and
braziers along its banks.

Over on the Ouse Bridge a narrow procession of
torch-bearing crowds and glowing pagonds still moved
away from the town in a seemingly never-ending
stream. So, she thought, they were still performing
round the city, well after dark. Oswinna had said they
did, and she was right. She breathed in lungfuls of the

cleaner air and searched the dark city for some sixth
sense of Jais's whereabouts. She could not expect Tom
to have sent a message to him for Tom was as anxious
to escape detection as Master Patrickson was, and it
was clear that he had stayed this long with her to
prevent another mauling of the kind she had suffered
this morning at the man's hands.

'Where are you, Jais?' she breathed. 'Please find
me.'

The air from the window was cool and refreshing,
helping to clear her head, but as she listened to the
crowds still bustling back and forth outside a change of
air-pressure within the room told her that downstairs
someone had entered. She moved quickly away from
the window, closed it softly and tiptoed to peer down
the staircase. A voice, deep and foreign-sounding,
floated up to her, combining strangely with the almost
falsetto squeaks of Patrickson. So, the Italian captain
had come to see the embroideries. Might this also be a
chance for her to escape from this dreadful place?

'Certainly, *signore*,' Master Patrickson was saying,
'Tom will bring them down. Yes, and the girl, too!'

He *did* want him to see her, then. She realised that
this was to be a critical moment for her: her resentful
compliance would determine the way in which the next
move would be conducted. To kick and scream would
only tighten their guard on her during a possible
transfer of her whereabouts. But perhaps a certain
meekness, even sulkiness, might lead them to relax
their security a little, and thus allow her to take
advantage of whatever situation arose.

She descended the staircase ahead of Tom, whose
arms were heavy with the embroidered vestments, her
eyes still red with the earlier weeping and the streaks
of grime on her cheeks showing clearly where the tears

had run. Through downcast eyes she was still able to observe the tiny room lit only by a lantern, the obsequious demeanour of Master Patrickson and the towering figure of the tall stranger, whose head fitted uncomfortably between the heavy wooden beams of the plastered ceiling. In spite of the long, dark cloak hanging loosely over his wide shoulders, Ginevra would have recognised him immediately, even at a distance, for his distinctive pointed beard and beaked nose made an impression which it would have been difficult to erase.

She noticed that he had replaced the figured gold tunic for a black one with gold highlights along its borders, presenting, as before, an effect of elegance and style. The room was suddenly crowded, for the table on to which Tom piled the embroideries left little room for manoeuvre. John leaned into the far corner, glowering and swollen-faced, keeping as far away from Tom as was possible, though he watched Ginevra's entrance with interest.

The captain held out his hand to her courteously, his deep-set eyes glinting in appreciation beneath the heavy dark brows. She placed her hand in his, wishing to acknowledge his gesture of gallantry, though she allowed the distress to show in her eyes.

'Ah, *signora*!' He had noted the ring on her hand, and touched the line of tears on her cheeks with a large finger. 'Who ees responseeble for thees, may I ask?' His voice was not unsympathetic, she thought as he looked first at Tom, then across to John's angry glance, then back to Tom thoughtfully. 'Yes. I see! A leetle competeetion!' He pulled himself erect, and studied her. 'I am not surprised. You are very beautiful, *signora*.'

Ginevra did not reply nor respond, but allowed him

to survey her from head to toe. Like a cow at the market, she thought, angrily seething inside at this game she was being obliged to play. Well, play the game for as long as it's convenient, and then we'll see who makes the rules! At least he was not a boor, like that creature there. She would be relieved to be removed from *his* custody, even though the consequences were unpredictable.

But where was Jais? Why had he not found her? Was it *so* difficult? Was he really trying?

The captain released her hand and turned with a smile to Master Patrickson, and she saw the glance of mutual understanding flash between them. The latter motioned to Tom with his head, and she saw him move to the door, leaning against it arrogantly, with folded arms.

'*Signore*, the vestments. Will you examine them?' Master Patrickson unfolded them and Ginevra watched the captain's reaction as he turned the mitre in his hands, causing the gold stitchery to twinkle in the soft light.

'*Molto buono*,' he murmured behind the black beard, '*Si, molto buono*!' At last he looked into the small eyes of the other man and nodded in satisfaction. 'Yes. They're good. Are we agreed?'

Patrickson's face quivered into folds. 'Indeed, *signore*. And the girl?' His piggy eyes widened.

The captain turned to Ginevra as though wishing to share a secret joke with her, his glance telling her quite plainly that he shared her disgust of this little man. 'The *lady*, sir, eef you please!'

'Yes, of course. The lady.' He looked uncomfortable at the rebuke. 'She is skilled, *signore*. You will find her useful, I know.'

The captain made no reply but looked at Ginevra

again, at her crumpled violet gown, the bruised forehead, her coppery-pale hair and huge golden eyes in the elfin face. Yes, he would find her useful. With her embroidering skills and that marvellous colouring he would get a far better price for her than he was about to pay to this stupid creature. He would not ask where she had come from. Best not to know on occasions like this. He knew that from experience.

Ginevra wondered whether he had been told who she was, especially as he had insisted on her correct title, but hoped that he had not, for he would then surely feel that it was too dangerous to abduct the wife of one of York's most prominent citizens, and a member of the city's wealthiest guild, too. That would certainly delay her departure from this place, and her chances of escape. But he must also know that no member of the aristocracy would allow him to escape the consequences of her seizure, a fact which seemed not to have occurred to Master Patrickson in his greed and bungling need for revenge. She would not disclose her identity in case he decided that the transaction was too dangerous, not worth the risk.

In fact, Patrickson was well aware of the need to get rid of her as fast as possible for those very reasons. He regarded her presence as something of a liability, though he was not going to throw away the chance of having an extra dagger to twist in the side of his enemy. 'You sail tonight, *signore*?' he asked smiling, and signalled John to repack the vestments. The sooner the better, he thought uneasily.

'*Si*, on the tide. Now, sir, I must request the use of your cloak for the lady.'

Ginevra's heart began to pound, anticipation welling up inside her at the thought of her one chance to escape. But he was big, and obviously strong. How on earth would she manage to evade him, and probably the others, too, if they were truly going to guard her closely? Would Tom go with her? If there were still plenty of people in the streets, even at this late hour, she would certainly have more chance of being hidden among them, and by her last look through the upstairs window it looked as though it would still take some time before the last wagon and its players reached its final destination back at Toft Green. So there was a chance! 'Courage,' Tom had said.

As the captain received an old grey cloak from Master Patrickson she stole a glance at Tom, receiving his tiny wink before she was encased in the foul-smelling garment, the hood pulled well up over her hair and the neck securely fastened. The large, strong hands were very sunburnt and deft, filling her with misgivings about being able to dodge their hold.

Two large pouches of money were placed on the table only moments before the two grasping little hands drew them away, prominent eyes almost bulging from their sockets with excitement as the weight was tested. A quick peep at the captain's face showed her the amusement written in his eyes, along with his contempt. 'Well, sir? Are you going to offer me the assistance of one of your brave young apprentices? Or do I have to carry the embroidery *and* the lady, too?'

Master Patrickson awoke from the contemplation of his newly acquired wealth and jumped to attention. 'Oh! Of course, *signore*—I was just about to suggest. . . Tom. . .you go.'

'No! Not him! Please. . .not him.'

Four faces in the room looked at Ginevra, hardly able to believe that it was her voice, after her previous silence. No one spoke. Then the captain bent his head to her. 'Your pardon, *signora*? You do not weesh this gentleman. . .?' He looked at Tom, amused and puzzled by her vehemence.

'No! He. . .he. . .' She knew that it was a dangerous game to play as her hand flew to her eyes to cover her apparent shame. But the more fuss she made about Tom, the more likely it was that they would insist on him being the one to keep a hold on her, and *that*, she hoped, would give her a better chance when the time came. Tom had not moved, giving her an indication that he understood her scheme.

'I'll go!' said John, moving out of the corner.

Ginevra's heart lurched into her throat. Holy Mother of God, she prayed. Please let my plan work. But she was saved, for Master Patrickson was more interested in safety, at this moment, than personal feuds over a woman. 'No, you won't! Tom knows how to handle her! Tom. . .!' He jerked his head towards her, and John slunk back.

'I agree,' said the captain. 'Since he's the one she fears, he should be able to keep her safe until we reach the boat. Tom?'

'Don't you worry, sir,' Tom said, coming to stand behind her. 'She knows I won't stand any nonsense.' He put his hand on the back of her neck and Ginevra flinched, turning her face away from him with a stony glare. She hoped they would notice her reaction. Tom's fingers signalled two sharp presses on her neck, confirming that he understood.

The night air felt like icy spring-water in Ginevra's mouth after the fetid atmosphere of the dingy room and its crowded maleness. It took all her restraint not to bound away up the street, but she knew that so many people would hinder her progress at this point. Apart from that, Tom's hand was now on her wrist and the captain was close on her other side with the precious bundle of vestments well-hidden under his long black cloak.

He pulled the big hood over his head, almost hiding his face, aware that he was hardly a figure one could ignore. It would be even harder to ignore him, he felt, if a beautiful woman was walking by his side. Now he was relieved of that problem, for young Tom obviously had her measure and would no doubt enjoy his guardianship for the brief journey.

Keeping his voice to a whisper, out of Ginevra's earshot, Patrickson reminded Tom to keep well to the opposite side of the bridge as they crossed, and to keep Ginevra's hood well down. But Tom had not forgotten about the de la Roche presence, and had every intention of parting company with both of these two well before then. He did not want to be seen with either the Lady Ginevra or with the receiver of the stolen goods, for his involvement was now indisputable. He had been paid, and this was a chance for him to flee, as well as for my lady. He was glad that he was to be instrumental in her safe return.

Almost immediately they joined the crowds on the busy street, many of them moving in the opposite direction now, away from the city centre, following the last of the pagonds across the bridge. Still they were riotous, full of high spirits and ale after a whole day of fun, and the three anonymous figures found it slow and difficult to walk against the flow in the darkness. Tom put his arm around Ginevra's waist to keep her by his side, motioning the captain to walk ahead. 'I'm behind you, sir!'

'No, my lad.' The captain stopped. 'This won't do! I want you both where I can see you. Here, come on ahead.'

They had now almost reached the corner of their

street, where it turned into Micklegate and the bridge ahead, and they were obliged to stop anyway, because of the throng milling around a huge wagon which had taken the corner too sharply and wedged itself against the wall. The actors and hangers-on were doing little to help, for this was the end of their long day and a laugh with the crowd before they reached Toft Green was not to be missed.

'It's the mercers!' Tom said, moving forward with the captain and Ginevra.

'The what? You mean, the Mercers' Guild play?'

'Yes, that's right. They're the last and the biggest. They show the Last Day of Judgement. . . Look, there's the black devil!' The crowd parted before them, shrieking and laughing in mock fear as the actors capered about—some like skeletons, with bones painted on their tunics, and none of them up on the platform of the wagon, for it now rested at a slight angle on the wall side. The horses were restless with the tilt of the shafts, neighing in alarm as their handlers tried to move them backwards. The long, floor-length curtain hanging all round the wagon and covering the wheels parted along one side, releasing a bright red devil from beneath the platform, howling and mouthing obscenities at the hysterical crowd.

Ginevra felt Tom's hand tighten on her waist and she peeped sideways at him, taking note of a slight nod of his head towards the opening. The two devils wrestled each other, to everyone's delight, but the captain was anxious to get past and on to the bridge, and he beckoned to Tom to bring Ginevra along round the edge of the crowd.

But at that moment the two devils spotted his tall figure, black-cloaked and hooded, and with howls of glee pulled at him strongly. He resisted, and his hood fell back to reveal the black hair, beaked nose and pointed beard. This was all they needed! Another devil! Yelling, they heaved him forward into the throng, pulling at his cloak and exposing the bundle underneath. In a flash, Tom broke through and wrested it from him. 'I've got it, sir! I'll keep it safe!'

The unfortunate man was now beset on all sides, and for all his size and power had no choice but to relinquish the precious bundle to Tom, rather than damage its contents in the skirmish. Tom turned to find Ginevra behind him. 'Quick, m'lady!' She could hadly hear him for the screams and shrieks of laughter, but she knew what to do.

Behind the crowd the wagon was still stuck, and in the next moment both Tom and Ginevra were through the opening of the curtain and underneath it without a soul seeing them. It was very dark, but Tom had already worked out what to do. 'Look, m'lady. Here's the costume box, fixed under the axle. This is where I'm shoving the bundle. See. . .' he whispered. Dimly, as the dancing shadows moved around the curtain outside, she saw what he was doing. 'Now, you go out of the back, and run as fast as your legs can carry you across the bridge. But *run*! No, wait. . .' He grabbed her as they stooped together beneath the wagon and kissed her hard on the lips. 'Now, run!'

'Tom, I shan't forget you!'

She parted the opening in the curtain at the back and poked her face out to look. Then she sprang, and ran blindly, madly, like a March hare.

It was some moments before she realised that she was not on the bridge, for now no one was about, and as she turned to look saw that she had gone straight across the crossroads instead of round the corner. She could not go back, for now the captain might be freed and searching for her. Panic filled her like a slow stream of ice in her arms and legs, threatening to hold her to the spot, immobile, frozen, helpless.

But at least she was free. She looked frantically across the narrow street. The river was on one side, dark and sleepy, and on the other the tall spire of a church was just visible against a dark blue sky. A church! Without another thought, she picked up her skirts and made for the narrow alleyway alongside the building, now deep in shadow. The tiny door was just visible, as was the huge iron knocker hanging above the latch. With trembling hands, and legs which shook with the effort, she pushed the door open, slipped inside, closed the heavy door gently behind her and almost fell down the three stone steps into the safety of the black interior.

The young groom in the green and black livery could hardly believe his eyes. At one moment he had moved his mount round to the back of the crowd, to see why the pagond was stuck in this strange position, and the next moment a frightened face had peered from between the curtains at the back. A second quick look had just been in time to see the cloak-covered figure fling itself across the road and into the darkness beyond. But was he dreaming? He could have sworn the face was that of the Lady Ginevra.

Before he had time to react, a second figure came hurtling out, too. But this time the groom kicked his horse forward, and easily caught up with Tom before he had time to get away. 'Tom! Tom Fuller! Wait!'

Tom stopped, and seeing the young groom whom he knew beckoned him over to the shadow of the nearby building.

'Tom Fuller!' The groom dismounted and held Tom fast by the arm.

But Tom shook him off irritably. 'No! Listen to me. There's no time to lose. Lady Ginevra. . .'

'Yes, I've just seen her, coming out from under the pagond. It *was* her, wasn't it?'

'Yes, it was! Go and tell the master. Did you see which way she went? Across the bridge, was it?'

'No, not across the bridge. Up *that* way. . .' He pointed along North Street, running alongside the river.

'Oh, God's *wounds*!' Tom groaned. 'The woman has no bloody sense of direction. She should have gone over the bridge, then the men would have seen her. I *told* her. . .! Oh, hell and damnation! Now what?'

'What happened? Is she all right?'

'No, not very. But at least she's free, though for how long is anybody's guess! Hurry and tell him. . . She's there, somewhere. I can't go back. I'm in trouble. And tell him this, too. Tell him that it's Master Patrickson he wants, and he's in that house down there. . .' He pointed to the street where the pagond had been heading before it stopped. 'It's the fourteenth house down. Tell him he'll find the evidence upstairs, and a lad called John who helped. Hurry!'

As the young groom flung himself on his horse Tom was away into the night, running on swift and silent feet, his role played out. The crowds were thinning now, but it was still well into the early hours of the morning before the young groom found Sir Jais and Master Mercer, with a band of mounted men, conferring near the Staithe. They had seen the departure of *Il Volpe*, the Italian captain's boat, had seen him board her, too, empty-handed and alone, looking exhausted and angry. There had been no reason to apprehend him, and they were still no nearer to finding Ginevra, until the arrival of her young groom, breathless after an almost complete circuit of the city, and overjoyed to see his master.

CHAPTER SIXTEEN

THE church was cool, the air inside still heavy with the
perfume of incense, and only an iron hoop bearing
candles providing a focus for her eyes in the darkness.
A leaden silence wrapped around her as she stood to
accustom herself to her surroundings, to still her
thumping heart and to control the shaking in her arms
and legs. The steady flickering of the candles helped to
restore her balance, beckoning her towards them,
comforting, telling her of safety and solace. New
candles lay in a neat pile at the side, inviting her to
take one, light it, and set it alongside the other with a
prayer.

'Holy Mother of God,' she prayed, kneeling on the
stone cold floor. 'Holy Mother, help me now, please.
You've helped me so far. Please don't stop now. Don't
take him away from me. I love him. I love him so
desperately.' Tears rolled slowly down her face and
dripped on to her clasped hands. She could think of no
more to say except, 'Thank you for protecting me.'

The darkness was so intense that she could make out
little except for the pale glow of the east window
beyond her. With a new sense of calm, her aching
limbs and bruised frame carried her towards the altar,
groping with sensitive fingers against the wall and
steering herself towards the tiny lamp which hung in
mid-air like a guiding star. Stepping-stones, she
thought hazily. I'm using stepping-stones to find my
way. Her toes touched the first altar steps in unison
with the thought and she halted, listening hard.

It was difficult, after all the events of her capture and escape, to believe that she was truly safe, to keep the demons of fear at bay, especially in the darkness and stillness of the church where she could summon no visual comforts to redress the balance. It was always possible that the captain, once he had been released by the revellers, would come to search for her, that he would alert Master Patrickson, that they would organise a search-party, make her tell them where the vestments were hidden.

She moved to the other side of the altar steps as far as the wall and sank down, exhausted. I can do no more until daybreak, was her last thought as she folded the rough cloak around her and lay on the steps, her nose now accustomed to the smell of the fabric and her senses too tired to care.

Sleep flitted past her, teasingly, stopping every now and again to spirit her away into a fantasy of faces and foolish absurdities before dumping her callously back into the cold darkness of the night, trembling with the shock. Time was lost to her. The world seemed to have disappeared.

She sat up, suddenly, the hairs on her head and arms prickling with awareness. Had she heard or only felt the tiny sound? Leaning back hard against the stone wall, ears straining, eyes searching for sounds, she waited. There *was* a sound. Hoof-beats. Was it dawn, then? Were these the usual noises of life beginning?

But it was not dawn. She looked above her for signs of a new light and caught, instead of a steady glow from the east, the faintest glimmer of torch-light, flickering and dancing against the walls above. With every muscle in her body tensed she heard men's voices, low and urgent, and more clattering of hooves on the flags at the side of the church. It was the search-

party! Come to search for her, to get her and the
vestments back. Master Patrickson, or the captain,
or. . .or Jais? Could it be? *Could* it?

As the fragmented sounds persisted and grew ever
closer she pushed herself even harder against the wall,
hoping that her grey covering would make her invisible
to her pursuer, hoping, too, that the pounding in her
breast would not be heard. Far away, at the end of the
church, the latch of the door clicked with a shattering
suddenness followed by a báng as it was thrown open
against the wall. Then more low voices, and a glimmer
of flames from torches.

Ginevra held herself rigid, hardly breathing, her
teeth now chattering uncontrollably with fright, cold
and pain. More voices, more lights dancing dimly on
the walls, and the heavy thud of feet on stone moving
in all directions. A light moved down the centre of the
church towards the altar, stopping every few steps and
then advancing again. The torch-bearer reached the
altar steps and moved the flames from side to side
slowly, and Ginevra caught the glint of a gold monogram on his breast, then an image of green and gold.
She gasped, and the light stopped.

'Shh! Quiet!'

All noises ceased while the figure moved the torch
towards her, outlining her bundled body, wide-eyed,
transfixed against the wall. 'Sir! Here!'

The racing of a man's feet, his cry, 'Ginevra!' like a
soft wail of rapture, his frame hugely outlined against
the torchlight behind him. It *was* him! It was his voice,
his arms. It was no dream. She did not remember how
she came to be on his lap, held like an infant against
his warm breast, rocked with deep cries, cradled and
kissed as though he would devour her. She did not
know which cries were his or which were hers, for they

flowed together in a duet of such anguished harmony that the old torch-bearer turned his head away, gulping back tears and halting the men who would have crowded forward.

'Jais. . .' she managed to whisper.

'My love. My dearest love. Darling little bird. You're safe now. Are you hurt, my love?' His hand fluttered over her face.

'Not badly, no. Darling Jais. Is it really you? Am I dreaming?'

'My darling, I love you. I love you. That's no dream.' His mouth was in her hair, on her cheeks, her lips, moaning with relief and happiness. 'Come, sweeting, we're going home.'

Home. Ginevra could not speak, for her heart was full to overflowing. His tender words of love, his joy at finding her, his strong arms around her once more — this was worth everything she had been through. Everything!

Easily he picked her up in his arms and, holding her tightly against him, carried her through the parted group of men and out of the church into the remainder of the night, where the first streaks of light were breaking through the eastern sky.

Richard and more men rode up at that moment; he was obviously overjoyed to see Ginevra safe at last in Jais's arms and embraced both of them together in one huge bear-hug with her in the middle. As he exchanged a few words with Jais Ginevra caught the word 'vestments', reminding her of the reason for the hunt. In the emotional reunion of the past moments, and the traumas of the ones before, she had completely forgotten the cause and the focal point of the incident, and she put an urgent hand up to Jais's chin as she lay bundled in his arms. 'Jais! The vestments.'

'Never mind them, sweetheart, they're not important.'

'Yes, I know where they are!'

Both men looked at her with incredulilty. Was she dreaming? 'You know?'

'Yes.' She smiled. 'You'll never guess. They're in the costume box under the front axle of the mercers' pagond.' Now she must be delirious. They frowned at each other in disbelief.

'Sweetheart. . .'

She felt Jais begin to turn, but she grabbed at Richard's arm. 'No, they *are*! Richard, go and look under the mercers' pagond, the one that got stuck on the corner by the bridge. In the costume box is a bundle. The vestments.'

His voice took on a new tone. 'Right! We'll go now, before they strip the whole thing down. Come on, you lot! With me.' He took some of the men and disappeared into the dawn. Ginevra knew that Jais was utterly puzzled, but this was not the time to go into details. Explanations would have to wait.

Wrapped tightly like a parcel in his warm cloak, she was passed up to him and tucked closely against his chest, with her head beneath his chin, feeling the rocking of Negre beneath her, the warmth and the smell of safety. She closed her eyes. Bliss, she thought, must mean this. To be held securely on Jais's saddle-bow by his strong arms, close to his body, secure and safe. He had said that he loved her. Then this *must* be what bliss was.

Jais looked down into her face grimly, and his arm tightened about her. She winced slightly. 'Did they hurt you, my darling? If he hurt you, I'll kill him!' His look was so fierce that Ginevra did not doubt for one moment that he would. She preferred not to elaborate, and for the rest of the journey through the city in the faint light of early dawn she was content to lie in his arms and feel the edge of his bearded chin on her forehead and the powerful rhythm of Negre beneath them. She would count this as the beginning of her life.

Messengers had been sent on ahead to alert the household and now, as they clattered into the courtyard, it seemed as though everyone had come to greet them, holding horses, clapping shoulders, tears of joy replacing the barren unhappiness of the previous day.

Marianne and Oswinna, speechless with relief and crying with delight, rushed down from the solar, where preparations had already begun, just in time to see Jais enter the hall with his precious bundle in his arms, her damp hair now clinging in dark strands to her face. Jais could not contain his grin of triumph as with purposeful stride he carried her up to their room through a crowd of applauding servants, more than happy to be woken an hour or two earlier than usual on this day.

Ginevra, smiling in his arms, had never felt so happy to be anywhere in her life—to see dear Marianne's glowing face and eyes filled with joyful tears, to receive a hug of welcome, like Richard's, between her and Jais—these were treasured moments she would never forget. Once again in the privacy of the solar, Marianne closed the door quietly behind them and tactfully withdrew, aware of their need to be alone together before attending to Ginevra's physical needs.

He laid her gently on the bed with great tenderness and sat by her side, seeing her now in a better light, noting the angry bruise on her forehead and the blue-grey shadows around the eyes, the grimy streaks of tears on the pale cheeks. He shook his head slowly, a steely-grey anger in his eyes, his mouth set in a hard line. Touching the bruise, and then her cheeks, he growled, almost to himself, 'I'll kill the swine who did this!'

'Jais. Jais, wait. Hear the whole story first. It's not what you think. . .' She could see what he thought and how he suffered and longed to comfort him, reassure him that she was harmed only superficially.

'Sweetheart, that I should have allowed you to fall into such danger. What a fool I am! What an utter fool!'

She held out her arms to him, enclosing his head against her breast, and stroked her fingers through his thick black mane. Now it was she who was the comforter. 'No, no, love. Hush. Don't say that. I love you. I love you. Nothing else matters. Nothing at all.'

If previously Ginevra had felt that she had never known such luxury, it was as nothing compared to the cosseting and fussing of Marianne and Oswinna and a bevy of maids who now administered to her. Her body bathed, her hair washed, wounds and bruises lovingly salved, and robed in clean white linen scented with lavender and roses, she now felt a sense of well-being which had been denied her for two nights and a day.

Although bursting to know about her ordeal, Marianne understood that Ginevra's bodily comforts were more important than the fufilment of her own curiosity, and so she wisely contained all questions until a more appropriate time. But her relief at seeing her sister-in-law safe and sound once more was not to be so contained, especially when she discovered that her sense of humour was still intact. Nor was she feeling sorry for herself—indeed, she appeared to be somewhat apologetic.

'You haven't *slept*, Marianne?' Ginevra was appalled.

'We couldn't, dearest. We knew that as soon as we put our heads down Jais would come bounding back with you. And we wouldn't have missed that for the world. Anyway, I couldn't have slept a wink.'

'I'm so sorry, dear one. I've put you all to a great deal of trouble. If I hadn't run off to the workroom at that moment. . .'

'Was it something we said?'

'No, Marianne dear, it wasn't anything you ever said. You've shown nothing but kindness to me. It was a look, that's all.'

'From me?'

'No, love. From Jais.'

Marianne did not at that moment want her to explain. She knew that it would no doubt become clear in time. This moment was for rest, food and peaceful comforts. So she found it strange that Ginevra, while warm oat porridge laced with honey and cream was being spooned into her mouth, should want to unburden herself to her at the same time, in spite of her physical exhaustion.

'You know Jais's looks, Marianne, don't you?'

Marianne smiled knowingly. 'I know his looks. Yes.'

'Well, that last one, during our discussion, quite clearly said, "Hah! One more step, my lass, and then I've caught you for good!"'

There was an explosion of laughter between them.

'But, Ginevra, he's already caught you, hasn't he? What do you mean, one more step?'

So as she lay back on the soft pillows with her friend's hand in hers the story was explained—how she had fought against any idea of taking part in Jais's embroidery business, even though it would have been her great delight, because she believed that it had been her skills as a broderer that had induced him to offer for her. She explained the circumstances of her betrothal, how she had felt manipulated, hurried to agree in a most unseemly fashion with a threat hanging over her head which involved her brother's future, too. How she had had little with which to retaliate except her refusal to show her love for him and to help with the workshop. And yet, she explained ruefully, he knew, he *must* have known, how she felt about him. It would have been impossible for him not to know.

Marianne agreed. It would indeed, for it was obvious to everyone, in spite of her air of wistfulness. He had known, too, of her feigned indifference to the idea of embroidering until, she emphasised, squeezing her friend's hand, until he had taken her to the minster, when it had been obvious that she could contain her ideas no longer and had allowed them to burst forth out of control. Then, like the devious fiend he was, he had told her and Richard of these new ideas, knowing how she, Ginevra, would be torn between discussing their implications more fully and letting them go, thereby missing her chance for good.

'And it was then that I saw him waiting to see which way I would go. And so I went. Rather than do as he wanted me to do and let him win, I went!'

'Ah! I see now.' Marianne smiled understandingly and stroked Ginevra's fingers. 'I had no idea it was quite like that. That's what all the wedding haste was about, then?'

'Yes, that was another undignified manoeuvre. . .'

'I can see why you were annoyed. I would have been, too. So when did he tell you about the workshop? Not until after the wedding?'

'He didn't tell me. . . I discovered it for myself. On the day of our wedding.' She looked sheepishly at Marianne's round-eyed look of surprise.

'And. . .?'

'And I was furious. I felt that it only proved what I'd suspected all along. . .that he just needed an extra hand with the embroidery. . .and perhaps. . .' She could not finish saying what was in her mind, but there was no need. Marianne knew.

'Oh, Ginevra! How could you think that? Jais wouldn't have to marry anyone in great haste to get either of those things, idiot! He's desperately in love with you. How could you ever have doubted it?'

The two friends were serious now, and thoughtful, both of them, for the first time understanding things which had seemed like mysteries.

'I suppose because, for one thing, I know so little about men. And for another thing, he never told me. Until now.'

Marianne felt that at this point the rest of the discussion should be continued with her brother rather than with herself, and she could see that Ginevra needed sleep. Other mysteries would have to wait to be unravelled.

'Is she asleep?'

'No, dearest. Waiting for you, I believe.'

With an embrace of love and gratitude, the brother and sister parted, and Jais went to the bed. He was exhausted. Without another word, their arms and bodies enfolded like hands clasped in prayer, and they slept in each other's arms, the bliss of completeness pushing the dark thoughts of the previous hours far away out of reach, the joy of their rediscovery pulsing through them.

As the full light of day flooded into the room Ginevra turned her head to look down at him, his mouth now relaxed in sleep against her breast, his black hair tousled like a young boy's, and her love for him poured out of her in a deluge of emotion. No more revenge, no more resentment or bitterness; these were now things of the past, like crutches flung aside once the wound was healed. She had his love; he had hers. Nothing more was needed.

Her hand caressed his face, sweeping gently over his brow, along his shoulder, and down his arm as it lay heavily across her, and she remembered its strength as he had curbed her wilfulness on so many occasions, its gentleness as she had melted in his embraces. Such sweetness. How could she ever have been so stubborn, so truculent? But there were still so many riddles, so many unresolved questions, which had done nothing to relieve these earlier grudges, and although the conflicts had now been discarded the cause of them would have to be discovered, if only to satisfy her curiosity.

Jais was as eager to discover the details of her abduction as she was to discover the reasons behind his initial interest in her, but his first investigations were of a more intimate nature. Marianne had told him of the bruises on Ginevra's body, filling him with a white-hot anger that she might have been abused, and so now, as they lay warm and at peace in the big bed, she was able to tell him what he needed to know. She did not see the terrible look on his face as he heard of her pretended swoon to escape the attentions of Master Patrickson, but once she had assured him that no real and lasting harm had been done, she was able to turn his attention to more pleasant topics.

Ginevra ran her hand across the breadth of his chest and found it captured against him by his hand. She spoke with her lips against his earlobe. 'Has it really taken this to bring our love for each other out into the open? Am I still dreaming that you love me, or is it real?'

He pulled her hand to his mouth and kissed the palm. 'I've loved you from the very first moment I saw you, my sweet one.' He laughed, turning his head to hers.

She sat up and leaned over him, her hair falling on him like a golden waterfall in the sunlight. Her eyes showed astonishment, regarding his twinkling ones closely while thinking back to that time. 'You mean, in the priory? Surely not!'

'Yes, my love,' he said, pecking the end of her nose. 'That was where I saw this wild bird flying down the hillside and felt a certain. . .emptiness. . .on my wrist!' He held out a strong brown arm, fist clenched as though to receive a falcon on the gauntlet. His eyes and white teeth flashed as she turned to look.

A gurgle of excitement welled up inside her as she peeped at him through her hair. 'And then. . .?'

'And then, little bird, I found it. Looking distressed. And so I teased it a bit, to see if it had spirit.' He grinned at her mischievously.

'Brute! That was despicable! Shame on you. . .'

He pulled her down to him roughly and kissed her hard. Then he let her go. 'And then. . .?' Ginevra asked again.

'And then, little bird, I told its keeper that I wanted it. Right then. Told her I couldn't wait. And I made her let it fly so that I could capture it again, all by myself!'

Laughter and disbelief jostled for first place so hard that for some time she could not speak. He watched her, enchanted. 'Jais de la Roche, am I to believe that you threatened the Reverend Mother, and you plotted all that. . .that estate business. . .just to. . .?'

He was looking anything but contrite. His handsome face glowed with delight at her discovery and his teeth parted as he threw back his head on the pillow in a rich bellow of laughter. Holding her tightly against her indignant struggles, he went on. 'I knew you wouldn't come willingly. They never do, the fiery ones. But I knew that once I had you I could tame you!'

Ginevra struggled in his restraining arms, her bruises reminding her not to try too hard, but he would not release her. He rolled, and pinned her under him, his face more serious now. She persisted. 'But you knew I was falling in love with you, didn't you?'

'I knew it, yes.'

'And yet you never told me you loved me, until now.'

'No.' His eyes were darkening with desire.

'Why, Jais?'

He studied her face, seeing a trust there which had been missing during those earlier days. The hurt and anger had now gone, too, to be replaced by a new warmth and sweetness. 'Well, for one thing, you didn't want my love. You wouldn't have believed me. You were feeling so insecure and hurt, after. . .certain rejections. . .that you preferred to believe that everyone was against you. Those you knew, as well as those you didn't know. Part of your defence, wasn't it?'

She was silent. Brother David. Prioress Claire. Alan and Johanna. Johanna's mother. Jais himself. Yes, she had been convinced of their enmity. His assessment was quite true.

'And the other thing?' she asked quietly.

'What did you tell me, after our betrothal vows were said?'

She knew. She ran a soft finger round the edge of his

chin and looked into his eyes, not wanting to repeat it, asking silently for his acceptance.

But he would not accept her silence as an answer. 'Come on!' he insisted gently.

'I swore to make you pay for taking me like that,' she whispered.

'And I swore to myself then that you would know me for master and want my love before I told you of mine.'

'But. . .?'

'But after losing you, and finding you again, I couldn't conceal it any longer. The thought that I might have lost you forever was more than I could bear. . .' His last words were muffled in her hair, his face now deeply buried as he rocked her in his arms in silence.

'Oh, Jais! Oh, my dearest love. Dearest master. How foolish we are.'

When she was able to speak, some time later, Ginevra sat across his lap, her arms about his neck, caressing the black hair which lay along her cheek. 'Jais?'

'What is it, little bird?' He smiled.

'You know that I've let it go now, don't you?'

There was a silence while her words were weighed. 'Tell me!'

'You said my heart wasn't in it, didn't you?'

He prised her away from him and held her, looking into her eyes with a knowingness that sent shivers through her arms, and though she tried to hide her face in his neck again, he would not allow it. 'Your heart wasn't in it even as you said it, wench!'

'How do you know that?' she asked in surprise.

'How do I know that? Because I knew you were lashing out on all sides—angry with me, angry with yourself, everybody. And because it was the only thing you *could* do, at the time. Promise revenge. Like a falcon being caught, beating its wings and screaming.'

'You didn't take it seriously, then?'

'Certainly I did. Falcons can do damage if they're not taken seriously.' He laughed softly, holding her as she tried to remove herself from his lap, ruffled that she should be so compared in this way and, more precisely, that the comparison should be so apt. She struggled against him in annoyance, thinking that he might at least acknowledge the validity of her vow, show some concern.

'And *did* I damage you, you great brute? Let me go!'

For an answer he picked her up, writhing but helpless. 'You'd like to think you did, wouldn't you, wench?' He was laughing as he put her down on the bed which they had only recently left. 'But, you see, I was wearing my gauntlet, as falconers do.'

She was about to make an angry retort, but her mouth was covered by his, her body stilled by the pressure of his chest, her arms caught and held by her sides. He raised his head at last. 'And now, little bird, you can show me how much you mean it.'

'What? Mean what?' She turned her head angrily to bite at him, but he laughingly moved his arm out of reach, releasing her hands.

'Your letting go. Show me!'

'No!'

He waited, feeling her hips move beneath him, seeing her eyes darken, and he smiled at the last remnant of conflict. But the next move must be hers. He would accept nothing less than total surrender.

'Jais,' she whispered. 'Please. . .'

'What?' he growled in her ear. 'Say it!'

'Take me, Jais. I love you. I want you. Please. . . please take me. . .'

He accepted her submission gallantly, tenderly and with infinite sweetness, taking and giving in equal measure. At last, putting aside her self-imposed restraints, Ginevra flew with him to new heights of ecstasy like a bird freed from the darkness into the light of day, swooping and tumbling, unfettered by chains of doubt. Paradoxically, her surrender was freedom. In giving all she had gained everything. In letting go of one vow she had strengthened the other.

CHAPTER SEVENTEEN

WITH the usual vigour of youth and rude health, Ginevra needed only to rest in Jais's arms to recover completely. Already the details of the past days were blurring, though Richard and Jais were both eager to know her account of events before she pushed them too far out of mind. Oswinna, proud of her direct access to the heart of the excitement, lost no time in telling Ginevra what she had heard in the hall about the capture of the thieves, how Sir Jais had knocked down one who pulled a dagger on him.

'Knocked *who* down, for heaven's sake?' Ginevra turned to look at the maid.

'The fat man, m' lady, Master Pat-something. As I 'erd, 'e 'ad a dagger up, and t'master knocked 'im across t'other side ert room. An 'e went down in a 'eap. An 'e didn't get up fer a bit!' she added.

Ginevra stifled an unladylike hoot of laughter. No, she thought, he wouldn't get up for a bit if Jais had knocked him down. Nobody would.

Later, looking refreshed and happier than anyone had ever seen her, she sat in the garden with Jais, Marianne and Richard, watching a family of young greenfinches learning to fly from the edge of the workroom roof. The small paved area was just large enough to accommodate them in private conversation without the danger of being overheard.

'Oswinna told me you knocked him down, Jais.'

'I'd have liked to do more than that, but we wanted him to talk!' He placed a strong hand over hers.

'And did he?' she asked, trying not to laugh.

'Only just!' Richard interjected. 'But what I want to know, Ginevra, is how the vestments came to be under the Mercers' Guild pagond in the costume box. Who put them there?'

'Tom, the apprentice, put them there when he helped me to escape,' said Ginevra, knowing that to prosecute Master Patrickson efficiently they would have to know the complete version—of Tom's ambiguous part in the theft and in his protection of her, and her eventual escape. They listened, enthralled, as she told them what had happened, but spared herself and them the details of how he had shielded her in the filthy little upstairs room. And now, she supposed, Tom would not be heard of again.

'Jais.' She placed her hand over his, holding it between her own. 'You won't pursue him, will you? If it had not been for him, I might have been somewhere on the ocean in that Italian man's boat and the vestments would be lost.'

Jais looked at Richard and Marianne with raised eyebrows, clearly requesting their agreement. They shook their heads and smiled. 'No, sweetheart, we'll not pursue him, I think. We have back what we sought.' He raised her hands to his lips and kissed the knuckles. 'I think he'll keep well away, by the sound of things, and it would be most ungrateful of us to punish him after his protection of you.'

'And Master Piers Patrickson is now being held awaiting trial, and I don't think he'll be heard of again, either. Did you know, Ginevra,' said Richard, 'that Tom left the maniple upstairs as evidence?'

Ginevra was puzzled. 'There were only three pieces. You mean that he actually left one of them behind, and *that* man never noticed?' She burst into a gale of laughter at Patrickson's greedy haste and at Tom's cleverness.

'Yes, and he also left behind a bolt of fabric and a list of the pieces he'd been given and where he was to take his share during the day. So we know who's got them.'

'And the others?'

'Yes, those, too. The lad John still had his list on him when we picked him up.'

'So, you got him, too?'

'Yes,' said Jais. 'How did he get the broken teeth and bruised cheek? Was it Patrickson?'

'No. It was Tom. Tom knocked him across the room when he. . .he. . .' Her hands clenched as she remembered, and she stopped, unwilling to go on. They looked at her expectantly, and Jais put his hand over hers again.

'When he would have raped you?'

She looked down at his hands on hers, so comforting and strong. Nodding gently, she had to agree. 'Yes, I suppose that's what he would have done,' she whispered.

'Well done, Tom,' murmured Jais.

'You've been so brave.' Marianne looked at her tenderly. 'We're all so proud of you. Do you feel strong enough to meet guests later on?'

'Guests?' Ginevra looked concerned.

'Yes. Family.' Marianne's expression gave nothing away. 'Will you and Jais come over to the house for supper? I hope they'll have arrived by then.'

It took Oswinna quite some time to achieve what Ginevra regarded as a satisfactory appearance. For all her wheedling she had not been able to elicit a sign from Jais of the identity of the family guests, and so her preparations took on proportions out of all keeping with the event. Her newest gown, a cote-hardie of soft russet velvet, fitted her trim waist perfectly, accentuating the roundness of her breasts and hips. Long dagged tippets fell from the sleeves to the floor, exposing tight undersleeves of black- and russet-figured brocade twinkling with gold threads. Instead of the caul for her braided hair, she chose her own style, a pile of copper curls on top of her head surrounded by her own gold fillet, which Jais had brought out of hiding to lend her. With the gold cross given to her by the Prioress Claire and the topaz ring on her hand, the effect was ravishing.

'Breathtaking!' said Jais, causing her to blush at his reaction. He was looking as devastatingly handsome as she had ever seen him in the gown he had worn on that day at Scepeton Manor when he had made his bid for her hand. The green bliaud, with its gold cypher on the breast, brought back memories so strong that she could clearly experience once again the confusion, surprise, anger and excitement of that evening. 'Do you remember, Ginevra?' he asked.

She nodded. 'Yes, I remember. I was so afraid of you.'

He took her into his arms. 'Or afraid of yourself, perhaps? Of new feelings you couldn't identify?'

'You were brutal!' she retorted hotly.

'I had to be.'

'*Why* did you?'

'Because gentling takes too long. And I had no time.'

'Then you were taking a risk, sir! I might have flown. . .'

'I knew you had courage. And I had aroused your curiosity, too.'

She pushed against him, her feathers ruffled once more. 'Insufferable! Arrogant. . .brute. . .!' But she was held firmly and kissed hard until her body melted into his and she trembled under his hands, just as she had done then.

'Jais de la Roche, you have still many questions to answer.'

'Ginevra de la Roche, you will discover the answers all in good time. But now we are expected to attend the family.' He grinned as she snuggled against him with a whimper of contentment.

'Must we?'

'What else did you have in mind, my lady?'

She wriggled again seductively. 'Sir,' she whispered, 'I believe the Lady Juniper has just arrived.'

Jais shook his head in silent laughter and tightened his arms about her, sliding one hand to the soft fabric over her behind. 'Then the hussy will have to wait until we return. Tell her, will you?'

'I'll give her your message. But she won't like it,' she pleaded softly.

'Neither do I! But she will do as she's told. Come!'

The ordeal of meeting new members of Jais's family was not at all what Ginevra had expected, for the face which greeted her in Marianne and Richard's solar was even more familiar to her than theirs.

'Reverend Mother!'

The white habit and erect posture of her beloved Prioress Claire could not be mistaken, even though her face was in shadow as she stood with her back to the garden window. At her side was yet another surprise.

'Rowenna!'

Many warm embraces and tears later, Ginevra found words to voice her confusion at this extraordinary turn of events. 'This is wonderful,' she said, wiping a tear from her cheek with a finger. 'But why. . .? Marianne, you said "family".'

'Yes, dear one. Aunt Claire *is* family.'

'Aunt Claire? You mean. . .?' she looked at them, one after the other, but their smiling faces told her nothing more. She became impatient. 'Richard, will *you* please explain to me what all this is about? I think there is something I need to understand.'

Richard laughed fondly and put a comforting arm around her shoulders, amused by her severe tone. 'Aunt Claire, Ginevra, is the elder sister of Sir Michael de la Roche, Jais and Marianne's father. Their mother and Aunt Claire went to the same convent as children, and learned to embroider, just as you did. Then Claire became a nun, and Isabelle Pomfrette married Claire's brother. Marianne was taught to embroider by her mother.'

Now it all began to make sense. As though the waters of a muddy pool had suddenly cleared to show its contents, so the tiny fragmented events of the past few weeks now came to light, to relate to each other, to take on a new significance. Even the cypher on the breast of Jais's green bliaud held a new meaning. 'Aunt Claire. . . Reverend Mother. . .*you* did that?' she whispered.

The prioress nodded. 'Yes, child. I did that.'

Ginevra looked at Jais, at his eyes brimming with laughter. Before she could speak he pulled her in to his side, and told them how at Scepeton Manor it had attracted her attention and set her thinking that she was destined to spend the rest of her life embroidering his gowns and the horses' saddle-rugs.

'Dear child!' exclaimed Aunt Claire. 'I knew he was a wicked tease, but I'm afraid he appears to be getting

worse!' The laughter was warming and kind, and
Ginevra felt a glow of happiness as she relaxed in their
company.

'But Rowenna here, too! Have you come home, dear
one? To stay?' What a coincidence, she thought, that
Rowenna should arrive at the very moment when her
skills as a broderer were most needed. *Was* it coincidence, or was there more to be revealed? she thought
that now might be a very good time to get a little of
her own back. Waiting for a lull in the conversation,
she remarked, casually loud, 'Do you remember,
Rowenna, in the dorter one day, how I told you I'd
just bumped into a horrid man talking to the Reverend
Mother?'

'Yes, I remember it well.' Rowenna clearly understood the game. 'You were very cross. Said he looked
like a trouble-merchant!'

'That's right. I still think my original impression was
not far wrong. What do *you* think?' She tried not to
laugh, but it was impossible. Everyone else did.

The meal in Richard's great hall was a hilarious
affair, the conversation and laughter flowing against a
background of sweet music and cries of delight from
the merry diners—so much news to exchange, exploits
to relate, questions to ask. Pages carried in huge
platters of skewered meats: venison—a gift from Jais—
pork, hare and tiny stuffed woodcocks. Then succulent
pieces of fruit, battered and fried in butter, and dates,
figs, and red wine brought back from Italy. And when
at last the company had washed sticky fingers in the
silver bowls and dried them, and the trestles had been
moved aside, then a troupe of jugglers were brought in
to entertain the guests. They were visiting York during
the feast of Corpus Christi, acting out their amazing
skills with firebrands, mallets and swords to such effect

that Ginevra and Rowenna were spellbound, for they had not seen anything like this before.

But questions were still forming in Ginevra's mind, faster than she could find answers for them, and so she was not disappointed when Marianne led the way out of the hall, leaving the revelry to fade as they approached the coolness of the solar.

'So, Jais was paying you a family visit on that day, Reverend Mother?' Ginevra kept hold of Rowenna's hand as they sat together.

'Yes, my dear, he was. He's been the chief source of our materials, you know. All as gifts. He had brought us more threads on the day you met him.' The picture of that small room flashed into Ginevra's mind—the words, the figure so familiar yet so ill-at-ease on that occasion, the glint of gold threads peeping out of the white linen bundle on the table.

'Have there been new commissions, Reverend Mother?'

'Ah, well, that's something we have to discuss. Rowenna and I stayed at Beesholme Abbey last night as the guests of Father Gregory. He told me that you'd stayed there recently on your way here. You remember the embroideries we did for them, all those years ago?'

Ginevra knew that Jais was watching her, but could not meet his eye. He broke into the conversation as though intercepting her thoughts of that night. 'We were shown the altar-frontlet that these two worked on,' he said, adding softly for Rowenna's ears only, 'And I heard how you sometimes had to work double-fast, too!' His smile made her grin. This handsome man did not unsettle her as he did Ginevra.

'I can see, sir, how you would appreciate *that*!' she retorted, twinkling her merry eyes at him. 'We have that much in common, it seems.'

He roared with laughter at her artful riposte. 'Well said, Rowenna. But what was it you wanted to discuss, Aunt Claire? A new commission?'

'Yes, Jais. Father Gregory tells me that the Abbot of Fountains. . .'

'He's still there?' Jais interrupted.

'No, dear. He went home last week, much to everyone's relief,' she murmured to one side, 'but he's told poor Father Gregory that he should commission a large altar-frontal now, after all this time! Says he knows they can afford it. The dear man asked if we could do one for them at the priory, but I had to explain that our numbers are dwindling and we can't take on anything of that size now. It's far too big a job.'

'We could, though!' The words burst out before Ginevra could stop them, surprising her as much as the others. The prioress turned to Ginevra and patted her hand with warm gnarled fingers which slipped hurriedly back into her sleeve again.

'Well, now. I was wondering if one of you might say that. Are you involved already then, Ginevra? I thought it would not be too long before you fell in love with Jais's workshop.' Ginevra exchanged looks with Jais, loaded with meaning. His grey eyes held hers steadily, as they had done on that previous occasion, but this time they asked not for a decision, for that had already been made. Only the declaration was now wanting.

Though she was speaking to the prioress, Jais knew that her answer was for him. 'Yes, Reverend Mother, Jais and Marianne have invited me to help and now I'm already deeply involved. I didn't think much of the notion of embroidering horses' caparisons——' she looked sideways at Jais, who laughingly caught the hand she waved in his direction '—but the kind of embroidery you taught me to do, I could never abandon.' Jais raised the hand to his lips and kissed her fingers next to his ring. Their eyes met again over the top of her hand and he knew what she was telling him. She turned to Marianne. 'Could we, Marianne? Could we manage it, do you think?'

'I think we'll have to give it some serious thought, don't you?' she answered. 'We shall need extra help, though, someone who can work to a high standard. . . A special friend, perhaps?' Her sweet face was turned towards Rowenna, her eyes peeping sideways at her guest, and everyone knew what implications were being revealed in her words.

'Do you think we might take Rowenna to see the workshop?' said Ginevra casually, to no one in particular.

Richard broke in quickly. 'You wouldn't care for that, would you, Rowenna?'

Rowenna turned to him, inclining her head coyly. 'Master Mercer, you obviously have something else in mind?'

'*Damoiselle*, if you must know, I am doing my best to even the score a little. Why does this handsome lout here——' he jerked his head towards Jais '—have no less than four lovely ladies, including my wife, anxious to do things for him, while I'm blessed with two spotty apprentices? Male ones, at that!'

Their laughter was mingled with exaggerated cries of sympathy and agreement. The handsome lout had done nothing to deserve it, they were in accord about that, but they would take Rowenna to the workshop just the same. If she preferred, she could always apply to become one of Richard's apprentices—even Aunt Claire agreed that this was only fair.

'Come, brother Richard,' said Jais. 'I'll tell you how

it's done. . .' And they followed the women out, Jais
grinning and quickly blocking a gentle fist to his chest
with one arm.

While Marianne showed Aunt Claire the newest
vestments, including the ones which had been stolen,
Ginevra escorted her friend round Jais's workshop,
now shrouded once more in the last light of the day.
Her openly declared involvement had generated a
strange feeling of peace and anticipation—excitement,
even—the resolution of so many indecisions of the past
weeks.

She had not known, for it had been kept a secret,
that Aunt Claire had been expected at some time in
the near future. Ginevra's suggestion, on that fateful
evening, that Rowenna would be the very person to
help with more work had been a coincidence and a
blessing, for they were not to have known that she was
the one Aunt Claire would choose to escort her, along
with her steward and servants.

Knowing how this would please Ginevra, the prioress
had not found the decision difficult in the least, for Jais
had kept her informed of events during the weeks of
negotiations with the tenants of Scepeton Manor.
Though the prioress had every reason to anticipate the
outcome of Rowenna's first introduction to a large
workshop like Jais's, she was prepared, sadly, to forfeit
her, too, knowing the economic realities of the situation better than anyone. It would help to solve a
financial problem for her parents if Rowenna were to
begin earning now, and, though she would live at
home, just off the Micklegate, work would be within
easy distance.

Rowenna and Ginevra linked arms and leaned
against the large cutting-table, their faces reflecting
their delight in each other's rediscovered company.

'You look wonderful, my lady!' Rowenna teasingly gave her title special emphasis.

Ginevra laughed and shook her head. 'Oh, dear one, I've missed you.'

'But you're happy. I can see that you're happy, Ginny.'

'I am, dear one. I am, truly. We fight, but. . .'

'But you lose?' And they giggled knowingly.

'Well, not always. . .'

'Nearly always. . .'

'Nearly always!' Their laughter erupted like a volcano, and Jais turned, smiling, guessing the reason.

'Richard,' he said, quite clearly expecting all to hear, 'I'm not sure how much embroidery would be done if these two were allowed to get together. Will you make me an offer for one of them?'

'*One* of them? Both, or none at all!'

'Damn!' He grinned.

Rowenna, however, had already made up her mind that she could get no nearer to heaven than this. 'Oh, Ginny. Mistress Mercer! This is. . .wonderful! Look, Reverend Mother, look at the space, and the light. . .' The wealth of materials, too, far exceeded anything she had seen before. No inhibitions of love or hate held her back as they had Ginevra. Her impulse was to begin immediately, on the morrow. Once again, thought Ginevra, the picture becomes clearer.

As the sky filled with the deep fiery glow of sunset Ginevra had a chance, at last, to talk with the prioress alone. As the others still discussed in the workroom, the two walked down through the vegetables into the herb-garden beyond, their thoughts flying back to their last conference in the sunset of the priory's tiny parlour. Then Ginevra had known the shock and distress of the impending change to her life, the suddenness, the unforeseen threat to her stability and security. She remembered her resentment and helplessness at the enforced redirection, and still longed to know the reasons behind it. Why the haste? Why the unceremonious rush to set her free? Jais's frivolous explanations had not been entirely convincing.

'You appear to be more at peace now, Ginevra. Am I correct?'

'I'm at peace *now*, Reverend Mother, as I have not been since you told me I must leave you. Do you remember how upset I was?'

'I remember only too well, my child. Do *you* remember how I said that there was a plan for you? That all would be well?' They stepped carefully over chamomile, spreading on to the path.

'Yes. But was there really a plan? Or were those simply words of comfort? You were not surprised to see me here with Jais, though my note told you that I was going to York. Nor was he surprised to see me at my brother's house so soon after our first meeting. How was this?'

'Steady, child!' The prioress laughed gently. 'Steady. I will tell you how that happened. I'm sure Jais won't mind my telling you.' She drew Ginevra into a recess in the long wall opposite the fountain and sat down on the bench. Patting the space beside her, she closed her eyes to find the beginning of the story. 'When Jais visited me that day I told him of the difficulties we were in. Not enough money coming in from anywhere. I told him that I might soon have to retire—close the priory, even, and send the girls home.'

'Is it that bad, Reverend Mother?'

'Yes, Ginevra. That's how bad it is, but no worse for us than for many another. Small priories have always found it more difficult to make ends meet than the larger houses.' She thought of the struggles over the past years—the isolation, the ever-present threat of Scottish raids which had often seemed terrifyingly close, the ever-decreasing number of novices, paying guests, paying pupils. And then the pestilence. 'So. . .' She took Ginevra's hand on to her lap and held it between her own. 'So Jais suggested that he should find a place for some of the girls who lived in York, like Rowenna. He needed help in his workshop since he'd lost some of his workers after the sickness, Marianne was to start a family, and there was too much work for only two pairs of hands.'

'So you're sending other girls to work here, too?' Ginevra said eagerly. This was even better than she had hoped.

'I agreed with him that this would be a solution to both our problems, and probably to theirs, too. But these things cannot take place immediately. Permission must be sought and obtained. That's why I've come here, to see some of the parents, among other things. To see you, mostly.' She smiled lovingly at Ginevra. 'I told Jais he'd have to wait several months for a decision.'

'But, Reverend Mother, why did *I* go immediately, then?'

'Wait, child. Not so fast.' She held up a hand. 'I told Jais of my most experienced broderer for a very good reason. And I arranged that he should see you. . . accidentally!'

'Accidentally?'

'Yes, my dear child. I, too, saw you flying down the hillside away from where Brother David was shearing the sheep. I'm not so unworldly that I don't understand the way men react, or not, to a woman.' She paused.

It was only recently that Ginevra herself had been enlightened on this point. 'And I realised that you were not ever to be one of us. On the contrary.' She waited for a little while in silence, listening to the drone of the bees on the lavender and thyme, gleaning a last burden of pollen before nightfall. No, Ginevra had many admirable qualities, but definitely not those required to be a nun. She continued. 'I've known Jais all his life, and loved him. And I knew. . .' she placed a hand over the well-worn habit where her heart was gently beating '. . .I knew that he and one of the other people most dear to me could find happiness together. And I believe I was right!'

Ginevra had had no idea that the Prioress Claire felt so deeply about her, nor even that she was allowed to, and on impulse she leaned towards the frail old lady and kissed her cheek. The prioress smiled at her and continued. 'So, of course, his reaction was immediate, as I knew it would be. He takes on a challenge as easily as breathing. He insisted that he couldn't wait several months. He had to have you *then*, Ginevra. You understand now why I had to let you go so abruptly?'

So, what he had said to her was true, except that he himself had not known that the hand of fate had been expertly manipulated by his aunt, the beloved prioress. 'It so happens,' she went on, 'that Scepeton Manor belongs to the family and he was due to visit your brother to sort things out. He knew Alan was having financial trouble. . .'

'*You* told him about my fees not being paid. . .?'

'Yes, Ginevra. I believe I did mention it.' Her mouth tweaked at the corners. 'Did he make things hard for you?'

The last light of the day was catching the fountain, glistening on the droplets as they rose and fell with a faint splatter on to the bowl beneath. It all seemed so far away at that moment, but not beyond recall. From the safety of this peaceful place, among those she had come to love, the painful process had gradually taken on a faintly amusing aspect, like an oft-repeated tale that ended happily, holding no fears in the telling when one was familiar with the outcome.

'Yes, Reverend Mother. Very. But I made things difficult for him, too!' And they laughed together, as women did.

'I thought you might!'

'But why could he not have told me of his feelings there and then? And wooed me, as other people do?'

The prioress glanced at her in mild surprise. 'Have you forgotten your first encounter in the herbarium, and how annoyed you were that he should have seen you like that? What chance would he have stood using conventional methods, I wonder? and, apart from that, the time element was a challenge to him. You must have discovered how he likes to win, and on his own terms.'

Gentling, he had called it, just as he would tame a falcon. No time—he had already added an extra day to his stay at her brother's house to negotiate the deal. They must both have been very sure of her courage to take such a risk. 'Reverend Mother, I've come to love him so desperately. Is it really possible that love can grow so quickly out of hate?'

'Indeed it is, my child, perfectly possible.' They sat together in silence as the darkness dropped like a fine veil of gauze around them, each deep in thoughts of love and the unaccountable way of fate. Eventually the lights of the workshop drew them towards the house, and the subdued murmur of voices and laughter led them once more into the arms of their family.

The reunion which had begun at the Mercers' house lasted well into the night, so late that Aunt Claire wondered if she might have to impose upon herself a small penance for missing both vespers and compline on the same day. Both Aunt Claire and Rowenna were escorted back home to stay with Richard and Marianne, leaving Ginevra and Jais to return to the peace of their solar, happy to be alone at last.

The revelations of the evening had passed through Ginevra's mind as though through a piece of muslin, straining new information to catch every detail with which to complete her complex picture. Now, at last, she was beginning to understand, though she thought her approval would take a little longer.

Rowenna was to help in the workshop and more girls were to come later. Now there were to be new vestments for the minster, and they had the commission from Beesholme, and there would be a baby for Marianne and Richard. Would the Reverend Mother come to live in York where they could all see her as often as they wished? There were designs to think about, a plan of work to make. . . The days were going to be packed from now on. . .

'Jais?'

'My lady?' He was lounging on the big bed completely naked, watching her take down the bundle of hair and noting the glints of new copper lit by the flickering candle beyond.

'I've done something I said I wouldn't do.'

'Again, my love?'

She whirled on her stool and threw her soft shoe at him, which he caught, laughing. 'I shall not tell you. . .'

'Do tell me, little bird. Is it serious?'

Picking up the embroidery frame which had been lying face down, covered by a pile of threads, she took it across to the bed and lay it before him. On the deep green fabric a tiny embroidered emblem of a wood anemone had been worked with great delicacy in silk threads, as real as though it had been freshly picked at that moment. He looked at it, captivated.

'It's to remind you of something I did which I shan't do again. And it's for the breast of your other green bliaud. This is what I said I would never do. Well, I said it to myself, anyway, but I expect you heard me.' Her voice, contrite, tailed off to a whisper. 'I bought the material and the hoop with your money in Richard's shop on the day before our wedding. I didn't know you had some already. I couldn't resist it. And Marianne couldn't tell me.'

'The wood anemone. Your first attempt to escape me.'

'And my last.'

His arms went around her. 'My dearest, my sweetest little bird. It's the most beautiful embroidery I've ever seen. It's exquisite. I look foward to wearing it against my heart, and only you and I will know its true meaning.' His deep kisses were all the thanks she needed. 'Now, I shall show you something.'

He rose to reach for a small leather-bound case with a golden clasp and, opening it, removed a piece of vellum, folded in half. Inside the fold lay the wood anemone which he had taken from her hands on the journey to York, now pressed flat but still white and pale green. Her eyes told him of her amazement that he should have remembered the incident just as clearly as she did. Now it was her turn to show her delight, lovingly and warmly, assuring him that her flights were now to be made only within the sight of her master.

Escaping from his embrace at last, she replaced the embroidery on the table and began the tantalisingly slow combing of her hair. 'Jais,' she said, 'what is the name of the little church where I hid? Did you tell me that it was on North Street?'

'Yes, it was All Saints on North Street, on the other side of the river.'

'All Saints,' she mused, combing the curling ends. 'Would you take me there soon?'

'Take you there?' He came across to her, puzzled. 'You want to return there, really?'

'Yes, I do. I have to pay for two candles. One which I used, and one yet to be bought. It's rather important.'

Jais caught something in her voice, a tone of seriousness which he knew must not be answered with flippancy. Taking the comb from her hands, he pulled her up into his arms. 'Of course I will, my sweet love. I'll come with you and light one, too. Now, is there anything else on your mind before we end the day?'

'Jais?'

'Yes, m'lady. It's time for bed.'

'Can we go and see Alan and Johanna soon?'

'Yes, we'll take Aunt Claire back home at the same time.' Without waiting for more questions, he picked her up in his arms and carried her across to the bed.

'And, Jais. . .'

His mouth and nose were already in her hair and on her throat, and he groaned and leaned on one elbow, looking darkly into her eyes. 'Ginevra. This is the last question. Do you understand me?'

'It isn't a question. I want to tell you something.' His hand had begun to explore her, but she caught it before it reached its destination. Her hair was spread out on the pillow and her half-closed eyes told him quite plainly that these were women's delaying tactics.

'Then tell me. Quickly, wench!'

'I've discovered the meaning of the topaz.'

'I could have told you. It means fidelity.' His hand became impatient again but she held it fast, out of the way.

'Yes. Fidelity.'

'Is that what you wanted me to know?'

'Partly. But there's more to it than that.'

'Ginevra!' His voice held a hint of warning that he was not to be delayed any longer. She giggled at his mounting frustration and nipped at the lobe of his ear.

'I believe it's also a cure for sleeplessness.'

He nodded, and his grey eyes narrowed at her, deep and intense in the dim candlelight. 'Then, little bird, if you're wearing it, I suggest we put it to the test. Now, is there anything else?'

There was a silence, and she released his hand. It flew to her breast like a hawk to the lure.

'Good,' he said.

LEGACY *of* LOVE

Coming next month

THE LAST ENCHANTMENT
Meg Alexander
Brighton 1813

To prevent her niece, Caroline, from marrying the notorious
Duke of Salterne, Aurelia Carrington took the girl away to
Brighton. As a means of escape, it was a failure, for Salterne
followed them. Deeply, if unwillingly, attracted to him,
Aurelia suspected he preferred her company to Caroline's, so
what had made him offer marriage? By the time she found
out, more was at risk than Aurelia's heart.

MARRIAGE RITES
Pauline Bentley
Essex 1694

Laura Stanton could lose Fairfield Manor on her
grandfather's death—and he was dying. In sheer desperation
she undertook a Fleet marriage with a prisoner, Matthew
Thorne, only to find her simple plan was fraught with
problems. Her grandfather unexpectedly rallied, and her
'marriage' *had* to seem real. But Matthew had his own
demons to fight, and answers to find, before he could think
about any future with Laura. Once he had his ship back, he
would be off to sea, and Laura wouldn't leave Fairfield…

LEGACY of LOVE

Coming next month

FORTUNE HUNTER
Deborah Simmons
Regency England

To save his inheritance, Leighton Somerset, Viscount
Sheffield, badly needed a wealthy wife, and lovely Melissa
Hampton was his target. Her coolness towards suitors had
earned her the name of Lady Disdain but, somehow,
Leighton slipped under her guard, even though hard
experience had taught Melissa to evade charmers like him.

Leighton wasted no time in manoeuvring her straight into
matrimony and, accepting her fate, Melissa was tempted to
lose her heart. But she was in more than one kind of danger,
for someone was stalking her—in deadly earnest—and it
appeared to be her husband...

HEAVEN'S GATE
Erin Yorke
Ireland 1567

Banished to Ireland, Regan Davies arrived at her new estate
ready for anything—except it's former owner! Connor
O'Carroll had sworn to kill the man responsible for taking his
lands, until 'he' turned out to be a woman. Unable to bring
himself to exact revenge on Regan, Connor planned to regain
his home by marriage. Simple enough—as long as Connor
didn't ruin all by giving his heart to his enchanting enemy...

Paperback Writer...

Have you got what it takes?

For anyone who has ever thought about writing a *Mills & Boon* Romance, but just wasn't sure where to start, help is at hand...

As a result of ever increasing interest from budding authors, *Mills & Boon* have compiled a cassette and booklet package which explains in detail how to set about writing a romantic novel and answers the most frequently posed questions.

The cassette and booklet contain valuable hints that can be applied to almost any form of creative writing.

There isn't an easy recipe for writing a romance, but our cassette and booklet will help point you in the right direction—just add imagination to create your own success story!

The 40 minute cassette and 28 page booklet are available together in one smart pack from most branches of WH Smith and John Menzies and other leading retailers. Price £9.99.

Or send your cheque (made payable to Harlequin Mills & Boon Ltd) to:
Cassette & Booklet Package, Dept. M.,
P.O. Box 183, Richmond TW9 1ST.